Fast Women

and

Neon Lights

Eighties-Inspired Neon Noir

Edited by Michael Pool
with a Foreword by Will Viharo

SHORT
STACK
BOOKS

Copyright

VALLEY GIRL by Kat Richardson
ALONE NOW by Patrick Cooper
BIG SHOTS by S.W. Lauden
THE DEEP END by Dietrich Kalteis
PARTS UNKNOWN by Sam Wiebe
BESTIES & BLOW by Sarah M. Chen
IT'S MORNING AGAIN IN LAKE CASTOR by Eryk Pruitt
WIDOWMAN by Matthew J. Hockey
THE ENVELOPE by Linda L. Richards
MEANTIME by Will Viharo
BIG HAIR, BANANA CLIPS, AND THE FIGURE-FOUR LEGLOCK by Nina Mansfield
DUTCH by C.S. DeWildt
IN THE SWIMMING POOL by Jen Conley
GETTING SECONDS by Greg Barth
CAUGHT ON VIDEO by Brian Leopold
FLECKMAN'S FIX by Preston Lang
LAST DANCE AT THE GLIMMER LOUNGE by S.A. Cosby
NIGHT THIEF by Michael Pool

Formatting by Rik – Wild Seas Formatting
Cover design by Dyer Wilk
Copy editing by Stacy Robinson - *The Next Chapter Editing*

ISBN: 978-0-9968552-7-3

Table of Contents

INTRODUCTION

By Michael Pool

The concept for this anthology came from a variety of sources. First and foremost, I've long been overly nostalgic for the eighties, which constituted the first decade of my life. Folks who are older than I am probably remember it through the lens of Reagan's "Morning in America", perhaps as the high-water mark of consumer culture, where nearly *everything* was commoditized in some way, especially film and music.

I simply remember the commercial campiness and bright colors, wearing my Jamz to elementary school, playing with slap bracelets, and watching MTV. And, of course, I remember the movies. Ridiculous commercial crime movies like *Adventures in Babysitting*, but also dark noir movies like *Thief* or *To Live and Die in L.A.* Oh yeah, and television shows like *Miami Vice* and *Magnum P.I.*, which I spent countless hours watching.

I was having a discussion with my good friend Will Viharo about the eighties one day, and afterward, I stumbled upon a reference in a review of Will's work by fellow noir author Rob Pierce, who had labeled it "Neon Noir." It was my first time hearing that term, though I soon came to learn a lot about what it meant. Bright lights, glass-block windows, dark cityscapes filled with unsavory elements all looking for an easy come up, only to discover that nothing in life comes easy. Femme fatales on the make. Wacky characters looking for success while inadvertently plotting their own doom.

Through my research of the term, I noticed that it was mostly applied to the neo-noir films of the 1980s. Almost immediately, I fell in love with the idea of a collection of fiction stories in the same vein.

Thus, *Fast Women and Neon Lights* was born, and I set out to invite some of my favorite modern neo-noir authors to contribute stories, as well as to open up *Crime Syndicate Magazine's* submission portal to submissions. Both efforts turned up stories that went above and beyond the call.

What you're about to read are eighteen of the darkest, funniest, and most criminally-nostalgic eighties crime tales ever written, pulled straight from the minds of authors who varied in age from preschoolers to full-grown adults when this most nostalgic of decades occurred, including my own rendition of a "one last job" story. It was an absolute honor to edit this anthology, and I have no doubt you'll enjoy reading these stories as much as I enjoyed working with the authors to polish them into a neon shine.

I want to express my thanks to you, the reader, for picking up this book, my thanks to the authors for writing such *totally rad* stories, and, most of all, my thanks to the eighties for all the amazing inspiration. This book is everything I thought it could be, and so much more. I hope you'll agree. Enjoy!

FOREWORD

By Will Viharo

Nostalgia for 1980's pop culture had always perplexed me until recently, when, as a middle-aged man, I began wistfully reflecting on my own misspent youth during that decadent decade. Not that *I* was decadent. I wish had been at least moderately hedonistic. Instead, I spent most of my late teens and twenties barely surviving via a series of odd jobs, getting my heart broken on a routine basis, and then writing (another) novel as my self-therapeutic reaction. I really should've just been out trying to score, like everyone else. Not dope, necessarily. But promiscuous, no-strings sex? Maybe. I often regret my self-imposed isolation, though in retrospect, considering so much promiscuity resulted in untimely death during the advent of AIDS, perhaps my celibacy was itself a matter of survival.

But I still have some fond memories of that era, mostly wasted in my little rented rooms, watching *Miami Vice* and reading crime fiction.

Growing up in South Jersey, my favorite authors were Damon Runyon and J.D. Salinger. In 1979, at the dawn of the eighties, I was booted out of the state by the right-wing guru cult that raised me, and found myself on my own at age 16. It was then that I met a rising young actor named Mickey Rourke via my own actor-father, Robert Viharo. In fact, it was Mickey Rourke who bought me my first car, a 1964 Thunderbird, when I was nineteen. Heady times, indeed.

In the eighties, the soundtrack of my life changed radically along with my environment, from disco and pop to punk and new wave. From Elton John, Olivia Newton-John and the Bee Gees, to Blondie, the B-52s, Devo and the Blasters.

I also discovered the works of L.A. bards Raymond Chandler, Charles Bukowski, and John Fante. Later, in 1985, I left L.A. for San Francisco, sick of the sun and drawn by the fog, living for a year in a residential hotel called the Europa in North Beach, above the Condor, where Carol Doda danced. I got a job as a desk clerk on the graveyard shift. I returned to L.A. In the summer of 1986, pursuing another hopeless romance and employed as Mickey's assistant, I returned to the Bay Area, eventually winding up in Berkeley, where my lonely literary lifestyle continued unabated into the 1990s.

It was around that time that Berkeley-based author Barry Gifford (*Wild at Heart*) reissued the vintage pulp classics of Jim Thompson, David Goodis, Charles Willeford (*Cockfighter*), and others in his now-legendary Black Lizard line. Meantime, Gifford and other modern hard-boiled authors like James Ellroy, James Lee Burke, Elmore Leonard, Carl Hiaasen, Robert B. Parker, and many others plied their lucrative trade, and I devoured every witty, world-weary word, naturally relating to the "noir" genre (in both literature and cinema) on several levels. The plots themselves were incidental to me, but the solitary lifestyles of the fringe-dwelling characters resonated with my own, because what always appealed to me most about crime fiction was the common voice of despair.

The subliminal influence of Thompson and Ellroy gradually began affecting my own artistic agenda, and I invented the private eye character of Vic Valentine, initially conceived as a cross between Holden Caulfield and Raymond Chandler because, as I said, I wasn't interested in the "mystery" being told, but the *way* it was being told. I was an outsider, like they were. But it was like we all existed within the same bubble, looking in at a society and culture whose apathy we mutually felt.

For these reasons, the 1980s were a seminal period in my development as a "pulp" writer. I self-identify as a "pulp" — rather than a "noir" or "crime" — writer because I've since expanded my output to include horror and science fiction, and most of my stories now are hybrids, not straight-up tales of cops and robbers.

But my characters are still essentially "criminals," whether the rules and laws they are flouting are legal or strictly ethical in nature. And even when they're committing self-destructive acts of desperation, they're doing it with style. That's what original film noir was all about in a nutshell: embracing one's self-made doom wearing sharp duds and drinking a cocktail while cruising down the highway to Hell in a stolen Cadillac.

That's what neo-noir is about too. And neo-noir was basically born, or at least came of age, in the 1980s, beginning with *Body Heat* (wherein my old pal Mickey made his initial splash), and continuing with Michael Mann's *Thief*, William Friedkin's *To Live and Die in L.A.*, the Coen Brothers' *Blood Simple*, David Lynch's *Blue*

Velvet, and even Ridley Scott's dystopian science-fiction classic, *Blade Runner*.

Most of the 1980s neo-noir films shared a common visual aesthetic and atmosphere, often combining the jump-cut editing and flashy comic-book construction of early MTV music videos with the cool, sleek, sometimes colorful, sometimes monochromatic, but always nihilistic mood associated with cyberpunk. They looked like beautiful moving paintings splashed with blood, and felt like elegantly dangerous nightmares, filled with garish imagery and pulsating music.

No wonder so many kids these days—especially those born after the 1989 cancellation of *Miami Vice*—romanticize the pre-Internet days of John Hughes-type innocence. They must think life in America was so much simpler and safer back then.

But it wasn't.

The difference between our present and the 1980s is the same time gap between the '80s and the '50s. The distant past always seems like a halcyon fantasy to those that didn't actually live through it.

We old timers know otherwise. Fashions change. Technology evolves. Human nature doesn't.

The stories in this anthology all hail from a similar place and period, though each voice is as distinct as the experiences that inspired and influenced them. Not all of the authors represented in this volume were old enough to truly appreciate the eighties as adults, but whether their impressions originate in memory or media, they're all authentic.

"The future is not what it used to be," Satan (Robert De Niro) tells private eye Harry Angel (Mickey

Rourke) in *Angel Heart*, one of several '80s neo-noir classics starring my old pal (*Rumble Fish, The Pope of Greenwich Village, Year of the Dragon, A Prayer for the Dying*, and *Johnny Handsome* being the others). The authors of these eighteen tales exist in "the future," even if their protagonists exist in the past. Perhaps their greatest advantage is in knowing what happened next. The next generation will no doubt look back on them with a similar mixture of nostalgia and pity.

And I won't blame them.

VALLEY GIRL

by Kat Richardson

The interrogation room smelled of Pine-Sol, Love's Baby Soft, and vomit. Detective Willet leaned toward the perfume and the slim teenage girl wearing it on the other side of the table. The social worker beside her glared at him. He ignored her. He wasn't touching the girl, or leading her, he was just ... trying to read her. Not so easy. Her thick makeup and wild dandelion-puff of blonde hair made the kid look more like a doll than a human being.

She wore a fluffy sort of short skirt over skin-tight leggings that ended in a band of lace at the knee, and a clinging black camisole that showed her bra straps under a tiny neon-yellow lace top that cut off just below her breasts. Plus five pounds of junk jewelry — mostly cheap chains and flashy crosses — and big, bright-pink hoop earrings. An expensive pair of leopard-print stiletto heels worn with lace-trimmed ankle socks finished off the outfit. The getup made her look like a cross between one of those big-eyed-kid paintings and a hooker with shiny, red patent-leather lips.

"Do you understand what you've done, Kim?" he asked.

Kim rolled her eyes. "Like, for sure. I set the bitch's hair on fire. Duh! I so totally 'get' that you're all pissed and stuff ... I'm not, like, some clueless dweeb, you know." She pursed her mouth and raised her hand to flip her hair back out of her face. Half-a-dozen bracelets rattled on her wrist.

She made an exasperated noise in the back of her throat. Her doll-like face was distinctly not pretty when she did. "Oh my God! This is just so bogus. Can't we talk someplace that's not, like, totally heinous? It's not like I'm going to run away, or whatever. I mean...*C'mon*. I'm from the Canyon—I'm not, like, some skank from Compton. It was just, like, y'know ... One of those things." Her hands fluttered like captive butterflies, then landed on the tabletop again, cuticles chewed ragged, red nail polish melted to blackened stubs on her right index finger and left thumb from proximity to burning hairspray.

"One of those things?" Willet repeated. "You set your friends on fire often?"

"Christie Damson is so not my friend." The eye roll again. "She's, like, such a total skeezer, and she narced me out. Seriously uncool."

The social worker reached out and patted Kim's hands. "You don't have to talk about this before your parents get here, you know. You're a minor, but you have rights."

"No doy," Kim sneered at her. "And stop touching me." She pulled her hands out from under the woman's reassuring pats. "Jeeze, what are you, some kind of lezzie or something? Gag me out the door."

The social worker drew back, looking offended. "I'm here to protect you and advocate for you in the absence of your folks, and make sure this officer—"

Willet sighed. "Detective. Michael Willet, Miss Sutherlin." They'd been at this for nearly an hour and he'd told her his name twice already. *What was with this woman?*

She glared at him. "Sullivan. And it's *Ms.*"

Willet pressed his lips together. He was hot, he was ticked off, and his collar felt like it was full of grit. He pushed up to his feet, smoothed his hand down his narrow tie, then picked up his pen and note pad. "I'm going to excuse myself until your parents arrive, Kim." He shot a glare at the social worker. "Just to be sure I don't violate your rights."

He didn't know which one he wanted to smack more: *Ms.* Sullivan or Kimberly Peterson. Either way, a break sounded like his smartest move. Let Sullivan swelter in the box with the bimbo — he was going out for a cigarette.

***

Kim slumped in her chair and rocked one foot back and forth on the long heel of her Donna Karan come-fuck-me pumps. The room was just so ... *butt.* Like grody to the max. And it stank. Now that Detective Cutie-Pie was gone, the Sullivan chick kept staring at her and trying to be all, like, friendly and whatever. Oh my God, it was just so gross. Like it was some big thing that she'd sprayed that skank Christie down with Aqua Net. It's not like she was actually hurt or anything. Bitch was, like, Teflon. The two-faced whore.

It had started okay. Christie was the new girl at school, but she hadn't seemed like a skeeze. At first. Not, y'know, *bangin'*, but not, like, totally heinous. And she knew how things worked. "You are so rad," she'd told Kim. "We should be bestest friends." *So* sure. Like that was gonna happen. But, y'know, they could be, like ... *almost*-best friends.

Even Kim couldn't make Christie utterly cool, because, like, Christie was just so ... totally from BFE. And the big hair was such a totally tragic look on her tiny little head. She really should have gone Molly Ringwald. But Kim just had to work with what was there.

At first Kim hadn't seen it coming. I mean, they were all, like totally cool together. Right? Her and Todd and Mark and Suzanne, all them. "The Galleria Gang," her mom called Kim's friends—the woman was such a ditz, even when she wasn't sleeping with Prince Valium or snowed to the max. But it wasn't like Kim was going to make a scene about including Christie. Not then, at least. Before *it* happened.

So she'd taken Christie on. Y'know, like a project. Like how Phoebe Cates had been helping Jennifer Jason Leigh get laid in *Fast Times at Ridgemont High*. Like that. Except not with the getting laid part. So gross.

"If you want to be totally rad, you have to have the Look," she'd told Christie while they'd walked through the Galleria.

"You mean, like ... Jordache?"

"No! Gag me with a spoon. Not like Jordache. I mean, like, proper. Y'know? Wicked style. Like, like ... a brand of you. But it also has to be, like, so totally fashionable and hip. And you have to have the right friends. But, y'know, you got that covered, 'cause you have me. So that's, like, totally awesome. Right?"

Christie had smiled and nodded. At the time, it had just seemed like a regular, friendly kind of smile. Like she so totally got what Kim was saying. But, of course, *not*. Looking back, Kim knew Christie's smile had been totally bogus. But, how could she have known then?

She couldn't, right? For sure. Totally right.

And they'd kept on shopping. Which Kim was super awesome at. Except Christie was broke. And Kim wasn't going to spend her money on somebody else. Totally not gonna happen. The 'rents were so cheap-ass about her allowance. They'd just have to shoplift to make Christie hip. No biggie. It wasn't like the stores were really going to miss anything.

***

The air was thick and brown. Better than the funk in the interrogation room, but bad enough to make Willet rethink his decision to go outside. He could have gone back to his desk where he'd left his jacket, but, instead, he'd leaned his shoulders against the brick wall that faced the parking lot behind the Sherman Oaks police headquarters, and tried to talk his frustration out while he watched Detective Sergeant Jerome Hagen chain smoke. It was only May, but, Jesus H. Christ, it was already hot.

Willet sighed. "Why the hell'd she do this? Her folks have money—she doesn't need to steal. She doesn't need to go ape on her friend for ... for what? Making a scene in the mall? Damn, I dunno ... she's just a kid. I mean, shit ... she's a mess, yeah. She's a spoiled brat, she shoplifts a little, but that's all she's ever done until today. And she's got a mouth on her, sure, but should we be treating a girl like her the same as a ... a gangbanger or a crack whore? She's got a few problems—"

"She's a seventeen-year-old kleptomaniac who set her friend on fire with hairspray and a Bic lighter." Hagen paused to spark a fresh cigarette from the butt of another and take a drag. "Over a guy, a can of styling mousse, and three tubes of lip gloss. You call that 'a few problems?'" Hagen dropped the spent butt to the ground to join its brothers, sending slow curls of blue smoke toward the burnt-yellow sky.

Willet—his fists stuffed into his trouser pockets— shook his head and stared at the asphalt. "I'm not saying it's not GBH, or aggravated assault, or whatever other charges the other girl and the store want to make. But all that 'get tough on crime,' 'tough love' crap ..."

Hagen shot him an ironic look. "Send her to Juvie, they cut her loose when she turns twenty-one and seal the record. Think that's fair?"

Willet hunched his shoulders defensively. "I'm just saying, technically she's still a kid, and kids do fucked up things they don't really mean to do when they get wound up."

"'Wound up.'" Hagen laughed. "Yeah, *right*. Let me tell you, my dad used to take his belt to my ass for a lot less. Maybe if Miss Valley Girl's pop had smacked her butt once in a while, she wouldn't have thought it was okay to point an improvised flame thrower at her friend's head just 'cause she was feeling a little pissy."

The door to the building opened and a female officer in uniform looked out, squinting against the glare of the sun stabbing through the San Fernando Valley inversion layer. "Detective Willet?"

Willet turned his head and frowned at her. "What?"

"Valley General called. The vic on that assault—the Galleria thing?—she didn't make it."

"Ahhh ... shit."

Hagen punched Willet's shoulder. "Hey, y'lucky dog. Had that gold shield six months, and you got your first homicide."

Willet rounded on him. "You think this is funny, Hagen?"

Hagen put up his hands, laughing in spite of himself. "No way, José. I just think you're fucked. And *that's* funny. Are you gonna go on being all Care Bear and touchy-feely about this poor misunderstood little girl, or you gonna get tough and nail the spoiled bitch for second-degree murder? Hey, you get it kicked up to Criminal instead of Juvie, they might go for murder one."

"Jesus," Willet muttered, starting to turn away.

"Go, get 'em Crockett."

Willet made a "what the hell" face back at Hagen.

"Y'know. Miami Vice?"

Willet's heartbeat stumbled. "Crockett?" *Did Hagen know?* He should never have gone to that damned party in the Canyon. He'd thought the whole "hookers and blow" thing was a joke, until he was in it.

Hagen chuckled and grinned. "Chill out, man," he said, and shook his head. "I'm just kidding with you. You're not cool enough to be Crockett."

"Fuck you, Hagen. Fuck you and the horse you rode in on." He smoothed down his tie and went back inside.

The Petersons hadn't shown up—they'd sent a lawyer named Chris Marberg instead. Willet had seen Marberg—one of those expensive, blow-dried reptiles in an Armani suit—before, but he couldn't bring the incident to mind. Or maybe he was just a type Willet was too familiar with. Didn't matter, really. Willet just didn't like him. And Marberg didn't seem to like anyone, judging by the way he scowled at everyone in the room, including his client.

"... This is totally, like, wigging me out. It was just, like, little stuff!" Kim protested, twining a stand of hair around one finger. "Make up, hair stuff ... like that."

"Little stuff that was apparently worth killing over," Willet said. "Christine Damson died an hour ago. So the current charges are second-degree murder—"

"God!" Kim gaped. "The stupid skank wasn't supposed to *die!*" Incredulity didn't look good on her: it left her shiny red mouth hanging open and creased her make up into ugly pinch marks on her forehead.

Marberg warned her, "Don't say anything, Kim," and the social worker on her other side glared at Willet, snapping, "There's no call to badger her, Detective!"

Willet shined them both on. "That's funny," he said. He flipped over a page of his notebook and glanced at it, though he knew what it said. "Because, according to one of the witnesses, you said—and I quote—'Die, you fucking skank.' And then you set your friend on fire, and said a lot of other things—"

Kim jumped up and bent toward Willet, punctuating her shouted words with a fist slammed against the tabletop. "She was so totally *not* my friend. She stole my boyfriend! She was a total two-faced backstabber, skeezing all over him and then being all, like, 'but we're, like, bestest friends' and all like that. Lying. Two-faced! WHORE!"

A uniformed cop rushed through the door and grabbed Kim by the arms, wrestling her back into her seat. She fought and kicked while Sullivan yelled, "Get off her, back off!" until Kim finally sagged down, and the cop retreated a step. Marberg leaned in and whispered into the girl's ear, and she glanced at the floor like she was trying not to spew.

The lawyer sat back in his chair with the hint of a smirk. Willet and Sullivan sat and waited.

When the silence was suffocating, Willet took a long breath through his nose and let it out slowly. "So ..." he started, looking steadily at Kim, "You want to tell your version, now?"

***

The detective-guy—Willie? Willis?—whatever. Him. Detective Cutie-Pie. He started some kind of recording and said a lot of stuff about her rights and the charges and all like that. And then he was all, like, "Go on, start talking."

Once she started, Kim just couldn't stop. Stupid Christie had gone and died and ruined everything, just like the selfish skank she was, so who cared any more anyway, right? It wasn't like Christie was going say anything.

"It was just, like, hair gel and mousse, and junk jewelry and stuff at first. Then, y'know, we'd, like, take clothes. We'd swap and then wear, like, a whole fresh outfit out of the store after we cut off the tags, y'know? We even did it at Magnin's once. She's all down with it—Christie, I mean—she's all, like, 'we should take a fur coat'—like one of those Blackglama minks? But they chain them to the rack. So harsh. But it's totally too hot to wear a mink in the Valley anyway, so, like, whatever.

"So we're, like, vegging out at the Galleria and Christie and I are, y'know, helping ourselves to a few things around the stores—no biggie."

The detective-guy asked, "Could you be more

specific about the things you took or the shops you took them from?"

Kim stared at him. Get real. She rolled her eyes. "No. Like, duh, I don't remember. Okay?"

Cutie-Pie sighed. "Go on."

"So, I'm, like, just coming out of the dressing room at Robinson's, and I can see Christie talking to Todd — he's, like, my boyfriend. *Was* my boyfriend. And Christie's all, like, totally skeezing on him. So I think I'll just, like, sneak over and dip on them. Right?"

"Dip?" the detective asked. Cute, for sure — but so dim.

"Like, listen in? Y'know?"

The guy nodded. "All right."

Kim looked at the table so she wouldn't, like, get all distracted or have to look at them being all 'concerned' and all like that, and kept talking. "So I do, and I'm all listening and stuff, and they're all sucking face, and talking, and all like that. And he's saying, like, she's so hot, and last night was so excellent, and blah, blah, blah ... And then I'm like," Kim looked up, just to see if Cutie-Pie was listening, not like she really cared or whatever, but, y'know ... "I'm like, oh my God, they've been doing the nasty behind my back! Gag me out the door! The total skank! I helped her out — she was such a big zero when we met and I was all, like, making her all Vogue. And she goes and does that! To *me*! How totally heinous is that?" Kim went all hot-and-cold, like she was totally going to spaz out.

She homed in on Cutie-Pie — he wasn't so old that he couldn't relate, right? "So I'm all, like, no way! So I come up and I go, like, You're such a total skank and you, like, so totally suck, you man-stealing klepto, wench.' And she goes and narcs me out to Todd about the clothes and stuff. Right in front of some clerk and everybody! Like she hadn't done the exact same thing! It's just, like, too much. Seriously, so *so* uncool and I just ... y'know, I wigged out. I mean, you'd be going totally mental too, right?"

Then she looked at all of them: the lezzie Sullivan chick, Detective Cutie-Pie, even Mr. Grabby-Ass Marberg, who, like, so totally skeezed her out always trying to cop a feel and like that. And they didn't say, like, anything. Didn't they get it? Oh my God ... She'd so have to explain everything. Like, to a baby.

"So I lit her up." She put out her hands like she could still, y'know, feel them. "Hair spray, lighter ... hasta la vista, bitch. Hasta. La. Vista." And she did like she'd done. Spritz. And flame on ... It had so totally messed up her manicure. And then, like, everybody had started screaming and stuff ...

***

"Kim," Marberg started.

Kim froze with her hands still in the air, posture brittle as thin ice. She made her scoffing noise and stared incredulously at him. "She so deserved it."

The lawyer grabbed her wrist to pull her toward him, muttering, "Kim, you should be a little more circumspect—"

Kim shrieked and jerked like he'd broken her. "Don't touch me, creepazoid!" she shouted and whipped around, yanking her hand out of his grip. "Like, seriously. You gag me out to the max! She hosed me! I was just being her friend and she so totally screwed me! She set me up and then she, like totally narced me out! It's not my fault! She's the one who should be here, not me."

"Kim, I advise you to shut up," her lawyer snarled.

"*You* shut up!" Her little fist smashed into Marberg's left eye and the slick bastard toppled out of his chair. A second uniform rushed in to help the first grab Kim, cuff her, and wrestle her back into Holding.

She was a tiny, blonde bundle of rage, and she screamed the whole way, "You total dickweed! It's all Christie's fault! She's the bad girl, you sleazeball! She's the one! She so totally made me do it! You're on her side, you scumbags! You fucking bastards! Fuckwad, dickface—"

The social worker skittered after her.

Willet sighed, shut off the recording, and helped the lawyer to his feet. Might as well. "You want to press charges?" God, the whole thing was sick and pathetic.

Marberg glared back at Willet as they walked out into the cleaner air of the hallway. "That little witch ..." the lawyer muttered. Then he clamped his mouth tight and shook his head. "I need to talk to my client."

"So, I guess that's a 'no' on pressing charges."

Marberg gave a poisonous smile. "I can handle her." Then he peered at Willet. "Wait ... I've seen you before, Detective ..." He looked up and down the empty corridor, then jabbed a manicured finger at Willet. "There was a party up in the Canyon a couple weeks back ..."

Willet felt the blood drain from his face. "Christ."

"Yeah ... *yeah.*" Marberg's smile oozed back onto his face.

Willet stepped back, shaking his head and smoothing a hand down his skinny tie. "I can't change the evidence to favor your client—it's in the record."

"I don't want you to change anything. I want you to stick right to the facts. My client is out of control. She's a spoiled little princess with a history of shoplifting, who thinks the world revolves around MTV, wearing the right clothes, and banging the right guys. Now her little antics have escalated from petty theft and bad taste to murder—those are the facts, aren't they Detective? And I want you to stick to those facts so hard that the DA moves this piece of crap from Juvenile to Criminal Court. Get tough on crime," he said, mimicking that goddamned commercial. Marberg's stare bored into Willet. "You can do that, can't you?"

Willet wanted to puke. "She's just a kid! Transfer this to Criminal Court and she gets sent up like an adult. Probably life for murder in the first. You'd screw up her whole fucking life over this?"

Marberg's face lit like a jack-o-lantern. He shrugged. "It'd be out of my hands."

"What'd she ever do to you?"

"Maybe she fucked the wrong guy. Maybe she stole the wrong fucking thing. Or maybe, I just don't fucking like her."

"Jesus." Willet gave it only a second's thought. "Screw it. No."

Marberg's nasty smile nearly split his face in half. "Detective ... is it worth torpedoing your career over one spoiled little brat? I mean ... doing *coke*? Hanging with dealers and whores? Looking the other way for your rich, sleazeball friends? That could be awfully hard on a young, ambitious guy like you, if it came out."

"They're not my friends—I don't know those people. It was just a mistake."

"Oh. A mistake. Yeah. And the rumors and suspicion might not be enough to send you to jail, but ..." The lawyer shrugged again.

"Whatever you can say about me, I can say about you," Willet shot back.

Marberg raised his eyebrow. "Do you think that'll stick? You think it ever has?"

Jesus, that smug smile ... Willet wanted to slap it off Marberg's face, but he stood frozen and stared, his mind reeling.

For whatever twisted reason, Marberg would do everything he could to send Kim to prison for the rest of her life. She was spoiled, and nuts to boot, but she needed help, not a prison cell. She wouldn't survive that. Christ, she was only seventeen.

Willet shook himself. Kim's folks had money—enough to hire a snake like Marberg in the first place. It wouldn't matter if he pushed it to Criminal or not—they'd spend whatever they had to to save their little girl. Wouldn't they? Kids like that always got off the hook. Jesus Christ... didn't they? While guys like him ...

He'd gone to the wrong party. Kim had gone a little crazy ... A moment's stupidity and they were fucked. She might land on her feet—if Marberg's spite didn't crush her—but he had to grab what he could, no matter how much it burned. Tough on crime—what a joke. Willet closed his eyes and rubbed his forehead. "Fine. You win," he muttered.

"I always do." Willet felt Marberg pat his shoulder as the lawyer said, "See you next time, Detective."

And the next and the next ... Willet had swallowed

his pride, but it felt like he'd just swallowed a bullet.

ALONE NOW

by Patrick Cooper

Trip Tryon fingered the payphone's coin slot. The key was waiting inside, just like his cousin said it would be. He cursed the Orlando humidity and wiped the sweat off his forehead as he jogged back to Nash Mastroianni's car, idling quietly in the shadow of the mall parking lot. The cold air gushing out of the Chevy Celebrity's vents was a sweet blast to Trip's face.

"Was it there?" Nash said, fingers drumming on the steering wheel.

Trip closed the car door and leaned forward, putting his face on top of the AC vent. "Jesus H. Christ, man. Dead of night and it's a goddamn swamp out there."

"I said, was it *there*?"

Trip soaked in the cool air for another moment, then reached in his jeans pocket and pulled out the key. He held it up to Nash and smiled. "My cousin's a man of his word," he said. "Alls we gotta do is dip in and out."

"And the alarm's disabled?"

"That's what he said. Cousin Harv is always the last employee in the store, so he locks up. And like I said, man of his word. The alarm is off, bet on that."

Nash nodded and looked out through the foggy windshield. Neon lights from the food court reflected off the damp pavement. He thought of the chain stores sleeping peacefully inside the concrete retail citadel. The stores that had killed his business.

Since that new corporate hair-cutting chain had moved in down the block last year, Nash's barbershop had been in the deep red. Even with loyal customers accrued over three generations of Mastroianni ownership, Nash couldn't compete with the corporate price undercutting. The tail end of the Reagan era spelled D-O-O-M at last for Nash's family business.

So there was no way in hell his wife Maria was going to let him buy the Air Jordan 2s, which dropped in the morning.

"Alarm better be off, is all I'm saying," Nash said. "Or tonight is all for shit. I'm not showing up on the court tomorrow without 2s."

"Don't be ree-dick-u-lous," Trip said, doing his best Bronson Pinchot. "You're gonna have the crispest J's there. Slick Dick Charlie's gonna shit himself when he sees you strutting."

"Don't do that again. Your Balki impression. Don't do it again. It sucks."

"You can do better?"

They traded Perfect Strangers impressions for a few minutes to lighten the mood. Finally, Nash said, "Let's get it on."

Nash pulled the Chevy up to the back of the Foot Locker and parked it close to the door. They pulled ski masks over their faces and got out of the car. Trip scanned the parking lot as he adjusted his mask. His long blonde hair poked out of the eyeholes.

"Shit, these masks really necessary?" he said, pushing his hair up and away from his eyes.

They'd been best friends since grade school, were

often compared to Lennie and George from *Of Mice and Men*, but reversed. Nash was the large one, but had the brains, while Trip was a slim, scrappy, uneducated man who worked as a janitor in the roller rink, a job his parole officer had found for him.

Nash tossed Trip a pair of black leather gloves and put on a pair of his own. He moved to the back of the car, opened the trunk, and took out a flashlight. He stuffed it in his back pocket, then he took out his aluminum bat.

"Hold up," Trip said. "Hell is that for?"

"Just in case," Nash said. He closed the trunk with one hand.

"I got an uncle named Justin Case, but what's he got to do with that aluminum fucking bat?"

"I'm not taking any chances tonight. Now let's go."

The back door opened with a groan. Nash and Trip held their breath as they moved inside the Foot Locker's stockroom. Music still played over the store's speakers. Trip eased the door shut behind them.

"Why is the music playing?" Nash asked.

"I dunno," Trip said. "My cousin must have forgotten to turn it off. Just be glad the alarm isn't on. Now let there be light."

Nash handed Trip the flashlight. The beam cast shadows up and down the rows of shoeboxes in the stockroom. They made their way to the front of the store. Their well-worn Jordan 1s didn't make a sound on the concrete floor.

"Right there, baby," Trip said, moving the flashlight over a display sitting in the middle of the showroom floor. There were black boxes upon black boxes of Jordan 2s, fresh off the truck, the red Jump

Man icon emblazed on them like a beacon.

Nash wasn't ashamed to admit the sight made his dick hard.

"Like fucking Christmas morning," Trip said.

Nash slapped him hard on the back and said, "Better than Christmas, man. You know how much we're gonna make selling these bad boys on the corner? Shit's gonna be worth more than coke."

"Speaking of coke, cousin Harv wants us to save him a white-on-white pair."

"Shit, he can have 'em. I'm calling dibs right now on all the blue and whites. That's my colorway."

"Hold up," Trip said. "That's *my* colorway. You know that. Don't be fucking with me now."

Nash laughed. He leaned the aluminum bat against the sales counter, clapped his hands, and said, "Let's get started then."

As he spoke, Tiffany's "I Think We're Alone Now" kicked in through the speakers, drowning out his words.

"What'd you say?" Trip asked.

"I *said*, 'Let's get started,'" Nash repeated, louder this time. "Think we can turn the music down? I fucking hate this song."

"Fucking kids love it, man. They play it alla time at the rink. Drives me nuts. Gimme a sec, I'll turn it down."

Trip went back to the stockroom and found the music controls sitting on a shelf next to the alarm system. The music receiver was a black box with two unmarked knobs jutting out of it. It looked archaic compared to the state-of-the-art dual-cassette player Trip had in his apartment. Trip normally wouldn't be able to afford such a model, but the guy in the alley behind the roller rink had given him a deal.

Trip shoved the flashlight in his armpit and slid the receiver forward to reveal a mess of colored wires. He tried to trace which ones were the receiver's wires, but it was all one big knot.

"God dammit," Trip said. He couldn't tell which wires went to the receiver and which went to the alarm. Not one to gamble, he pushed the receiver back in place and turned one of the knobs, hoping it controlled the volume. Nothing happened.

"What's up with the music?" Nash called from the front of the store.

Trip shrugged and turned another knob just as Tiffany's song got to the synthesizer solo. This turned out to be the volume control. The synth blasted through the speakers at a deafening volume.

Trip's heart jumped into his throat. When he shot his hand out to twist the knob back the other way, the flashlight slipped out of his armpit. In the sudden darkness, he felt the knob snap off.

"Fuck!" he said. He bent down to get the flashlight. His forehead smacked against a lower shelf. "Agh!"

Nash bolted around the corner into the stockroom. "What the fuck, man? The music!"

"The fucking knob broke off," Trip yelled, holding his pulsing forehead.

"Well, do something!"

"All the wires run together with the alarm. We're liable to set the damn thing off!"

Tiffany asked if they could hear her heart beat.

"Just be cool," Trip said. "This is the end of the song. Trust me, I've heard it a thousand times."

He was right. In a moment, the song faded out. Nash let all the air out of his lungs and said, "Thank Christ. C'mon, let's get the J's in the car and get the hell outta —"

The opening beat of "I Think We're Alone Now" exploded from the speakers again. Trip felt the bass drum in his bones.

"Are you fucking kidding me?!" Nash yelled.

Trip put his hands over his ears and said, "Fuck! I think it's busted!"

"No shit!"

As Tiffany mocked her elders' warnings about the trappings of young love, Nash and Trip turned to head back to the front of the store. In the dark, Trip's foot caught against a shelving unit's leg. He stumbled and put his hands out to take the fall. All of his weight drove into his left thumb. He didn't hear the bone snap over Tiffany's seductive vocals, but knew it was broken right away.

Trip clutched his left hand to his chest. "Fuck! I broke my fucking thumb, oh Christ!"

Nash helped Trip to his feet and said, "Lemme see."

Trip aimed the flashlight at his thumb. The sight of the appendage in an unnatural crooked position almost made him throw up. "Oh shit, man," Trip said.

Nash pulled his ski mask off and rolled it up as tight as he could. "Bite down on this," he said.

"What?"

"Just do it!"

Nash put the acrylic fabric between Trip's teeth. "Ready," Nash said, "On the count of three ..." Trip bit down and tensed his entire body.

On one, Nash yanked Trip's thumb back into place. Trip screamed and the mask fell out of his mouth as his knees turned soft and he dropped to the floor. Despite his cries of agony, Tiffany claimed that the beating of their hearts was the only sound.

"Wait here," Nash said into Trip's ear. He ran to the front of the store, careful of the fixtures, and grabbed the first sneaker he came to on the display wall. He unlaced the sneaker with dexterity gained from years of haircutting and moved back to Trip, who had managed to stand and lean against the shelving fixture. Nash wrapped Trip's thumb securely with the laces.

"How's it feel?" Nash said.

"I dunno," Trip replied, breathing heavy. "I can't feel it no more."

Nash took the flashlight from him. "Well fuck it, let's just grab everything and get it in the car."

As Tiffany wondered what people would say, Nash held out his arms and Trip, using one hand, started piling shoeboxes into them. Arms full, Nash ran to the back door. Trip trailed him, lighting the way.

Trip tugged on the back door with his good hand. It didn't budge. Tiffany repeated her mantra as the song faded out again.

"It's not opening," Trip said. He pulled on the handle again. "Why isn't it opening?"

Nash placed the shoeboxes on the ground and pulled on the door, to no avail. "What the hell? Does it lock from the *outside*? That doesn't make any sense!"

As the song started up again, Nash and Trip felt the bass in their guts this time.

Trip clutched his stomach and said, "Why is this

happening?"

"Try the key!"

Trip fumbled with the key. He picked it off the ground and tried again. It wouldn't turn in the lock. He made a kind of animal sound in his throat as Tiffany suspected that there wasn't anyone around.

"We have to make that fucking music stop!" Nash said. He took the flashlight from Trip and started shining it around the stockroom in desperation. "Up there! Up inna corner! A speaker!" He traced the beam along the ceiling and found another speaker in the opposite corner. "If we rip the speakers out, she'll stop singing!"

While Trip held the flashlight, Nash scaled one of the shelving fixtures. The higher he climbed, the louder the music got, until it vibrated inside his skull. The single flashlight beam cut through the dark, making Nash feel like he was climbing through a tunnel pulsating with mall pop music. He must have become disorientated as Tiffany's vocals bubbled through the shelves.

"What's happening?" Trip called. "Are you okay?!"

Tiffany did not care if Nash was okay or not. Nor did she care that he lost his grip and fell ten feet to the concrete floor below. She just opened up her black jaws in the darkness and swallowed him whole.

***

By the time Nash regained consciousness, the music had stopped. His vision crept back in, or maybe it didn't. Everything was dark and Nash couldn't tell. He looked around for Trip. Felt a throbbing pain on the back of his head. Touched where the pain was. His skull felt wet.

Nash thought maybe he was in Hell. That the fall had killed him. Or maybe he'd died before they even made it to the mall. They could've been in a fatal car accident on the way here and crossed on over the River Styx. If not Hell, then purgatory, or some space rested on the edge of the world they had once known.

Before Trip could say anything to him, the opening beat of "I Think Where Alone Now" rang through his skull like church bells. Nash screamed.

"You bitch," Nash yelled at Trip. It came out as a gurgle. Nash dragged himself to his feet and reached for the aluminum bat, still leaning against the sales counter.

"Who are you talking to?" Trip asked, confused.

"Fuck you, Tiffany!" Nash yelled, the storm in his mind raging from the fall.

Tiffany continued to sing. Trip was confused as to why Nash would be holding the bat, taking up batting stance, but then he realized: *He thinks I'm Tiffany.*

The first swing connected with Trip's ribs, breaking three. He keeled over and wheezed as Nash swung again. The bat bounced off of Trip's skull and he crumbled to the ground.

Ten minutes later, when the police battered their way through the glass front doors of the Foot Locker, guns aimed and ready, Nash was cradling Trip's head, sitting atop the pile of Air Jordan 2 boxes. Blood trailed down from Trip's skull, over the Jump Man logos. Nash was pointing to the speakers above and singing along to the music in a shrill voice. Along to Tiffany. Like no one was there to hear him sing. Like he was alone now.

BIG SHOTS

by S.W. Lauden

Gary leaned against the boarded-up doors of the old Hollywood theater. A blank marquee jutted out into the grey sky looming above. The air was still and stank of trash.

He scratched at the scabs on his arm while watching the liquor store across the street. A cigarette dangled between his chapped lips. Thin wisps of smoke clung to the contours of his sharp cheekbones and sunken eyes.

A young tourist couple wandered past him, clearly lost. The guy's outfit was a bad mixtape of black Reebok high-tops, acid-wash jeans and a corduroy fanny pack cinched tight around his waist. His girlfriend's mop of curly hair was held in place with a sparkling scrunchie that matched her huge hoop earrings. A map of stars' homes was unfolded between them. They took one look at Gary and quickly moved along.

He snarled, shoving a hand into the pocket of his leather jacket to fish out a quarter. A Chrysler LeBaron full of yuppies almost ran him down as he shuffled to the pay phone across the street. The receiver felt cold against the piercings in his ear, just like the rest of his dope-sick body. He waited for the pager to pick up and punched in his code. The dealer would be at his apartment in thirty minutes. The clock was ticking and he was miles from home.

A bus crawled along the gutter and Gary caught his reflection in the windows. His hair was a mess of short spikes, like it had been for years. *Pretty good for thirty*, he thought. *Somebody has to keep punk rock alive.*

He'd had the same look since wandering into his first punk club a decade before. That was 1978, back when bands like the Screamers, the Bags and X ruled the local music scene. Now it was all those ridiculous hair metal clowns up on Sunset Boulevard.

Gary wanted to puke whenever he thought about those cavemen in their zebra-print T-shirts and spandex pants. He shook his head in disgust while walking down to the liquor store. It was a tiny mom and pop run by a Korean family. He'd been in there once or twice over the years as a customer, but never to work. He pulled a ski mask on before stepping inside.

Framed headshots of wannabe actors lined the walls. The man behind the counter saw Gary's small 9mm and took a step back, almost knocking a few bottles of vodka to the floor.

"Godammit! Please don't shoot me ..."

"The only God you should worry about is down the barrel of this gun. Now give me the money."

The clerk jabbed at the buttons on the register. Gary almost pulled the trigger when the drawer sprang open. He brought his voice down to a growl.

"All of it. And two cartons of Camels."

The man did as he was told, sliding a paper bag across the counter. Gary pushed it back.

"Wrong cigarettes. I need the ones with filters."

***

Gary ran all the way back to his decrepit apartment building, bounding up the stairs. His front door was unlocked, like it always was when he was working. The cockroaches scattered as he raced across the tiny living room and into the kitchen. He pulled the bag out of his jacket and started counting. The haul was just over three hundred dollars—more than enough to get him through the night.

A welcome knock came at the front door. Gary was heading over to open it when the wall phone rang. He guessed it was his business partner, Murphy. It was a call he couldn't miss.

"Yeah?"

"Ready for the big show?"

They'd recently started managing a new band from Seattle, and their first L.A. showcase was happening later that night. Gary was the public face of their team, while his partner was the no-nonsense number cruncher. Murphy was also the closest thing that Gary had to an ally in his cold war with addiction.

"Rumor has it that a few major labels are coming to the show tonight."

The knocking became pounding. Gary guessed his dealer wouldn't wait much longer. And he knew that Murphy wouldn't stop talking long enough to let him answer the door.

Gary grabbed a hundred dollars from the stack and stretched the curly phone cord to its limit. He held the receiver in his left hand, reaching to open the door with his right. Murphy's voice was a muffled buzz in the background for a moment. Gary extended the money out into the hallway and came back with four plump balloons full of tar heroin. The transaction should have

S.W. LAUDEN

been done, but his dealer yelled out at the last moment.

"You want works?"

He slammed the door shut in response, squeezing the drugs in his sweaty palm. Adrenaline coursed through his veins in anticipation of the high. But first he had to get Murphy off the phone.

"Sorry about that. What were you saying?"

"Who was that?"

"At the door? Just the pizza guy."

The line went silent. Gary thought his partner had hung up.

"Murph? You there?"

"You better not be using again. Not tonight. Not ever, but especially not tonight. There's way too much riding on this show."

"Chill out. It's just pizza. You want to come over and have a slice?"

"Very funny. You know I'm in New York trying to get these kids a record deal."

"Then you'll just have to trust me. Now finish telling me about the labels."

Murphy obliged. Gary went over to a drawer in the kitchen, the phone wedged between his shoulder and ear. He pulled a spoon and lighter out, setting them down on the counter next to a syringe. The small knot in the first balloon was too tight, so he went at it with his teeth. His mouth began to water as the familiar scent reached his nose. He inserted a couple of "mm-hms" into their conversation while dropping a chunk of tar into the spoon. It took him a beat to realize that Murphy was practically screaming.

"Did you hear me?! It's all coming true. Everything you always said about punk making a comeback. And we're gonna get rich off of it."

Gary let that sink in.

"I don't need to be rich. I just don't want to be broke any more," he said.

"Take it easy. Nobody's telling you to sell out. But you've been talking about getting out of Hollywood for years. This could be your chance."

"Maybe one of these days. Not until hair metal's been completely destroyed."

Murphy laughed for the first time since he called, but was soon back to business.

"Amen to that. You got enough money to put the band up in a hotel tonight? You'll probably need to fill up the gas tank in their tour van too."

Gary looked over at the disappearing stack of cash. The gun was right there next to it, reminding him that he could always get more.

"I got it covered, Murph."

"Good. Call tomorrow and let me know how it went. Don't fuck this up."

Gary hung up, giving his full attention to what mattered most — getting well.

***

His mind was a little fuzzy that evening, but he felt okay after a long nod that veered into a nap. A hot shower and a couple of drags from the foil was all he needed to get straight. He slipped the remaining two balloons into his leather jacket, along with the gun, then stuffed a fresh pack of smokes and the rest of the cash into the other pocket.

Gary went downstairs and headed east on Hollywood Boulevard. He stopped at a convenience store a few blocks from his apartment to grab a cup of coffee and a donut for dinner. His eyes scanned the ceiling for cameras out of habit. There's no way he'd ever rob a place that brightly lit or so close to home. You don't shit in your own backyard.

He got to the club shortly after the sound check. A sign out front said the show was sold out. Gary smiled as he walked around to the artist's entrance at the back of the club. The lead singer of the band he managed was still on stage, writing out a set list. Gary called to him as he approached.

"How's it going, Kyle?"

Kyle pushed greasy brown hair from his eyes and stood up. The sweat on his forehead glistened in the spotlight. They'd only met in person a couple of times, but something about him was different. His skin looked pale, and he was impossibly thin, even for a budding rock star.

Gary frowned.

"Rough time in San Francisco last night?"

"Gig was great, but the after party got a little out of control."

"I hope you got some sleep in the van. This is a big show for you guys tonight."

"I'll be fine, I just need to ..." His voice trailed off, but Gary finished the thought in his head: *Get well.*

"Where's the rest of the band?"

"They went out to eat. Hey, got any cash for a hotel? I could use a shower."

Gary could almost hear Murphy in his head, screaming at him about giving money to a junkie right before a label showcase. But he also knew from experience that the show would probably be terrible unless he did something about it.

"Go get your stuff. I'll walk over there with you. It's right around the corner."

The place was a dump, but it wasn't cheap. This was Hollywood after all. Gary paid for two rooms and they rode up in the elevator together. Kyle leaned his head against the paneled wall and closed his eyes as the car rumbled upward. They'd almost reached their floor when Gary cleared his throat.

"You got a rig in your bag?"

Kyle didn't move, except to open his mouth. "I don't know what you're talking about, man."

"Fine. You want to keep feeling like crap, that's up to you."

The doors slid open. They walked down the hall in silence until they reached the first room. Gary slid the key in the lock, swinging the door open. Kyle slid past him and threw his backpack on one of the two beds. He pulled the curtains open to reveal LA sprawl. It was just after dusk and lights twinkled all across the basin.

Gary watched Kyle from the doorway, silhouetted in the suburban glow, the whole world spread out before him. *I wonder if he has any idea how much his things are gonna change after tonight?*

"Well, I'll let you take that shower. See you back at the club."

Gary was turning to leave when Kyle spoke up. "Yes."

"Huh?"

"I've got a rig in my bag."

Gary sighed, stepping back into the room. He shut the door behind him.

***

The tiny club was packed when the band took the

stage later that night. Screaming and applause heightened the electric waves of anticipation surging through the crowd. Gary was a little antsy since Kyle shot the last of his dope, but at least one of them would make it through the show. Besides, a few of the eager record label reps had open tabs at the bar. Gary was halfway through a free cocktail when the band finished their first song.

He leaned against the bar, watching the sweaty mass pulse in time to the thunderous drums. The guitars growled and the bass boomed while the singer hypnotized the room. Gary watched it unfold all around him, everything that he'd dreamed about since the original LA punk scene had withered and died. This wasn't the same music from ten years ago – it was heavier and more melodic – but anything was better than the vapid crap they were pedaling up on Sunset Boulevard.

Gary was waving a bartender down when the head of A&R for one of the major labels put a hand on his shoulder. His white linen sports coat and pastel T-shirt almost glowed in the darkness of the club.

"How they hell did you find these guys? They're incredible," the AR guy said.

"Lucky, I guess. Glad you're digging the show."

"We're planning to make a serious offer. We'll fax the paperwork to your partner first thing tomorrow morning."

"Great. I'll tell Murphy to look out for it."

"You two are gonna be big shot managers now. You'll have to fight the bands off with a stick. Can I buy you a drink?"

Gary had similar conversations with four other

label reps by the time the band played their encore. And every one of them bought him another drink. He might not be feeling any pain as the club cleared out, but he was beginning to jones. It would have to wait until he could share the good news with the band. Then he could slip out and page his dealer.

The easiest way to the dressing room was across the stage. He'd almost reached the door behind the drums, but turned to look at the club. It was a familiar view at another time in his life, back when he played in bands himself. Before he hocked most of his guitars for dope. He'd traded the final one for the gun in his pocket. Music is a young man's game, anyway.

Gary laughed at himself and moved on. He wound his way through the amplifiers and cymbal stands until he was in the cramped dressing room. Both guitarists had already disappeared with a couple of girls, but the singer was slouched on a ratty sofa against the graffiti-covered wall. The bassist and drummer sat on either side of him, drinking beer and smoking cigarettes. All three of them looked up like lost little puppies when Gary walked over.

"Great show! The labels loved you. I'm pretty sure you'll have a couple of record deals to choose from tomorrow."

The rhythm section exchanged high fives, but Kyle didn't budge. His eyes were busy boring into Gary's, silently pleading with him to produce another balloon. He practically leapt up when Gary reached into his jacket pocket.

"I just want to make sure you have gas money to get to your show tomorrow."

Kyle extended a shaking hand, palm up. Gary

hesitated a moment before handing over his last sixty dollars.

"Make sure you guys get some rest tonight."

He grabbed the singer by the chin, squeezing hard.

"You understand me? This is your shot. Don't blow it."

Kyle slapped Gary's hand away and stormed off.

"Whatever, man. I need to go get some smokes."

Gary told the bassist and drummer to call him when they got to San Diego the next day. They promised they would and said their goodbyes.

The club was empty as Gary passed through on his way out the front door. There was a bus stop pay phone a half block down on the right. He dropped a quarter in and punched out a familiar series of numbers. The only thing left to do was get more cash.

***

It was close to 2 a.m., so most of the liquor stores were already closed. Gary picked up the pace, taking a couple detours on his way home. He considered knocking over a popular twenty-four-hour diner, but the place was too crowded. And cops were always hanging out there at night.

There were only fifteen minutes left when he got within a couple blocks of his apartment. Gary started looking around for somebody to mug, but the only people out were hookers and junkies like him. Then he saw the convenience store he'd stopped at earlier that night. It looked like a glowing junkie's mirage.

Gary would normally hang outside for minute to make sure the place was empty, but time was tight. He reached into his jacket pocket for the ski mask, realizing too late that it wasn't there. But at least the gun was.

He cursed under his breath, pushing through the front door. The cashier recognized him immediately.

"Back so soon?"

Gary rushed to the counter, leveling his gun.

"Give me all the cash."

A look of disbelief came over the cashier's face as he brought his hands up. Gary was practically screaming now.

"Put your fucking hands down and open the register!"

He lunged closer, jabbing at the air with his gun for emphasis. The cashier did as he was told, shoving the cash into a small paper bag. That's when Gary heard a voice coming from the back of the store near the magazine rack.

"Gary?"

He spun around at the sound of his own name. Kyle was walking toward him with the latest issue of *Creem* magazine in his hands.

"What the hell are you doing?"

There was nothing Gary could say. This wasn't just some terrible coincidence; it was a God that he didn't even believe in totally screwing with him. He stepped away from the counter and lowered his gun, but Kyle froze. His eyes went wide as he focused on the cashier over Gary's shoulder.

Gary dove to the floor as the first shot echoed in the small space. He heard a groan and watched Kyle collapse. Gary sprang up and fired twice. The force of the bullets sent the cashier spinning backwards through a cardboard cigarette display.

The silence that followed was punctuated by Kyle's gurgles and gasps. Gary moved to help him, but stopped when he saw the gaping hole in his neck. A thick pool of blood spread out around his head. He fixed Gary with the same pleading look as before. Their eyes remained locked until Gary was alone in the store.

Sirens were already wailing in the distance. Gary went back to the counter to grab the cash. He shoved the gun into his jacket pocket and ran out into the electric night. It looked like he might be leaving Hollywood after all, but not until he got well.

Maybe tomorrow, he thought.

THE DEEP END

by Dietrich Kalteis

"You sure make that look like work." His words rang cool, Connie Jackson bowing over, doing justice to the hiphuggers, flipping a stone from her path, using the spade. Scrunchie holding her perm back.

The wide gate on the temporary fence hung open, enough for him to look past the muck swaths where the backhoe and dump truck had rolled across the grass. A couple of guys working inside, one guy fitting aluminum sheets, making the frame, another anchoring the stiffeners. Trying to get it done ahead of the long weekend.

"Hard on the back," she said, coming up and arching, showing the curves. Clapping muck from her gloves, she leaned the spade against the fence, stepped to the passenger side of the Riviera, its top down.

Emmett Granger reached the radio knob, Tina Turner asking "What's love got to do with it." Turning it down.

Leaning on his passenger door, Connie waited, seeing what he wanted, this guy not bad looking, with a nice car.

"Looks like you'll be cooling off pretty soon," Emmett said, pointing to where the pool was going, seeing mostly fence, but he could picture it. The Craftsman sitting on a good-sized corner lot, the hole facing the side street. Emmett guessing she was trying to rescue the yew hedge, digging it up with the spade, getting plenty of root ball.

"Just needs a pour of concrete and a pool full of water," she said. Man, that smile was something.

Emmett nodding, picturing her in a bikini, nice build with the long legs.

"Just glad there's some summer left," she said, glancing at the side yard. "Would have started sooner, but with Ed's schedule ..."

"Your husband, huh?" Emmett nodded, guessing a payout on the claim she'd filed was what they were really waiting on. One big enough to take care of the pool, walkways and the new cedar fence to boot. Emmett a senior investigator for NorthWest Lifeco. Connie off work the past two months, claiming cervical injury and something else Emmett couldn't pronounce. His boss Doris Bender sending him to get some shots. Enough to kick back the claim, maybe even charge the woman with falsifying. Doris living up to the nickname Maneater, loved nailing the cheaters. The office staff dubbing her that after that Hall and Oates song came out. Behind her back, anyway. Somebody scratching the name and a phone number on a stall in the men's room.

First thing this morning, Doris left the file with a copy of the doctor's report and CT scan, Connie Jackson seeing a physical therapist twice a week. Doris saying something about the lengths people would take, cheating their insurance. Shaking her head as she said it. Told him to get some telling shots.

"Ed's always off on a business trip," Connie was saying, her hand on his passenger door, "you know, when there's *real* work to be done."

Man, that smile ...

"Convenient, don't you think?" she said, letting him know there was a husband, letting him know he wasn't around, her eyes going to the Minolta on the passenger seat.

Picking it up by the strap, he said, "Yeah, sorry, guess I was hoping you wouldn't mind ..."

She lifted a brow.

"See, I love a good Craftsman, and yours ... Well, right out of the Sears catalog. I had to guess, I'd say about nineteen o-eight."

"O-nine, but close enough," she said, then narrowed her eyes. "Tell me you're not a tax assessor, something like that?" She checked out his ride. "But, if the neighbor's complaining again, the permit's taped to the window."

"Nothing like that," he said. "I'm a student, third year, architecture, over at Cap U. Researching styles. Was heading home," Emmett said, "and, well ... spotted yours."

"Student, huh?"

"Thinking a little old, right?" Emmett smiled back. "Story's I got tired of playing in stocks, standing watching that screen, get an ulcer by the time I'm forty." Emmett thinking he was spinning it well enough. "This is me making a career change. Better late than never."

"Nothing wrong knowing what you want."

"Saw you digging up your hedge and figured I should ask first."

Hand still on his door, she was reading him, still smiling, telling him to snap away. Standing up, she arced her back again, looking at the house. "Not like you'll steal its soul or anything."

"These old gals sure got them, a soul, I mean." Emmett grabbed the camera strap, getting out.

"Fell in love with the place, first time I saw it. Ed, not so much. Took some coaxing, but a fresh coat of paint, new roof, kitchen cupboards, second bath, the pool, he's coming around."

"Plus real estate values shooting up."

"Afraid Ed just sees a lot of work and a mortgage. Jokes how they'll be burying him out back before it gets paid." Telling him to watch where he stepped, she went to the fence, took the spade and went back to stabbing at the earth, the line of yew planted where the new walkway would go.

Emmett made like a student of architecture, clicking and cranking the winder, taking his time shooting a roll, getting the porch and posts, the portico detail, the river rock chimney, the shake roof. Feeding the leader, he wound in a fresh roll, dropping the exposed one in a pocket. The telephoto lens not much use for shooting the house, but perfect for sneaking shots of Connie Jackson. Bracketing shots of her jabbing the spade around the roots, putting her back into it.

The digital watch reminded him Ed Jackson usually came home in about an hour, giving Emmett plenty of time. Doris had attached a Post-it note to the file, warning that Ed was an easily agitated son of a bitch. A bull with no neck, going a good two-fifty, having tossed Joe Lightner, the claims adjuster, from the very porch Emmett was standing on. Joe also on disability leave, his being legit.

Emmett snapped one more of Connie grabbing

hold of a root. The phone inside rang. Connie clapping her work gloves, going past him, stamping her feet, taking her shoes off on the mat and going through the screen.

Seeing her in silhouette down the hall, phone in her hand. Connie winding the dangling phone cord round her finger. Emmett taking a shot of the rail detail, inspecting the spindles. He cranked the winder, getting the gist of the call, Ed, the husband, burning the midnight oil. Connie not happy about it, something about firing up the barbecue, the pesto and chicken she'd marinated. Taking a shot of the rock chimney when she came out, looking for something else to shoot. Knowing he had more than enough to get her workman's claim tossed.

"Got a pitcher of Kool-Aid," she said, from the other side of the screen. That smile again. "Interested?"

"Kool-Aid, huh?"

"Always liked the grape."

"Who says no to grape?"

She pushed open the screen.

Looking up at the cloudless sky, he bent and took off his shoes, following her to the kitchen.

Connie setting her work gloves on the counter, getting glasses, going to the fridge, Emmett watching the way she moved. Filling glasses, she handed him one, cold fingers touching his, Connie saying, "Could've offered you something more adult."

"This is good," he said, taking a sip, remembering the taste from when he was a kid, looking into the family room, an exercise bike and one of those rebounders.

"Sorry to keep you from your hedge."

"Been at it all day. Trust me, I could use the break."

"Could lend you a hand. I mean, if you want."

Looking past him, down the hall, saying, "Those shoes in my muck? I don't think so, but it's nice you offered.

"Think I moved enough of them." Connie telling him they were pouring the concrete tomorrow. "The pool anyway. Won't get to the walkways for another week. Plenty of time to move the rest." Looking at her half-empty glass, saying, "So, how about it?"

"What's that?"

"Something stronger?"

Setting the Minolta on the counter, he checked his watch, saying, "Guess a quick one can't hurt, thanks."

"Sunrise, White Russian, something straight?"

"Have what you're having."

His heart jumped, Emmett watching her take a bottle of tequila, one of grenadine, a couple of highball glasses, dropping in ice, pouring, topping each with OJ.

Handing him a glass, she said, "I'm Connie, by the way."

"Nice to meet you, Connie." Emmett clinked his glass against hers.

"You got one, a name?"

"Right, sorry. Emmett."

"Emmett, nice and old fashioned," she said, sipping, pointing to the wicker chairs by the fireplace in the family room.

"Yeah, my grandfather liked it. Emmett Julius Holmes is the whole thing."

"How's your drink, Emmett?"

He said it wasn't bad, thanking her again.

"From the accent I'm guessing California?"

"Toronto."

"Nobody's perfect." She smiled, going to the stacked sound system on the wall shelf, flipping a couple of switches.

Going through some LPs, choosing the new Pendergrass, putting on *Love Language*.

"Still going with the vinyl, huh?" Emmett making conversation.

"Cassettes are for the car. Vinyl's for the house. One of Ed's rules."

By the time "Hot Love" came on, Connie had let her hair down, topped up his drink, and was showing him around the place. Connie smiling, pointing out the backyard, the English garden, two-car garage off the lane. Swaying her hips, she was humming along.

Girl let's not waste time.

Connie looking at him. "So how about it?"

He looked at her.

"The real story," she said, "why you're here."

He just looked at her, part of him wanting to tell her.

Moving down the back hall, she shrugged like it didn't matter, pointing out a bedroom Ed used as a home office, IBM PC on the desk, next bedroom set up as a guest room, frilly sheets and pillows, then the master.

She opened the door, still swaying with that dreamy look, could've been the Pendergrass, could have been the tequila. A king bed, a tribal duvet covering it. Danish nightstands and dresser, a fern by the window, wallpaper border running around the room.

"Ever try it?" she said, glancing at the bed.

Second time he couldn't find words.

"Waterbed."

"Seen them, but no, never."

"Go ahead," Connie said, taking the empty glass from him, leaving him and getting him another.

Not sure what was next. Could be she was playing with him, knowing he wasn't a student. Sitting on the edge, Emmett felt the movement of the water under him, felt warm. Watching her go down the hall. A wedding photo next to a heart-shaped jewelry box, looked like it was brass.

Coming back, she handed him a fresh drink. "So, what do you think?"

"Well, if I told you that ..." Emmett looking at her, swirling his drink, taking a sip.

Taking his glass, she set it on the nightstand, sliding next to him, Emmett feeling the water slosh under them.

***

Lying next to him, she turned to him. "Store calls it the 'Wet Dream.'" She ran fingers along his arm.

"Hardly notic–"

The bang of the front door had them both jumping.

A man calling her name, saying he didn't smell no chicken.

"Oh, shit, Ed!" She shot out of bed, looking around, panicked.

Grabbing for his pants, Emmett remembering his shoes by the front door. The waterbed frame going down to the floor. Thinking the window was his best bet, pushing at the sash.

Footsteps, then Ed was filling the doorframe.

"The fuck ..." Ed didn't wait for something like 'not

what it looks like.' Cocking back his fist, he charged and threw a punch. Ducking under it, Emmett went for the door, Connie trying to stop Ed.

Shoving Connie aside, Ed swung Emmett into the dresser, knocking over the fern, a wedding photo flopping to the floor. Glass breaking.

The next punch put Emmett on the shag rug. Planting his knees, Ed pinned Emmett's arms, slamming his fist down. Rage in his eyes.

Not sure how many times he'd been hit, Emmett hearing Connie yell, feeling Ed wrap his fingers, digging them into his throat, squeezing, lifting and slamming his head down.

Clawing at the grip, Emmett thinking this was it. Then Ed's grip relaxed, his eyes rolled up and he slumped on top of Emmett. Sucking in air, Emmett pushed the big man off.

Connie dropped the jewelry box, necklaces and chains spilling out. Her hand over her mouth, tears in her eyes.

Emmett got his feet under him, hand at his throat, tongue going around the inside of his mouth, tasting blood, his bottom lip split.

Ed lying there, blood staining the shag.

"Where's your phone?"

She blinked tears at him, shook her head.

Emmett bent down, took Ed's wrist, feeling for a pulse. "Needs an–" Emmett looked at blood dripping from the gash, the man dying, wedding photo of the happy couple next to him.

"Would've killed you." Connie wiping away tears.

Looking up at her, he checked for a pulse again, shaking his head. She walked from the room, Emmett thinking she was making the call. Couldn't have the man looking at him like that, the rage gone from his eyes, Ed looking like he was surprised. Emmett closed the eyes. Blood puddled on the rug.

Connie came back, ice clinking in two glasses, handing him one. Emmett taking it, his hand shaking.

"They coming?" Emmett drained the glass it in a swallow, thinking his stomach was going to heave it back.

"We'll roll him in it." Connie sounding composed now, tapping a foot on the rug.

Draining the glass, Emmett felt the burn down to his stomach, trying to think.

"You need another?" Connie reaching for his glass.

Emmett shook his head.

"Drive home, Emmett. Come back tonight, say nine, but leave your car a block over, come in through the back."

Giving her a look.

"You drive his car, put it in long-term at the airport."

"Can't just ..." Emmett looked at the body.

"We have to." Her eyes serious, Connie telling him to go to the bathroom, clean up his face, pull himself together.

***

Textbook workmans' comp case. Connie Jackson claiming a severe back injury suffered at work, lifting file boxes weighing significantly less than her yew hedge. The folder on Emmett's desk held the claim, the medical reports and x-rays. Would have held the 35 mm shots he was sent to shoot, the two exposed rolls from the Minolta under Connie's yew hedge. Emmett digging the hole at the deep end, next to the drain, the two of them dragging Ed out, rolled in the shag rug, flopping him in, smoothing the ground after, the concrete poured the next day. Curing now, weeks until the final inspection, the pool filling with water, the chemicals added.

"Grainger?"

He nearly jumped from his chair.

Doris Bender stood in his doorway, that sour look on the Maneater's face, saying, "What happened to you?"

"Took a tumble jogging, crack in the sidewalk hooked my shoe, you believe it?"

Doris shaking her head, telling him he ought to be more careful.

"Worse than it looks." Connie did a good job with the makeup, hiding most of it. The turtleneck covering the bruises on his neck. "So, what's up, Doris?" Smiling at the assistant department head.

"You got my message, right?"

"Which one's that?"

Her nostrils gave a bit of a flare, Doris pushing her glasses up her nose. "Left it right there." Pointing to his desk.

Emmett smiling, saying, "You want to tell me, or write another one?"

"Said we're dropping the Jackson case."

"Yeah?" He sat up straight. "This about the shots? I can go try again."

"Comes from the top. The Jacksons just filed a misconduct case against Lightner."

He couldn't believe it.

"Claiming he acted inappropriate," Doris clearing

her throat, "with the missus."

"Mrs. Jackson?"

"Allegedly."

"Huh."

"Against Lightner in the loafers, if you can imagine," she said, looking like she enjoyed it.

Emmett leaned back, having to smile.

"This is serious, Grainger." She went on, saying Mrs. Jackson just reported her husband missing. Apparently went to see Lightner, couldn't let it go, and never came back. The cops asking questions, found Jackson's car in long-term parking, possible foul play."

"And they think Lightner — "

"They're not saying. Ask me, Ed Jackson just ran off. It's what they do." She glanced out the window, then, "Anyway, upstairs wants the whole mess dropped, settling this one out."

He pushed the file across the desk. "Case closed then."

"They're out there, Grainger, the cheaters." Shaking her head, she turned for the door, telling him to put it where he got it. "Give you something to do." She turned for the door. "Another one on my desk. Auto accident, whiplash, a real winner. Guy spotted at his jazzercise class," Doris said from the hall. "And get some shots this time."

"Right."

"And Grainger?"

"Yuh?"

"Check your messages." Her heels clicked down the hall.

"Jawohl," he said, waiting, then picking up the phone, pushing a button, getting a clear line. Picturing

Connie by her pool, sipping tequila in her bikini, lubed in Coppertone, getting brown. Wanting to stop by after work.Connie answering, sounding glad he called. "Doing anything?"

"Talking to my lawyer."

"Yeah, just heard, nice touch."

"Thought so."

"Want to see you." Emmett knowing they had to wait.

"Me too, but ..."

"Stop by my place, grab my trunks."

"Won't need them."

"Won't, huh?"

"Rub on some lotion, places I can't reach."

"Yeah."

"Four weeks. You can pick up a bottle on your way, something with bubbles."

"Four weeks, huh?"

Hanging up, Emmett guessed he'd need more than something with bubbles to steady his nerves, seeing himself going off the diving board, cutting through the water, feeling the cool close around him, swimming to the bottom with his eyes open, looking at the drain cover, remembering the look when he closed Ed's eyes.

PARTS UNKNOWN

by Sam Wiebe

The guy who trained me used to say there's only two things real in this business: the money and the miles. I already had the miles, long before I arrived in New York to work the Garden. For the last year I'd been in the Georgia territory, Portland before that. Trips to Japan, England, Germany. In Mexico, I'm known as Corazon de Tigre; in Montreal, le Maître de Lutte. If your town has a veteran's hall or bingo parlor that runs wrestling, chances are I've lost in it.

Losing is my business, losing and making the other guy look good. We call it doing the job. You put the other guy over right, you make him more of a draw in his territory. There's an art to it.

Of course, nobody goes in thinking they'll end up a jobber for life. When I broke into the business up in Seattle, I was in a tag team that held the belts for almost six months. Jose and I headlined shows, drew money. Not big money, but we packed those three-hundred-seat venues, from Vancouver to Spokane.

For most of my career I've been what's called a mechanic. A good hand in the ring, technically sound, capable of working any style from lucha to catch to straight-up brawling. I can go twenty minutes with anyone, and with a halfway decent opponent I can give you something special. One match I had with the

Dynamite Kid up in Calgary, we tore the house down. Afterwards, all the boys in the locker room wanted to shake my hand. That entire summer I drank for free.

A few years in, I caught a bad break, working down in Texas. I was curtain jerking with the promoter's nephew, a good kid, but green as goose shit. Naturally the promoter wanted me to make him look like a million bucks. We worked out this spot where I dove out of the ring, and the kid was supposed to catch me, slam me on the concrete, and roll me back in for the one-two-three. What power! What brutality! Nothing I hadn't done before.

But the nephew was nervous, got out of position, two steps too far from the ring. I tried to adjust, but not much I could do in midair. I ended up hitting the steel barrier that keeps the audience back. The way I landed, I could feel my knee blow out, and pain poured from between my ribs where the steel caught me.

The funny part? As I was laying there, a guy in the front row leaned over and stubbed his cigar out on my shoulder blade. He yelled, "Get up you phony, get up you fucking fake."

Since then I've needed the knee brace, and I've been doing the same job every night. Hundred bucks a show when I'm lucky, sometimes forty, or ten, or a shrug from the promoter if it's an empty house.

So it happened I was in Red Hook for an afternoon show when I ran into my old tag partner Jose. Turned out he was working the New York territory, by far the biggest in the country, and they had a show that night in Newark. There was a thirty-man over-the-top-rope battle royale, and they could use a few more bodies. Paid a hundred and fifty bucks. Did I want the job?

Hell yeah I want it.

That night, I was the first to be eliminated, tossed out by the Giant in under a minute. He picked me up one-handed, somersaulted me over the ropes to the concrete. If you take it right, land flat on your back, it spreads the impact out somewhat. Still hurts like hell though.

The bump to the outside must have impressed someone, because the booker asked could I do the same spot again, the next night, at the Garden?

The Garden. The one place I've never worked. I've been in it, though, as a fan, the night Ivan Koloff took the belt off Bruno, and I was there a month later to watch the Russian Bear lose to Pedro Morales. And so now here I am, getting ready to work there.

I drive into New York, get to the Garden four hours early. The head of security tells me my name's not on his list, he can't let me inside. I wait forty minutes till the booker arrives and straightens things out.

But then I'm in.

I discover pretty quickly that the Garden is a venue like any other. It doesn't even have as much history as you'd think, since the original Garden is long gone. Walking the dirty, narrow halls, seeing how much smaller it is than on TV, part of me is disappointed.

The other part is ecstatic, because this is the place. Everyone who laces up a pair of wrestling boots wants to be here tonight, on this card. Hogan. Tito. The Junkyard Dog. Wendi Richter and Sherri Martel. And I'm in the opening match, doing the job for the Giant.

As I walk the halls and the others arrive, it starts to feel real. I see a guy in his forties flexing his biceps for a couple of girls who might be eighteen. I see the Iranian in a supply closet, smoking a cigar-sized hand-rolled of the harshest dope I've ever smelled. I see a French Canadian gently nuzzle the neck of another wrestler, both wearing blue-sequined warm up jackets. None of which is new to me, but it's the Garden, and I'm here, walking among the gods of my business.

I look in every door, try to meet everyone. I grab two meals at catering. This could be my only chance to be here.

There are private dressing rooms for the stars, each with their name printed on a card taped to the door. Most of them haven't arrived yet, so the doors are unlocked and I can walk around the rooms. It hurts to think about, but I can't help it—one less bad bump and my name might be on one of those doors.

There's one locked dressing room, no name on it. My first lap around the building I try the handle and keep walking. The second time though, I knock. I wait a minute to see if anyone will open it. No one does. I start walking, and as I start, the handle turns.

In the doorway is the most beautiful woman I've ever seen, and she looks frightened out of her mind.

She scans the hallway timidly. Once she sees me, she draws the door closed, till all I can see of her is one blue eye, a tangle of hair, three scarlet-tipped fingers pushing against the jamb.

"I'm sorry," she says, faint trace of a Georgia accent. "I thought you were someone else."

"Are you okay, ma'am?" I hope I sound chivalrous. Since my wife decided she preferred Portland to the road, my only companions have been girls from bars. I haven't met many ladies, let alone conversed with them.

"I'm all right," she answers, but her lashes flutter down to shroud her eyes. There's something she wants to say but doesn't feel she can.

"Can I help you at all?" I ask. "With anything. It's really no trouble."

"I'm okay, I'm just ..." For a moment she seems to consider closing the door. Then, for some reason I can't comprehend, she decides I'm not a threat, that I might be able to help her.

I don't know what her problems are, but I'll try to solve them all if she asks me to.

"I mean it," I say. "Anything I can do, Miss —"

"Cynthia," she answers. "Thank you."

She lets me in.

I notice two things about the dressing room. One, it's a wrestler's room, and one of the top guys, because who else would have a private space? And two, it's neat and decorated like no dressing room I've seen. Flowers, framed photos, the costumes and dresses hung up in dry-cleaning bags. That tells me something about the standards of the woman who stays there, and it tells me she expects to be there for a long while.

She has an electric kettle. She offers me a cup of tea. "Sorry I don't have milk and sugar," she says. She pronounces it 'sugah.' When I say we could grab some from catering, she says it's all right, black is fine with her. With me as well.

We talk. I expect her to come around to her problem. Instead we converse about other things. Airports, waffle houses, getting sick, hitchhiking in Canada. As she talks, she teases out her story, hinting at what she's allowed to do, when, and what and when she can't.

Erik, the man she married, is a good man. She stresses this more than once. He gets angry, sure, but never violent, not to her. But he is possessive. Jealous. Erik doesn't trust anyone, least of all other wrestlers.

It hits me she's talking about Erik the Red. I've heard the name. We broke in around the same time, and for a few years we were both considered top prospects. Now he's an upper-mid-carder in the New York territory. Not a star like Hogan, not yet, but clearly on his way up. And I'm in his dressing room, talking to his woman, sipping his Black Darjeeling.

Erik doesn't trust Cynthia to stay by herself at home. He says it's for her safety. So Cynthia travels with him, stays in his dressing room or hotel, speaks to no one, sees nothing of the towns.

"I don't even know where we are tonight," she tells me. When I say New York, the Garden, she looks at the off-white ceiling and nods at its familiarity. "Of course," she says.

Right now Erik is at a radio station, doing an interview to promote tonight's show. He's in the semi-main, wrestling King Kong Bundy. We've got three hours till show time, two hours till she expects her husband back. A hundred and twenty minutes to do whatever she wants.

I shouldn't get involved and I know it. Erik's much higher up the card than I am. I tell myself Cynthia's not asking me to cross him, to help her run away. Everyone else in the company is afraid, she says. All she wants is to talk to someone for a little while.

I tell her we can get out of here, go for a walk, grab a bite, a drink. We could stay in. Or go out only for a little while—I could make sure she's back before Erik returns.

She decides she wants to stay in.

She has a radio. She puts on soft country music, Tammy Wynette. All real innocent, just us hanging out, and would I like more tea? Her head falls to my shoulder as "Forever and Ever, Amen" comes on. Randy Travis. "I love this song," she says.

And then that innocence is gone, evaporated, and she's in my lap. She's uncaged, warm, taking control. I feel her lips on my cheek, her teeth seize my earlobe.

It's a small dressing room, but there's a bed, and we make use of it. We make use of the shower too. Her hands work the knots of soreness out of my shoulders. She kisses and purrs. For one hour I forget my wretched life and imagine I belong here. The dressing room, the Garden, the woman. All mine.

I'm lovestruck—well, struck by *something*—but I can tell I should get going, while there's still a good forty minutes before Erik is due back. We're lying on the bed, both without a stitch on. I'm considering how best to occupy those last minutes, and that's when I hear the knocks.

Four loud beats on the door, then the jiggling of the handle. I'm thankful we remembered to lock the door. The pounding increases. "Cynthia." That famous voice, each syllable its own separate stab. "Cynthia, open up."

She's sitting on the edge of the bed. "What do we do?" I ask.

Instead of answering, she sits up, swings her legs down and, naked, walks to the door. I'm about to protest when she throws back the bolt. I'm groping for my socks when he barges past her.

There's yelling and hitting, and I can't remember

which comes first. I think he kicks me before asking what the hell is going on and why the hell I'm in here. He's in his full outfit—Erik the Red, fur-lined trunks and vest, long red hair and beard running wild.

Before the kick lands, I brace myself the way you do in the ring when someone's going for a stiff chop. Half-thinking it's a work, that it's pretend. By the third kick, when my ribs are broken, I'm convinced he's not holding back.

Maybe it's shock and maybe it's guilt, but I take the ass-whupping without fighting back. Not even when he throws the table at me. I feel a Howitzer go off in my skull, and then he's pulling the broken halves of the table off me, clearing the way to throw punches and knees.

As I ball up to protect myself, I catch a glimpse of Cynthia, standing in the far corner of the room. She's slowly pulling on her dress, observing me with a scientist's calm.

When Erik is out of breath, he pauses, then calls for security to get this piece of trash out of his dressing room. The guards enter and obey. As they drag me along, I realize something: it's not shock or guilt that kept me from fighting back. It's seniority. He's top of the card, and weird as it sounds, hurting him would be unprofessional.

My skull cracks against the doorframe as I'm dragged outside. Security asks if I want an ambulance called. I tell them I don't have that kind of money.

What feels like an hour goes by. I've propped myself up by the loading bay doors. That's where Jose finds me.

"Hell happened to you?" he asks.

I tell him the story as he cleans me up. By the end, he's laughing at me. "Shit," Jose says, "and you fell for it? Well, you're not the first, but I thought you were smarter than *that*."

He tells me it's Erik and Cynthia's thing. They've been doing it since the Memphis territory. Seeing her with another man turns him on, while she gets off watching him break bones. Anyone in the locker room could've told me not to knock on that door.

The good news is, other than the nose and the left cheek, there's not a lot of blood. I can stand on my own. Breathing hurts, but I can manage it.

"Guess you'll know better next time," Jose says. He checks his watch. All the New York boys have fancy watches. "Time I get ready," he says, making like he has to go. "Can I call someone for you? Taxi cab, maybe?"

I tell him no, just help me to the dressing room.

"You don't mean—shit—you're not going back in there?"

"Far as I know I ain't fired."

"But your ribs," he says. "Your nose."

I could tell him I've worked hurt before, with worse injuries than this. Could say I need the money. Could even tell him the truth: that it's the Garden, and I won't give this up, no matter how much my head's pounding, how my vision isn't right.

But I don't have to tell Jose. He knows what it means to me. Together we convince the security guard that I'm no threat. I'll wrestle the opening match and be gone before Erik leaves his dressing room.

I change into my gear, then walk-limp to the curtain. I can hear the crowd on the other side. Near me

67

are the other entrants in the battle royale. I've worked
with most of them. It's clear from their expressions that
my story's already made its rounds. Normally they'd
be joking with me. Tonight though, there's a distance,
but also, maybe, a touch of respect. Everyone's worked
hurt before, and seeing someone ready to perform
despite their injuries reminds the rest of us we're part
of something special.

I see the Giant lumber up, still clutching a wine
bottle. Even his massive head does a double take when
he sees me.

"Same spot as last night, boss?" I ask him.

He nods and smiles, says something I don't catch. I
can hear the crowd on the other side of the curtain, a
teeming, echoing, many-mouthed scream, growing
louder, waiting for the show we're about to put on.

For a second, I let myself close my eyes and take it
in.

It's possible I'm bleeding out on the loading bay,
that that sound is a siren, that the light behind the
curtain is, well, the light behind the curtain. It's
possible, but I don't believe it. This is my moment, my
night in the Garden. Real or not, this is what I'm doing
forever.

BESTIES & BLOW

by Sarah M. Chen

"I can't believe you didn't buy tickets," I said, shifting my weight from one foot to the other. I should have expected this from Tiffany, dumbass that she is. But, like, *seriously*? The Oingo Boingo show at the Greek Theater tomorrow was totally sold out. I'd flown all the way back home to L.A. from New York because Tiffany wanted me to. Oh and because Danny Elfman is, like, totally fucking hot.

"I didn't think it'd sell out," Tiffany whined. We were standing outside Amanda's Bel Air mansion on the circular driveway in front of the concrete water fountain. While a party raged inside, the Bangles' "Walk Like an Egyptian" blasted through wide-open windows. "And there's something I didn't tell you."

"You mean besides the fact that you didn't get us tickets?"

Tiffany said in a low voice, "Amanda and Zachary are, like, a *thing* now." Her gaze shifted to something behind me.

I whirled around to see Amanda Bennett, my former best friend, and Zachary, my ex-boyfriend, walking arm in arm toward us. I sucked in my breath.

Zachary and I had a totally toxic relationship. He dumped me when I left for NYU last year. The guy would be super sweet one minute, then ignore me for days. But I put up with it because he was totally babe-alicious. We were the best-looking couple at Fairfax High. Plus I have a tendency to like the bad boys.

And boy was he *bad*. Or at least he thought he was. He always had one scam or another going. But they were dumb scams. Like the time he sold copies of the AP History exam but didn't bother to check that it was the right one. Thirty-two juniors were furious after shelling out fifty bucks to Zachary for last year's test.

I always knew when he was cooking up another scheme because he'd get this smug look on his face. I called it his Gordon Gekko look. Greed is good, motherfucker, he'd say.

"Aaaand she's back," Amanda said, eyeing me up and down. Big dangly gold earrings caught the bright light emanating from her house. Her lips shined with sparkly gloss, and I got a whiff of clove cigarettes.

Zachary still made my breath catch in my throat with his button-down shirt, black tapered pants, and suede leopard-print Creepers. Like, *total* hottie.

"Hey, Pia," Zachary said with that sly grin. *Omigod, there it was. Totally Gordon Gekko.* I wondered if Amanda was wise to it. "You look great," he added with a wink.

"Hey," I said, ignoring the cartwheels in my stomach. I tried to come up with something clever to say, something to show that I didn't want to jump his bones, but all I could come up with was, "Thanks."

"You going to the concert tomorrow night?" Amanda asked.

"It's gonna be totally rad," Zachary added. Oingo Boingo was his favorite band ever.

Tiffany glanced at me. I sighed. "Not unless you have extra tickets," I said.

"Sorry, Pia, just got two tickets for me and my baby here." She squeezed Zachary's butt. He flinched. I glared. Amanda pulled out a small vial that dangled from a thin gold chain around her neck. She unscrewed the top, shoveling out as much coke as she could on the little spoon. She snorted it up one nostril and frowned. "This goddamn blow sucks." She yanked the chain from around her neck. "Total baby powder shit."

I was surprised. Amanda always had the best blow. Stuff that made you feel like you just cleaned out your insides with diesel fuel. We used to do it at her house every day before school — and after school too. Yeah, so what? I mean, I needed it to get through the day. Like, who didn't? But I wasn't Amanda, who sent her drug dealer Christmas presents.

"What happened to your guy?" I struggled to recall his name.

"Constan," Amanda said, rolling her eyes. "If you bought your own coke instead of mooching off me all these years, maybe you'd remember his name."

I smiled. "But that's what everyone uses you for, Amanda. It's certainly not your fun personality."

She shot me an evil look, which was pretty much how she always looked at me since I was voted prom queen over her. *Like get over it already, bitch.* She didn't. Instead, she'd keyed my brand new convertible Rabbit. I had no proof, but I knew it was her. And she called my parents in the middle of the night and told them I was a slut and fucking the Driver's Ed teacher, Mr. Oberle. And now she was dating my ex-boyfriend.

Amanda finally broke our stare down and tossed her curly hair behind one shoulder. "Well, anyway, there's no good blow in Hollywood right now. The

LAPD just did a major bust, took down all the major players. Constan said everyone's laying low 'til the heat's off. How do you not know all this, Pia? Oh, duh." Amanda slapped the side of her head. "I forgot, you're a *nobody*."

I felt my face flush red. "I've been in New York for the past year, doing something besides snorting all my daddy's money up my nose." I did my share of blow at NYU, but like, no way was I telling her that.

She rolled her eyes. "Oh puh-*leaze*. You were a nobody long before you ran off to the other side of the country."

"Then how come I can get the best cocaine, no problem?" It just came out. Like I had no control over my mouth. That happened a lot.

I had everyone's attention now. Amanda and Zachary looked like I'd just announced Duran Duran would arrive any minute to perform a free show. Tiffany's brow wrinkled up like she was trying to think but not having much luck.

"Like tonight?" Amanda looked skeptical.

"Yup." I nodded, feeling sweat trickling down my temple.

"Who?" Zachary asked, suspicion clouding his face.

"I'm not telling you," I said.

Amanda smirked. "Because you're lying."

"No, I'm not," I said. "It's, like, totally primo stuff." I could sense Tiffany's stare but refused to look at her. I was doing this. "If I bring you an eight-ball, then how about I get your tickets to Oingo Boingo?" I knew Amanda had front-row seats, probably the pit. Only the best for my former bestie.

It was as if everyone sucked in their breath at the same time. All eyes on Amanda. I couldn't tell if it was the bump she just did or the anticipation of an eight ball, but her teeth clenched so tight the tendons in her neck flared out like an iguana.

"If the coke is as good as you say, then the tickets are yours," she said. "I want it by tonight though. Before my party's over."

I swallowed. *Omigod, like, there was no way.* "No problem. How's three a.m.?"

"Deal." Amanda stuck out her hand.

I shook it. Her hand was damp with sweat. Or maybe it was mine.

***

"Why are we leaving, Pia? That totally hot babe, Todd, was so into me," Tiffany whined as I dragged her by the arm to my Rabbit parked in the street in front of Amanda's mansion.

"Only 'cause he knows what a total slut you are," I said.

She gasped. "Omigod, I'm so sure."

We climbed into my car, and Tiffany turned on the radio. Terence Trent D'Arby's "Wishing Well" blasted from the speakers. She squealed and cranked it up. I turned it off.

"Hey, I love that song," she said.

"Forget the song. What am I going to do?" I looked at her. Her forehead wrinkled. She had no clue what I was talking about. Big surprise.

She studied me with her blue eyes until realization dawned. "Oh! You mean the coke? Like, I had no idea you even knew where to get good blow. But you saved us, Pia. We're going to see Danny Elfman!" She bounced around in her seat like a five-year-old.

"That's just it, I don't know where to get good blow. Or *any* blow, actually."

She stopped bouncing and looked at me. "What do you mean?"

"I made it up."

"But why would you make something like that up?"

I wanted to whack Tiffany in the head with my giant Dooney & Bourke purse. "It just came out, okay? Now I have to get it. I'll look like a complete dweeb otherwise. Amanda will laugh at me for the rest of my life." *Omigod, would I be around that backstabbing, blood-sucking whore for the rest of my life?* The thought made me seriously want to kill myself.

"You mean we may not be going to the Oingo Boingo show?"

I ignored her. "You've got to know someone, Tiffany. Think." Which I knew was asking a lot.

Tiffany chewed on her cuticles. She shrugged. "All I know is Constan."

"Yeah, me too." I sighed. We had to start somewhere. Hopefully I remembered where Amanda's drug dealer lived.

***

When the door opened, revealing a bald dude with coffee-colored skin who was built like the Terminator, I thought maybe I remembered wrong. The Constan I met a year ago was short, scrawny, and pasty.

"You're not Constan," I said.

The Terminator glared at me. "You're goddamn right I'm not that motherfucking snitch." He stared me up and down, then did the same to Tiffany. "What do you bitches want?"

"We want to talk to Constan." I heard a car engine rumble behind me.

The Terminator watched it cruise by with a scowl on his face. He stepped back and waved us inside. "Get in."

Tiffany and I looked at each other. The last thing I wanted to do was be in the house with this freak, but I had a feeling we had no choice.

"Sit." He pointed to a dirty couch in the middle of the filthy living room and we sat. Discarded fast food wrappers and empty pizza boxes littered the coffee table, spilling onto the stained brown carpet. It reeked of pot and piss.

It also appeared as if someone had torn through everything looking for something. The couch cushions were ripped apart, foam sticking out of them. Random gouges were hacked into the drywall.

The Terminator peered out of the curtain that covered the big living room window.

"What's going on?" I asked.

He marched over and hovered above me. He smelled like sausage and onions. "That's what I'd like to know," he said. "You the new partner Constan told me about?"

I shook my head. No wasting time. "No, I'm here for some blow." I noticed Tiffany giving the guy goo-goo eyes and arching her back, pushing her boobs out. Christ. The girl was a walking libido.

The Terminator chuckled this freaky laugh that reminded me of a cartoon villain, going "mwah mwah mwah mwah." When he finally stopped, he said, "Yeah? Funny, I'm here for the same thing." The big dude clenched his fists. His muscles bulged and got all veiny.

I gestured to the vandalized living room. "Is that what you were looking for?"

"Place was like this when I got here." I must have looked skeptical because he glowered at me. "You know who I am, bitch?"

I shrugged and looked at Tiffany. She giggled and said, "A total hottie?"

Oh for the love of God. Sure, he had these gold-flecked green eyes that, yeah, I had to admit, were gorgeous, but everything else about him was, like, totally fucking scary. He had on a wife-beater shirt with tats up and down his arms and chest. His biceps were bigger than my head.

Dude didn't seem to know what to make of Tiffany's comment. He must have decided that she wasn't joking around because he broke out into this, like, totally goofy grin. He pointed at her with a finger that had this giant gold ring on it.

"You're a cool chick. I'm Reese."

Tiffany giggled again. "I'm Tiffany." She uncrossed and re-crossed her legs just enough to give him a good view up her skirt. She never wore panties.

It was like watching *Love Connection.* All we needed was Chuck Woolery to announce the location of their date.

"So, like, where's Constan?" I asked.

Reese finally tore his eyes away from Tiffany's tits and scowled at me. "You think if I knew that, I'd be sittin' here with my thumb up my ass for two days?"

"Two *days?*" I figured he'd been here for, like, two hours.

"Yeah, two fucking days. The cops released me on Wednesday, and when I got home all my blow was gone."

"Maybe the cops, like, confiscated it," I offered.

He shook his head. "No way. I hid that shit good. Cops popped me for pills, weed, some guns they found. Big whoop." Reese's upper lip curled. "No, that motherfucking rat Constan is the only one who would know where to look, and who's dumb enough to take it."

I stood up. No coke here. We were wasting time. "Well, thanks for the chat, but we gotta go." I nudged Tiffany. The bitch full-on ignored me.

Reese wasn't having it anyway. "Sit the fuck down. You're not going anywhere. Not until Constan comes back."

I swallowed. "But you've been here for two days already. What if he never comes back? He probably knows you're looking for him."

"What if you know where he is and you're going to go warn him, huh?" He inched closer to me. "I think you're lying about being his partner."

"Look, we just came here to buy coke. If you don't know where we can get it, then we'll just get outta your way—"

"Sit!" He pointed back down to the couch.

No way was I sitting back down. "I gotta pee," I said.

He seemed to mull that over, then pointed to the back of the hallway. "Make it quick. No funny stuff."

I glanced at Tiffany and raised my eyebrows as in "you wanna come with?" She hesitated, looked back and forth between Reese and me, then shook her head.

Suit yourself, slut. I slung my purse over my shoulder and scurried to the bathroom as I heard Tiffany's high-pitched giggle.

The first thing I checked was the bathroom window. Like if I could crawl out of it. No luck. It was super tiny and high up. Unless I found a ladder and steam-rolled myself, I was never squeezing through.

"Shit." I yanked my panties down and squatted on the toilet seat, then thought better and hovered directly over it instead. The bathroom was totally disgusting. Like, layers of black mildew on top of green stuff that I didn't even want to try to identify.

I thought about what to do while my thighs burned from crouching. I had no idea how I'd get Tiffany to leave now that she had a cock practically waving in her face. *Fuck her. Danny Elfman was my priority right now.*

After I peed, I reached for the toilet paper and ended up grabbing the cardboard roll. A sliver of toilet paper dangled, mocking me.

"Figures," I muttered. I crab-crawled over to the sink, my panties stretched across my knees, and opened the cabinet underneath. Nothing but various bathroom cleaners, which obviously Constan never used and, like, twenty boxes of Kleenex. *Bingo.*

I reached for a box and almost dropped it. It weighed more than a book. That had to be some thick Kleenex. I noticed the perforated piece, the one you rip out to open a new box, was just sitting on top, like someone had opened it and stuck it back on. I threw the top off, unveiling something inside that wasn't facial tissue. It looked like plastic wrap and duct tape. I ripped the box to shreds, which was pretty easy because it was, like, poorly Scotch-taped together.

Suddenly I was staring at a kilo of cocaine, at least.

I grinned, my heart hammering in my chest. I was tempted to test it out right there but didn't have time. I stuffed the brick of coke in my purse and wanted to grab the rest of the boxes, but no way would I be able to carry them all. I grabbed a second box, then heard a high-pitched shriek. *Tiffany.*

I wondered if he was hacking her up into little pieces. I kind of didn't give a shit. I just wanted to get out of there with the blow. I crept down the hallway and noticed that they'd dimmed the lights. How romantic. I heard moaning but didn't see anyone. They must be lying on the couch, fucking their brains out. Tiffany's shriek confirmed it. It wasn't a "Help me, I'm being murdered!" shriek but an "Oh yeah baby, keep doing *that!*" shriek. I'd been around Tiffany long enough to know what fucking her brains out sounds like. Not that I'd heard her being murdered. Not yet, at least.

I tiptoed to the kitchen and noticed all the drawers were flung open, the cabinets too. I found the back sliding door and snuck outside, careful not to make any noise. The backyard was tiny with weeds growing through the cracked concrete. I took off my heels and ran around the house to the side.

I turned the corner and stopped. The narrow walkway to the side gate was covered in a layer of dead leaves, like, five inches thick. Guess Constan didn't do much yard work either. I made sure to step carefully, as I didn't want the crunching leaves to alert the two horndogs inside. The side window to the living room was wide open. Tiffany's shrieking told me they were still going at it.

Crunch, crunch.

I was about to say "screw it" and charge the rest of the way through when I tripped and almost face-planted into the leaves. My Kleenex fell and I reached to pick it up. Instead of the cardboard box, I felt something gross and stiff. I screeched and immediately clamped my hand over my mouth. Luckily, Reese was now yelling, "Oh! Oh! Oh!" so they probably didn't hear me.

I kicked at the leaves, revealing a pale hand, then a hairy arm. *Omigod, it was, like, a person.* I scattered more leaves with my foot until a face appeared. It was Constan. Despite his head being bashed in on one side and dried blood everywhere, it was definitely him.

I squealed and hurdled over Constan's head, praying I wouldn't land on the rest of his obviously dead body, then sprinted through the gate. I leaped into my Rabbit, turned the engine over with shaking hands, and peeled out of there as fast as I could. That was, like, totally the grossest thing ever. Even grosser than seeing Mr. Oberle make out with Cindy Moorehouse in the school gym last year.

***

"I said, hot *damn!*" Amanda screamed as she threw her head back and snorted.

We were in her room with the brick of cocaine. I'd left the second box of Kleenex tucked underneath my passenger seat. Amanda had sliced open the plastic wrap with her sterling silver letter opener. It was, like, seriously, the best shit ever. My body pulsed with energy and my brain felt like it had been electrocuted. I couldn't tell if it was from the coke or from seeing Constan's mangled face over and over in my head.

"Omigod, we're totally going to have the best fucking time at the show," I said as I dipped my pinkie nail into the coke and snorted it up my right nostril. The fact that I'd arrived over an hour late didn't even matter. We were at the peak of that cocaine high, where everything is totally awesome and you just want to chatter as fast as you can about all the fun shit you're going to do together because you're, like, *total besties.*

I fanned myself by pulling my shirt away from my chest over and over. My hands were clammy and my teeth ached. I rubbed some coke on my gums until they were numb.

Amanda giggled. "We got front row seats, of course." She spoke in a staccato rhythm.

"That's so fucking awesome." I felt the bitter taste in the back of my mouth and snorted again, feeling the coke drip down my throat. I wanted to tell Amanda about Constan, but then she'd know where I got the blow. *But was that such a big deal?* I wasn't sure yet. My mind was a frenzied mess of thoughts and tingly sensations. I didn't feel like sorting them out yet. I just wanted more blow.

Amanda covered her letter opener in coke and hoovered the entire line up her nose. She threw her head back and snorted hard. "I've missed doing blow with you 'til dawn, Pia." She handed me the letter opener.

"Omigod, I know." I meant it too. Nobody in New York wanted to talk to me about all the shit Amanda and I always talked about when we were coked up. Like surfer dudes and how fucking hot Rob Lowe was and how, like, totally awesome it was when Sean Penn and Madonna got married. I dipped the letter opener into the coke, plugged my left nostril, and snorted a big fat bump. *Fuckin' A!*

"What are you two doing?"

We both whirled around to see Zachary in the doorway. When he realized we were snorting lines, his eyes practically bugged out of his head.

"Hi, babe," Amanda said cheerily. "Look what Pia brought me." She held up the brick of coke. "Totally righteous shit too, just like she said."

"Where the fuck did you get that?" Zachary spat out.

"Take a chill pill, dude." Amanda laughed at him.

"Have a bump." I held out the letter opener, now coated with white residue, toward him.

He didn't even look at it, just kept staring at me. "Where did you get this?" he repeated through gritted teeth.

"She won't tell me," Amanda said. She looked at me. "Come on, spill, Pia. Where'd you get it?"

"From Constan." I blurted it out because I couldn't take it anymore. It was probably the coke too. Made me fucking ballsy. My head was going to explode from keeping my secret.

Both their mouths fell open. Amanda had that bitchy jealous look, the same one she had when she found out I was voted prom queen. "But ... but that's *impossible*. Why would he sell me that baby powder shit?" she stammered.

I ignored her. I was totally transfixed by Zachary's reaction. It was like disbelief and shock. His entire body went rigid. Then his gorgeous lips, like, pinched together until they were all white, and his eyes flat lined into these little slits as he glared at me.

"That's impossible," he said. He barely opened his mouth to say it and it came out, like, "thatsumpuzzable."

Amanda looked at him. "Right, babe? Constan would never lie to me. He told me he was laying low. I don't know why he'd sell to *you*, Pia."

I wasn't listening. The way Zachary was staring at me, those hollow eyes, made me shiver despite the layer of sweat coating my skin.

I'd seen that look before, when Tanya Burkowitz showed Zachary her Benadryl tablet and how it was just like the Ecstasy he'd sold her. She threatened to blab to the entire school, but then Zachary got this deranged look where his eyes went dead and suddenly he smashed her face into her locker. Wham!

I moved to leap off the bed but it was too late. Zachary grabbed my arm and squeezed. "Where's the rest of it, bitch? That's my fucking blow!"

Amanda screamed and scuttled away from us to the hallway.

I yelped and tried to pull my arm away, but this, like, inhuman growl exploded out of him and he yanked my hair back with his other hand. My scalp burned. Maybe it was all the coke, or seeing Constan's dead body earlier, but I had this, like, crazy out-of-body experience where I watched myself stab Zachary in the thigh with Amanda's letter opener, like plunging a meat thermometer in a raw turkey.

I wasn't sure if I actually did it or not, but he howled and let go of me. He gripped the letter opener that stuck out of his thigh and made this weird grunting sound like he was struggling to take a shit. His face flushed pink. Amanda screamed from the hallway for someone to call 9-1-1.

I grabbed my purse and the blow and sprinted down the hall. I ran down the stairs so fast I practically somersaulted. I bolted past a few people sprawled in Amanda's living room watching MTV and flew out the front door. Zachary's cursing and Amanda's yelling trailed behind me.

***

"Hello?"

"Is this Reese?" I asked.

There was a pause over the phone and then, "Yeah, who the fuck is this?"

I turned around in the phone booth, making sure no one was sneaking up on me, like, especially Zachary, but all I saw were excited concertgoers trudging up the steep hill through the grassy picnic area to the front gate of the Greek Theater. "It's Pia."

"You." A low growl or laugh, I couldn't tell. "You've got a lot of nerve calling me, bitch."

I heard a familiar giggle through the phone. *Omigod, Tiffany was still there with him.* I wondered if I'd be the maid of honor at their wedding. "You like Oingo Boingo?" I asked.

Another pause. "What the fuck kind of question is that?"

"Just tell me. Do you like Oingo Boingo?"

A sigh and then, "Not really. I'm an N.W.A. or Slick Rick kind of man."

"Too bad. The guy you want, Constan's partner, is sitting in Row BB in seat nine. In the pit section. His name is Zachary."

"What? Where?"

"I'm at the Greek." I hung up and stepped out of

the phone booth to join Amanda, who was waiting for me at one of the picnic tables. I wasn't sure how Reese was going to get inside without a ticket, but I figured a guy like him would have his ways.

"He coming?" she asked. She took a snort from the vial around her neck.

I nodded.

"Good. I'm out of blow. Let's motor," she said. She stood up and we walked arm in arm down the hill to the lot where my Rabbit was parked.

Amanda hadn't kept her promise of giving me the tickets, especially since I was over an hour late, but she did something even better instead. While waiting with Zachary at the hospital all day to get stitches in his thigh, she called me. Wanted the low down on what the fuck was going on.

I told her everything, including the plan I had cooked up. She agreed to help me. All she had to do was convince Zachary to wait until after the concert to hunt me down. Wasn't too hard since he had a gnarly man crush on Danny Elfman. Once they were seated, Amanda snuck away and met me at the picnic tables. I knew it had nothing to do with being my friend and everything to do with being freaked out by Zachary's Gordon Gekko side, but that didn't matter.

Not to mention I was the one with at least twenty Kleenex boxes of coke. At least I would be soon. Constan's place wasn't too far from the Greek.

We were missing Danny Elfman, but, like, Amanda was totally right. More coke was the priority. I mean, like, why *wouldn't* I want to do lines all night with my bestie, that backstabbing, blood-sucking whore?

IT'S MORNING AGAIN IN LAKE CASTOR

by Eryk Pruitt

They pulled Jessi Spangler's body out of Blood Holler on a dark, grey morning in September of 1985. She'd been half-buried, just deep enough to discourage the coyotes and buzzards, and the Lake Castor police might never have found her had they not received an anonymous tip in a phone call the night previous. The girl was seventeen years old, beautiful, and very popular in high school.

She'd been in that hole for two weeks.

I know because I helped put her there.

I didn't kill Jessi Spangler, but I know who did. Hell, half of Lake Castor knew who did it. You could step into Grady's Barbecue on Broad Street or Charlie Fetter's barber shop downtown—or anywhere else, for that matter—and be hard pressed not to hear folks whispering behind cupped palms about "That Dix Boy" or "Those Brothers" or "That Family Out There." Conspiracy theories ran wild and the police ran up one tree and down another, but at the end of the day, nobody doubted Randy Dix had been the one to choke the life out of that girl.

What they *didn't* know was what to do about it. Randy and his brother Billy didn't have much by the way of parents. Their momma took off a couple years back with some guy in a Jeep Scrambler and never looked back. Their daddy fell simple after a bad batch of shine. The boys and their sister did all right for themselves, thanks to a lack of God and a connection with some black boys up in Baltimore. For years, folks blamed the steady uptick in production at yonder mill because of what they smoked, snorted, or shot, coming from their little trailer on the edge of town.

The police could do little about it either. Time and again, they'd sent an officer to roust them, but the Dix boys were cagey. They had hideaways all over town where they kept their stashes, and usually enjoyed a good twenty-minute head start on the cops, because they always knew they were coming. They hauled both brothers to the station several times after digging Jessi Spangler out of the hollow, but never found anything they could pin on them. Both boys stuck to their story. To keep folks at ease, the cops rolled down to the Back Back where the blacks lived and busted a few heads, said they were running down a few new clues. Nothing ever turned up.

Alvin Spangler went on a tirade and swore before God and everyone that he would not rest until he found justice for his little girl. Night after night, he'd go on a toot then stand before everyone at the 809 or Dixie's and blame folks for turning their backs on his baby girl. He'd point his finger toward the other side of town and say he had half a mind to go down there and seek justice on his own. After a while, even he grew tired of it, and went back to work at the mill like everybody else.

Eventually, things settled down and folks quit talking about it. They knew the Dix boys sold drugs and they knew there was little they could do about it. They knew (more than likely) that Randy Dix killed the Spangler girl. And they knew he'd never be punished.

What they didn't know was *why*.

***

"It was a sex thing." Noah Spencer, eighteen years old in 1985. Dropped out of Lake Castor High his sophomore year. He drove a Z/28, held the *Galaga* high score in the arcade at 7-Eleven, and was best friends with Billy Dix.

He also had been there the night Jessi Spangler died.

"That girl ... Folks think she was one of the good ones, but that's far from the truth. She took up with Dave Albany and he was what ... Twenty-two, twenty-three? What do you think they did together, go to church? If you ask me, that girl was a freak."

Noah only put to words what everybody was thinking anyway: "If she was such a good girl, then what was she doing over there to begin with?"

"The girl was there to score." Jaron Little, eighteen years old. Black. Once caught four touchdowns in a single game against Whitfill, yet entertained no scholarship offers from area colleges. Instead of carrying the pigskin at UVA, he carried ounces of cocaine from the Dix Brothers to the Back Back. "You could see it in her eyes, man. She'd near-abouts do anything to get it."

"It wasn't for her; it was for me." Dave Albany, twenty-four years old. LCHS Class of '79. Laid pipe at the mill since the day he received his diploma. Parked his Celica across the street every day after school and jammed hair metal while waiting to pick up his girlfriend. "It's all my fault. I work hard, so I play hard, and I wanted some for the weekend. I told her it was real important to me to score. I told her—"He cleared his throat and steadied himself, before continuing. "I didn't want to be seen around those boys, and I knew she went to school with a couple of them, so I sent her to fetch it for me. I had no idea it would end up ..."

Dave too, would eventually put it behind him. At Jessi's funeral, he sat with her best girlfriends, on account of her parents would let him nowhere near the rows reserved for loved ones. Allison Wabash particularly took a shine to comforting him, and soon the Celica returned to its 3:30 vigil across the street from school.

Still, he was adamant. "It wasn't a sex thing. She loved me. We loved each other. If she had sex with one of those boys, then she was drugged or raped, one."

"It was contractual ... I mean, it was constru— I mean ... She was *willing*," Noah said. "Maybe she didn't want to do it, but when push came to shove, she handled her business like a champ. She got it done."

"She didn't want to do it," Jaron said. "But she did it."

"Fuck yeah, she did it." Billy Dix, twenty-four years old. Second oldest of four children by Wayne and Phyllis Dix. Drove an old Ford pickup and lived in a trailer on the far side of town. Estimated to be the second or third wealthiest citizen in Lawles County. "Randy's a maniac, for real."

As a rule, no one talked about Randy and Jessi in front of Billy Dix. However, from time to time, Billy would get zonked to the max and start bragging on his brother.

"An apple don't fall far from its tree."

Billy himself had a reputation. Folks said he was the reason why the school cafeteria used plastic cutlery, and why James Hampton had that scar down the middle of his hand. They said he beat the Mexican out of Hector Martinez. Word had it that if the cops looked long and hard enough, they'd find plenty more bodies up and down Blood Holler, all of them folks who got on the wrong side of Billy or his daddy or their other brother Ricky.

But if Billy's chest puffed up over what Randy done to that little girl, then it was more on account of Randy's reputation than his own. You see, Randy wasn't known around Lake Castor for being brutal. Where words like "violent" and "terrible" were often linked to the Dix clan, Randy got good grades. Randy stayed after school to study, not for detention. The youngest Dix boy had a gentle side to him.

Which was why his older brother hated him.

***

I got there after ten that night. You could count on four hands the places I'd rather be in Lake Castor than the Dix trailer, but none of them sold good snow. By the time the shit made it to the Back Back, it'd been stepped on so many times it was barely white, and these days, the blacks preferred to smoke it in pipes. I was a long way off from that.

Me? I got the taste for it one night after a Lake Castor Tigers basketball game. Everybody spazzed after a buzzer beater in overtime took down Tucker and we didn't want the night to end. Lucky for us, Mal Henry had a taste he scored off some seniors and we kept the party going all weekend. By Sunday, we were couch potatoes, zoning out to MTV, brains melting to puddles on the floor. But what a weekend.

I never looked back.

Sure, I had some issues, but it wasn't like I was going to make it on an episode of Donahue. Me and mom didn't get along, my grades had gone to shit ... I could play a little guitar and me and a couple boys liked to jam in the garage from time to time, but only recently had I come to realize it would never be anything serious and, best case scenario, all I could hope for was a full-time job at the mill when I wrapped up things at the school. Grass and booze were baby food compared to the sweet release I got from the coke. Where better to get it than the source?

No matter how much it sucked going to the source.

The Dix trailer never had any shortage of drama. If someone was lucky, the only thing they left with was hurt feelings. Mostly, it was a tattoo or something pierced. Billy grew bored rather quick and often needed something to keep him entertained. He didn't understand folks wanted convenience from a drug dealer: a quick in-and-out was asking far too much. He had shit stashed all over the woods around his trailer, so a quick raid from the police would produce nothing. All he asked was that you wait a minute while someone ran to fetch it.

And while you waited, why not stick around a bit for the show?

The night Jessi Spangler died, all I wanted was a gram. I told myself over and over I didn't have time for Billy Dix's bullshit. If he made a production out of it and things lasted longer than one side of a cassette tape, I was out. With or without the shit. I wasn't in the mood for it.

Man ...

***

"Shhh, shhh."

Noah Spencer answered the door with a finger over the shit-eatingest grin I'd ever seen. He led me by the arm into the trailer and closed the door behind him. Also in the room: Jaron Little, Bryce Franklin, and big bad Billy Dix. All of them tried their best to stifle their laughter as they listened intently to the silence in the room.

"What's going on?" I asked.

"Shhh!"

Billy held up a finger, then tip-toed across the shag to a closed bedroom door. He put his ear to the wood paneling and listened.

"What's going on?" I whispered.

Jaron Little looked none too pleased. He rolled his eyes and shrugged his shoulders. A thin sheen of sweat slicked his forehead and he hitched a thumb toward Noah and Bryce, giggling on the couch.

"These honkies," he said. "It's always something."

"I ain't heard nothing for five minutes," whispered Billy.

"Maybe he's licking her snatch," Noah whispered back.

Billy grabbed a cassette case—*Invasion of Your Privacy*—and threw it at Noah's head. Missed. Shattered against the coffee table.

"My brother ain't no faggot," he hissed.

"I didn't say—"

This time Dix caught him in the ear.

"Say it again and I'll cut off your head."

Billy quit wearing shirts in April. He spent most days lifting barbells under the carport next to his brother's broke down Mustang. He drew on himself with India ink and a safety pin. He'd gotten better with it over the past couple months, but he still wasn't Nagel. He'd pierced himself in nearly every imaginable spot on his body, and then some that weren't.

If Billy said shut up or he'd cut off your head, you shut up.

"If tonight proves anything to you barf bags," he growled, "it's that my brother ain't no faggot. You hear anybody at that school say it and I want you to bring me their name."

When he put his ear to the door again, I turned to Jaron and asked what in good hell was going on.

"You know that white girl Jessi from school?" He motioned to his head. "The one with the big hair?"

He could have narrowed it down a little more, but I nodded.

"She rolled past, looking to score a little toot. Only Billy raised the price on her and she didn't have enough. He said she could work it off and she told him to gag her with a spoon. He said he'd gag her with more than that and if she didn't do what he said, he'd make sure she couldn't score nothing else in Lake Castor."

"Lame."

"For sure. He said she had to pick any one person here and spend ten minutes with them in the bedroom, then she could get the coke."

"She got to pick?"

Jaron shook his head. "Man, I can't tell you how scared I was that she was going to pick me. I can't have that shit right now. I got too many problems without some coke-starved white girl."

"Wait. You're telling me she picked Randy?"

"That's what I'm saying."

The math didn't add up. "Really?" I repeated. "She picked *Randy*?"

"Hey man, maybe she thought it was the one dude in the room who—"

Billy hissed from the door. "Will you two fairies shut your yaps?"

We did.

"For real, Billy," said Bryce. "Maybe we ought to open the door and check on them."

A new grin took hold of Billy. Nothing could send a person off their lunch easier than a new smile from Billy Dix.

"Oh, that's bonus," he said. "That's fucking grand."

With Noah and Bryce saddling alongside him, he put his hand to the knob. Again, he held up a finger to shush the room, and with the flourish of a magician, threw open the door.

***

When the cops found her, nobody knew what to make of it. She'd been stripped naked and thrown in the bottom of a shallow hole, then covered with dirt, leaves, and muck.

"By all accounts, she had been a very pretty girl," said Deputy Lorne Axel, of the Lawles County Sheriff's office. "You couldn't have told as such by what we dug out of that holler."

"There was blunt force trauma to the back of her head," said Graham Maloney, the county coroner. "But most likely what killed her was strangulation."

Some of the other police talked about the smell, or what time and the elements do to certain parts of the body after death sets in. Some even talked about how long a hike it had been to get to the grave, and how much further it'd be carrying a dead girl. Not Lorne Axel. He'd gone to school with Jessi's daddy Alvin, and when it came up in discussion, he'd look up or down, but never in anyone's eye.

"It's a damn waste," was all he'd add.

***

"What the hell did you do?"

Randy was inconsolable. He'd huddled himself into a ball in the corner of his bedroom, knees tucked beneath his chin. His face had run red from bawling, and his shirt had been ripped to tatters. His chest looked like it had been worked by a bobcat.

"She wouldn't shut up," he said through the sobs. "I told her to shut the fuck up and she wouldn't shut up."

He looked to the center of the room.

"Why wouldn't you shut up?"

I remember my first thought was *Oh, that Jessi.* How I'd thought the whole time it was Jessi Carroll in the room with Randy.

No.

They'd meant the other Jessi.

They meant the one who sprayed maybe three different kinds of hairspray into her hair every morning. The one who kept extra purple cans in her locker to freshen up between classes. The one from my third-period History class last year, who sometimes would have at me in the hall, and sometimes wouldn't. The one who dressed preppy and had eyes the color of a summer lawn.

That Jessi.

The one lying on Randy's floor with eyes gone cloudy and neck twisted at an unnatural angle. Her tongue lolled half out of her mouth and a light froth of foam gathered at the corner of her lips. One of her legs was propped against a small beer fridge in the corner. Her hands balled into fists. The skin around her throat had been rubbed purple, and she wore a polka-dotted skirt which now bunched around her ankles. I tried— tried real hard—not to look, but my eyes went all the way up her legs to where she'd quit shaving and how ...

Jaron made a break for it. He bolted like a rocket and cleared half the living room before Billy Dix shut him down with nothing but his voice.

"Don't you move, boy," Billy growled.

Jaron's eyes like to pop out of his skull. "Look, Billy, man ... This shit ain't got nothing to do with me. You don't understand—"

"I understand you're about to run out of a trailer where there's a white girl dead on the floor."

"I got walk-ons next week at State," Jaron pleaded. "I got nothing to do with this shit and you know it, man."

"You got everything to do with this, boy." Billy yanked him back into the room and closed the door behind them. "All of you do."

***

Jaron never made the team at State. He was faster than anyone else and certainly had the hands. Jaron could light up a room with his smile and couldn't nobody smooth talk the ladies better. Somebody somewhere at that university didn't think he had what it took to hide his grades, and he came back to Lake Castor to run coke for his cousin.

Two months after we dropped Jessi Spangler in that hole, he turned up dead in a creek bed, shot twice through the chest. It was big news, on account of how big a star he'd been for the football team.

"It was all that shit he was driving into the Back Back," my daddy said after reading about it in the paper. "Cocaine is real bad among the blacks."

"It's a shame he couldn't just say no," my mother added.

"I heard it was because somebody wanted his shoes," said a kid in class. "They're always shooting each other for their shoes."

"So long as they keep it on that side of town."

At no time did the cops bust any heads when it came to Jaron Little. Nor did anyone ask questions. One day it was big news, then it was forgotten the next.

"Best to let them sort it out on their own," said an old man at the barber shop where I got my hair cut.

"They say they want to be treated equal," said one person to another in the supermarket checkout. "But you don't see white folks acting like that to one another, do you?"

***

Two months later, Noah Spencer drove his Z/28 into the concrete wall at Old Man McCarthy's place going about fifty miles per hour. While he lay in a closed casket, I sat in a funeral pew with Bryce Franklin. It was the first time we'd spoken since that night.

"You and me," he said in a low whisper.

"What do you mean?"

"Out of all the people who buried that girl," he said, "you and me are the only ones still alive."

He smiled when he said it, so I shrugged it off.

But one thing bothered me: Billy and Noah had been thick as thieves since grade school and Billy was nowhere to be found at the funeral.

"It's because him and Noah were super tight," Bryce said, much later. "He didn't want nobody to see him cry."

"I hear it's because the cops put the screws to him over the Spangler girl," said Welch Thompson, another guy we knew.

"He can't take a shit without three deputies wiping his ass," said yet another.

Still ...

***

Me?

I got worse with the coke. However, I didn't want to go around the Dix house for it anymore. Instead, I rolled down to the Back Back to talk to Anton or G-Cru or Smooth Baby Pop. I went up to the hills to see the Mullins crew, who everybody knew cut that shit with rat poison. I even scored a couple grams off Mr. Canary, the theater teacher, who needed a couple bucks to tide him over before his paycheck.

I did nearly everything in my power to keep from rolling back over to the Dix house, until the day I had to roll back over to the Dix house.

I came up the gravel rock path to the carport on yonder side of the Dix trailer. I found Randy bent beneath the hood of his Mustang, where he'd been for the better part of six months. He'd surrounded himself with posters of Heather Thomas and Kelly LeBrock and Catherine Bach. He'd wiped oil and grease alongside his cheekbones and neck. He'd worked a good spackling of sweat down his back.

"Billy's not here."

I didn't look him in the eye the night we put Jessi Spangler into that hollow. Nor did I that February afternoon beneath his carport.

"He said I could talk to you or your sister, one."

Randy wiped grease from a socket wrench. "You here to score?"

I nodded.

Randy wiped his hands with a sooty towel and led me in through the back door.

The first line leveled me out. It had been a while since I'd had shit that good straight up the nose. The second one got me where I wanted to be. I considered a third, but I needed to save something for when I finally got the fuck out of there.

Randy popped open a beer from his small fridge and offered me one. I sat on the couch in his bedroom and stared at the spot where we'd found Jessi Spangler all those months ago. My leg shook like the dickens and it took both hands for me to calm it.

"I really don't think I should stay —"

"Have one."

I did.

"You don't come around much anymore."

"Well ..."

On his wall: posters of Whitesnake, Motley Crue. The poster for *Heavy Metal*. Susan Anton in a red swimsuit. Loni Anderson. The cast of *Charlie's Angels*.

"I don't see you much at school anymore," I told

him. "I heard you dropped out."

"You heard?" Randy replaced his wry grin with a furrowed brow. "What good is school going to do anyone in Lake Castor?"

I tried to think of an answer, but instead I choked up another line off the back of his *Pyromania* cassette case.

"I know what the President said ... It's morning again in America." He set his beer down on one of his stereo speakers. He'd hardly drank a drop. "Maybe it's morning in America, but it ain't morning in Lake Castor. In Lake Castor, the goddamn sun is setting."

"What are you going to do if you don't go to school?"

Randy turned to me. "I'm going to be like my brother."

I didn't mean to laugh. I'd been running my finger along the back the cassette case and sucking it clean. I stopped myself and apologized, but the damage had been done. Randy looked at me with several shades of "et tu" shrouding his face.

"I didn't mean—"

"You don't think I can be like Billy?" he asked.

"Randy, I—"

"Go ahead, say it." Randy hitched his button flys at the waist. He squared his shoulders. "You don't think I got what it takes to be a Dix."

"I didn't say that. I—"

"You don't remember what I done to that girl?" Randy paced the floor. "You don't remember how I done that to her with my bare hands?"

I didn't want to hear another word. I wanted to clap both hands over my ears and shout out the noise. I wanted to run free of that trailer and not stop until I'd reached town. I wanted to do a great many things to keep from hearing about that night, but instead I fixed my eyes upon a collection of empty Sundance Sparkler bottles and kept them there.

"It was so simple," Randy shouted. "She didn't want to be in here and neither did I. She could have picked any guy in the room. I did what I was supposed to, so why couldn't she? Instead, she kept talking about how me and her were the same. Over and over, she's saying 'We both got secrets, Randy. We both hide who we really are.'"

"Randy ... I don't—"

"I told her to shut up. Just do what we were sent back here to do before my brother—" Randy eyeballed the door to the living room like someone might hear. "Just shut up and do it, but she kept wanting to talk. She kept wanting to say how we were the same. Guess what? We ain't the same. One of us is alive and the other one ..."

If I laid out another line—even a tiny one—I'd only be left with two or three skinny rails for later. If I saved it, I'd start a heavy comedown and I'd need more to kick-start me again. But if I did it now, I'd be down in the Back Back at all hours, howling through the streets for more until—

"She didn't know shit."

I shook my head, then nodded. Then shrugged my shoulders.

Randy watched me shake out a little more dust onto the back of the Def Leppard cassette. I scraped together a line with the edge of my driver's license, then tooted it up my skull with a rolled-up two dollar bill. I sat back on the couch and watched his ceiling fan oscillate.

Randy took a seat on the couch next to me. He smelled of sweat and motor oil.

"I'm like my brother, goddammit."

Without looking to him, I said, "I know you are."

"Just like him."

I nodded my head again.

"When my brother wants something," he said, "he reaches out and takes it."

"That's what you should do."

"Really?"

I nodded my head again.

Randy grabbed me by the cheeks and pulled me to his mouth. He tasted of corn chips. His tongue reached me well before his lips and he used it to shove aside my lips and make his way inside. He was half on top of me, swinging a leg over my lap and pinning me to the couch. He panted through his nose, blowing hot air across the stubble of my face.

"Ran—"

I wasn't much, thanks to the drugs. I tried to muscle him off me, but he had me by a few pounds. *When did he put on pounds?* He held tight to my face and I could feel his stiff cock against my rib cage as he positioned himself atop me. I wondered if this was how it was going to happen, if this was where my life would change, if this was the line of fucking demarcation.

I opened my mouth wide to scream, but that only let him further into me.

When the garage door opened, Randy hopped off me and pulled his pants taut at the front. He raced to the opposite side of the room and pretended to fuss with the cassette deck. Billy Dix wandered in, smoking a Winston and eyeing the two of us.

"What are you homos doing?" he asked.

"Kurt came by for some coke," Randy said, half out of breath.

"Did he get it?"

Randy nodded.

Billy looked to me. "You need anything else?"

I didn't trust my own voice. Instead of saying a word, I shook my head.

"Then get the fuck out of here."

I did.

Man ... Did I ever.

***

Bryce Franklin ran his motorcycle into a telephone pole. He was still alive when they loaded him into the ambulance, but somewhere on the trip to the hospital in Tucker, he died.

"I heard he told the paramedics it was Billy Dix who done it," said Harold Creamer, a kid from school. "I heard he talked the whole way, but ain't none of it good in a court of law, since he had a brain injury."

"I heard they ran his motorcycle into the telephone pole."

"I heard it was because he was about to go to the cops over the Spangler girl."

"I heard ..."

Honestly, it didn't matter what anyone else heard. Never did anybody in this town ever get a damn thing right.

Know what I heard?

I heard a branch break outside my bedroom window. I heard a car start somewhere down the street.

Sometimes I'd hear the tick, tick, tick of a time bomb, and I'd spend the rest of the evening wondering when it was going to go off. Even now I hear silent footsteps behind me, wherever I go.

But I'm pretty sure I won't hear it for long.

WIDOWMAN

by Matthew J. Hockey

Roppongi, Tokyo – 1984

Aki woke on a strange couch to keys rattling in the lock. Swatches of another woman's shredded clothing fell away from her lap as she reached for the gun on the end table. Stupid to fall asleep here. Careless. Crazy. She was asking to get caught. Begging.

She took her sneakers off and held them in one hand as she crept over the bare floorboards to the door. She used the pistol butt to knock the lights off.

The door swung inwards, sending a wave of white hallway fluorescence crashing onto the stacks of books piled around the room. Junko walked inside, closed the door with her heel and dropped her bags on the floor.

Without bothering to turn the on light, Junko felt around blind in the junk by her TV set, clicking something and muttering under her breath. She produced a lighter flame and lit an incense stick, let it burn for a moment before blowing it out and drawing the fragrant smoke deep into her lungs.

Aki hit her on the back of the head.

Shibuya, Tokyo – Earlier that day

Aki had it all worked out. She would be ready and waiting out on the balcony in her favourite Versace, a metallic silver cocktail dress, the one she'd made Shoji, her late husband, promise to bury her in if she died before him. When the Widowman rang the bell, she would buzz him inside with the hand fob, count three seconds, hear the door open, and click two more buttons to dim the lights and activate the record player. That way, the white glow would bounce ghostly off the Versace while throwing every inch of her exposed skin into shadow, making it look for all the world like a disembodied dress standing out on the balcony.

At the very instant the Widowman set foot in the apartment, the record player's stylus would land in the pre-programmed groove and the sound of Joy Division's "Transmission" would fill the penthouse suite. She'd dance with it in her disembodied dress. *Dance, dance, dance, dance, dance to the radio.* Then she'd come inside, delightfully sweaty from the exertion, and pour him a Glenfiddich. What kind of man could resist a scene like that?

She'd never gone to so much effort for a man before, had never needed to. She saw one she liked and without consciously thinking about it—finger snap, she had him.

That's how she got Shoji, and the two since his murder. Not that either of them had been worth even that much effort. One of them had locked himself in the bathroom crying after she'd slapped him during sex.

But the Widowman was different. She'd made several plays for him, and he'd parried them all. He was much older than her, and ugly. Which begged the question, *why did she want to win him in the first place?*

At first she'd assumed it was some sort of dormant daddy issue brought to the surface by her grief. But her therapist saw straight through that, had his own theory. Aki had been somebody with Shoji. He'd validated her, taken her to parties and top restaurants, movie premiers. She'd rubbed shoulders with enforcers, hitmen, corrupt politicians and police captains, not to mention TV actors, musicians and chefs. Without a man like Shoji, who was she?

Except just now, the Widowman was late and it was cold on the twenty-fourth floor balcony in nothing but a tiny, silver cocktail dress, not to mention *boring*. She put the music on early. When the Widoman finally rang the bell twenty-eight minutes later, she'd already listened to the whole of side A and didn't have time to flip record back over, reset the stylus exactly where it needed to be, and climb back onto the balcony to buzz him in. So, instead, she just opened the door and went through the whole sorry routine they'd been perfecting since Shoji's funeral.

"Good evening, Yamagawa-san. What a pleasant surprise. Won't you come in?" she asked, knowing that he wouldn't ever accept her invit—

"Yes please," he said, pushing by her, barely pausing to put his shoes in the cupboard in the entrance hall.

She didn't even think to close the door behind him she was so shocked. This had never happened before. He was *supposed* to say, "Thank you for the offer, but I'm afraid I couldn't possibly intrude," then hand her the envelope with her monthly allowance and leave.

"Take a seat," Aki said. "Can I get you something? A tea?" Aki playing the dedicated housewife in the face of this most terrible breach of protocol.

"A cold drink I think. Yes. A cold drink." He slumped back on the futon.

She poured him a glass of water from the kitchenette. This man who would never have been granted his role as the Widowman excepting that he had performed admirably for the family in his youth, who her husband had drunkenly told her had a penchant for dispatching his enemies by pushing heated guitar strings through their eyes. His hand shook as he reached for the glass.

"Is anything the matter?" she asked, and the Widowman—who had a near perfect circular scar cut deep into his scalp—gulped the water as he spoke.

"I'm sorry I'm late. I hit a dog on the way here." There were tears in his eyes.

On top of everything else, it was just too much. She couldn't help it. She laughed in his face.

He wrenched the envelope out of his satchel and made a face.

She took the envelope from where it lay on the coffee table beside a copy of Helmut Newton's 'World Without Men' and knew immediately that something was wrong with it. It was light. Emptying it into her palm she saw why - there were exactly one-third as many bills as there should have been. It only came to one hundred thousand Yen. A mistress's wage, rather than a wife's.

She flipped it over. There was another woman's name and address written there instead of her own. Junko Fuminora from Roppongi near the subway station.

Nothing unusual about him carrying an envelope for another woman. He was the Widowman, after all. There'd been a war. There were a lot of widows to take care of. Nothing unusual at all. No reason for this icy hardness in her stomach. No reason she felt like a belt was slowly tightening around her neck. She teased her finger against the edge of the envelope's flap. The dead man's name would be written there.

She didn't want to look. Didn't want to know. So of course she looked and immediately spat on her own floor. There it was in thick, black calligraphy pen. Shoji Hachrobei. Her husband. The bastard. If he was here now she'd cut his balls off and feed them to—

The bands squeezed even tighter around her neck. She shoved the bundle of yen back into the envelope, dumped it on the table and mopped the puddle of saliva with her bare foot.

The Widowman, looking distressed again suddenly, leaned forward and picked up the envelope, shoved it back in his satchel and said, "Oh, my mistake. I gave you another lady's package."

"Quite alright," Aki said, pretending she hadn't already opened the flap, hadn't been waiting behind the door for it since the last one came. As if it wasn't the only connection to her old life, to anything like normalcy, that she'd had since they shot Shoji in the face on an Okinawan beach.

Yamagawa stared into her eyes as he gave he the correct envelope. Any trace of his former emotion a moment ago submerged beneath his usual unreadable blank.

"Is there something else?" She kept her smile dialed up to manic proportions, head tilted forward in mock subservience.

"I'm sorry."

"Whatever for?"

Long pause with that same piercing stare, trying to

get inside her head, to see if she'd noticed anything was wrong.

"For taking up your time with my lateness," he said as he stood up and went to the door.

After he was gone, she didn't even have to think about it. She just went into the bedroom and slid the cherry incense box from under the bed. She blew the dust off the lid and took out the blue steel Walther PPK automatic pistol from inside.

She threw some street clothes on over her gaudy dress, a US M1A1 flight jacket with extra shoulder pads and venting, torn steel-grey fishnet stockings with ladders and gaping holes held together by safety-pins and loose stiches, and a pair of Nike high tops with great looping bows, all capped off with a Sony WM DD-2 cassette Walkman and headphones like industrial ear defenders, twenty feet of cabling wrapped around her left arm and her imported albums marked with a yellow exclamation points in a tote bag she hung over her elbow.

She chose *Swordfishtrombones* by Tom Waits for the subway ride out to Roppongi. She kept her eyes closed for as much of the journey as she could, knowing when to get off only by counting stops and breathing through her nose to wrestle down the urge to shoot Shoji's whore on sight.

***

Seeing the shithole they had her stashed in almost made Aki feel sorry for her. It almost made her wish she'd brought the girl a box of instant ramen and bottle of water instead of the pistol.

Shoji's mistress lived in a dull, grey apartment complex that looked as though it was just waiting for the next earthquake to come along so the owners could claim on the insurance and get out.

She ducked into the alleyway, changed the tape out in her Walkman — *From Her To Eternity* by Nick Cave and the Bad Seeds — turned it up so loud she couldn't hear the panic in her own head as she shimmied up onto the fire escape that clung to the outside of the building.

Six floors up. Eight windows along. She took the pistol out of her tote and slammed it two-handed against the glass door. She punched a hole clean through, reached inside, lifted the latch and opened it.

The apartment was cramped and stacked on both sides with hardback books with no dust jackets and handwritten stamps on the spines. A formal portrait took pride of place on the wall. Junko; a plain girl in white makeup and fitted kimono, with big eyes, a straight nose and a scrawny neck.

The whole apartment was one room. Living space with sofa that doubled as a bed, kitchen nook in one corner, bathroom in the diagonally opposite corner that was little more than a toilet and a drain in the floor with a rubberised curtain on a track.

Nothing to personalize it but the books, the portrait and the heady scent of cherry incense — Shoji's favorite — that clung to everything. Hundreds of burnt incense sticks stood upright in a glazed pot by the TV.

She took a fish knife from the kitchen drawer, sliced through the plastic wardrobe bag. She pulled it wide, popping the zipper. All of the girl's clothes were pastel. All plain. Good girl. Preppy girl. Bow in her hair. Clean bra every day. Home the minute her father told her to be. *What the hell did Shoji see in her?*

She lashed out with the knife, splitting cotton, wool, fabric, blouses, skirts, cardigans, sweaters and that fitted kimono from the picture. Again and again. Imagining the slut was wearing them, imagining the cream and pastel linens were her cream and pastel skin. Imagining the threads of cotton were strands of her hair.

She swung until the tape heads crackled and her breath wheezed in her ears. Not a scrap of clothing remained whole.

Aki sat down on the couch, looked around at the piles of scattered books and shreds of clothing. She closed her eyes for a moment. Just long enough to get her breath back ...

***

Junko moaned and stumbled forward, though she hardly seemed surprised to have been attacked in her own home. She didn't scream or try to defend herself.

Aki lashed out with her foot, connecting with the back of the girl's knee and sending her tottering towards the bathroom. She kept her back turned as though she didn't want to look at who was hitting her. That pissed Aki off even more.

She picked a hardback book off the nearest pile and threw it. Junko turned at the sound of the pages fluttering through the air and caught the corner of it full in the teeth.

Her head snapped back and her shins crashed against the toilet bowl. She weaved for a moment before righting herself. Aki tackled her round the waist and the pair of them fell, tangled in the rubber shower curtain.

Aki pinned the girl down using her knees and

clawed at her neck. Even then, the girl didn't bring her hands up to protect herself.

"Just kill me already. Get it over with," Junko said.

"What?"

"Wait ... who *are* you?" Junko's eyelashes fluttered open against the shower curtain.

Aki closed her thumbs over Junko's windpipe before she could scream.

"Shoji was my husband."

Junko stopped struggling, eyes wide with realisation. Slowly, Aki relaxed the pressure on her throat until she could speak.

"I know ... who killed ... him."

"Everybody knows. Those Okinawan dogs—" Aki's hands loosened, let Junko grab a shallow breath.

"No, no, no. It wasn't. That's what they're saying, but it's—"

"What are you talking about?"

"I was ... there. I wasn't supposed to be. I flew out to surprise him, found out what hotel he was in. I put this Ursula Andress bikini on, you know, the white one, from Dr. No? You know he liked to play James Bond—"

"I know."

"When I swam out to his cabana—do you mind?" She peeled the curtain off her head and waited. When Aki made no move to stop her, she hauled herself to a sitting position with one hand in the toilet. "I got out there and he was talking with his bodyguard, the one with the missing fingers—"

"To."

"Yes. And another man too. He had a tan and an Aloha shirt. Looked like a local, though he still had his

Tokyo accent. When Shoji saw me, he shook his head slightly so I'd see it while the others weren't paying attention. I knew it was serious. I hid in some trees. Next thing ..." She trailed off, sobbing.

"Next thing *what*?"

"I don't think you want to hear it."

Aki pressed the gun between Junko's legs.

"You don't get to tell me what I want to hear and what I don't want to hear."

"The local guy started shouting. Shoji tried to get to where his jacket was hanging on the back of the chair. I think he had a gun in it."

"Was it his pink jacket?"

"I don't..." She squeezed her eyes shut, lips pursed. "Yes. I think so."

"It would have been a knife, not a gun."

"The local picked up a shell. A nautilus or a conch—"

"I don't give a fuck what kind of shell it was."

"He threw it and it hit Shoji in the neck and he slipped on the tiles and the local and To both got a hold of him under the arms and held him in the pool and ..."

***

Aki hit rewind and play on her Walkman so all she could hear was that horrible squeaking as the cassette spooled back onto the heads.

When she opened her eyes again, she was sitting on her haunches with Junko cuddled up beside her, a blanket thrown around their shoulders.

"I prayed for you." Junko got out from under the blanket long enough to light another incense stick.

"The first time in history that the mistress prayed for the wife."

"They wouldn't let me go to the funeral."

"I can see why they thought it might have been a problem," Aki said, and for the first time, Junko scowled at her, anger doing strange things to her weak brow.

"I made my own shrine at home. Whenever I tried to light the incense it wouldn't burn, and I had to light it off the gas. Tonight I finally decided to stop praying for mercy on his soul and to start praying for vengeance. It lit the first time."

"That means something to you, I suppose?"

"I know how to get revenge. I just needed someone cra— *willing* to do it. And here you are. If you want vengeance, that is?"

Aki didn't even have to think about it.

***

To took a demotion after Shoji died. The family couldn't very well keep him as a bodyguard after he let his boss die, even if Junko was right and they'd ordered it. How would that look to the other families?

They had him running security for their gaming arcades instead. It looked like a step down, a slap in the face, but there was a lot of money in it for somebody who knew how to work the angles.

And To knew all the angles, if his car was anything to go by. On the few occasions he'd come by the apartment to talk to Shoji, he'd driven a second-hand Suzuki Cultus.

"You're sure this is his?" Aki asked, pointing to the only American car in the lot. A Chevy Camaro.

"I'm sure," Junko said.

Junko worked nights at the library. A job which, according to her repeated claims, came to little more than putting the day's returned Murakamis back onto the shelves and sleeping six hours in a hammock. It left her free all day to follow To around, see where he went, who he met with, learn his routines. Today, the Sunday after Aki gave her the beating, was a Shibuya mega-arcade day. Four floors of video games, slot machines, air hockey, and rigged hoop shooting games that paid out in tickets that could be exchanged in units of tens, hundreds or thousands for worthless stuffed toys and plastic crap.

"He stays in his office until midnight, eats some noodles in the Hunanese place on the corner, sees a girly show, then comes back to his car."

The plan was for Junko to keep his attention by looking like a streetwalker. Baker boy hat pulled low over pigtails, high school skirt cut ass-short, denim jacket open over a bra, stiletto heel boots. Either he'd tell her to get lost or he'd go for it and she'd quibble over price, anything to keep his focus long enough for Aki to come up on the other side of the car and put three in him through the passenger window.

That was the plan they'd settled on. It had seemed pretty good the six or so times they'd gone over it at the all-night McDonald's during Junko's three-in-the-morning 'lunch break' from the library.

Now, crouched in a fish-gut stinking alley, fighting stray cats for a spot amongst the trash bags and empty jerry cans of cooking oil, it was starting to seem like a very, very bad idea.

She wasn't sure she could even pull the trigger when it came down to it. Sure, she'd almost shot Junko the other night, but she'd been in the moment then. She'd only just found out Shoji had been fucking around — the rage was still fresh, the anger over his murder was almost nineteen months old. The fact she was angrier about the sex than she was about the death spoke volumes about her messed-up value system, she knew that — it didn't mean she could do anything about it, other than pencil it in with her therapist.

She was in the alleyway and Junko was in the papered-over fire door of a closed-down rock pub, lit by the buzzing red light above. She might as well have been on the other side of the moon. They hadn't come up with any way to signal each other and Aki couldn't think of anything short of stepping out into the middle of the lot waving her arms over her head.

Which is exactly what she did.

No sooner had she come out of hiding than To and two other guys stepped out of the mega-arcade stairwell.

To had half of his head shaved like a samurai, a heavy linen safari suit and a silk zebra-print shirt. The cleats of his shoes scuffed up blue sparks on the asphalt. The taller of the other two men wore an electric blue suit over a black oxford shirt with a popped collar. The third guy was short and stocky and had his yellow polo shirt cut tight to show off his arms, very hairy for a Japanese man of his age.

Thank God for that. No need for her to call anything off. There was no way Junko would try anything with all three of them there.

Except ... *Of* course *she'd have to be that stupid.* No sooner had they climbed into the car than she came sashaying out from her doorway. Aki and Junko had calculated her route to skirt the very edge of the streetlights, catching the barest curve of her hip as she swayed between the cars. In that outfit. In that place. Three men. They'd be looking. *What was she doing? She must have seen them. Who did she think Aki was? The Terminator? The gun started to feel very small in her hand. How many bullets did it even hold? Five? Six?*

"Little late to be out on your own," To said from the driver's side window.

"I could use some company." Like a prostitute in a movie, Aki thought, all innuendo and doublespeak instead of just saying it like it was. *I'll suck your dick for so much, with a condom this much, without this much, in my ass for so much extra.* The men in the car all bobbed back and forth, sensing fresh meat.

Junko looked over the top of the car at the place where Aki was supposed to be hiding. *Walk away, walk away now, we'll get him another way!*, Aki screamed in her head. It didn't do any good.

"So, you game?" To asked.

Take a pass. Take a pass.

"Sure."

Aki kept in a crouch and moved from the alley between two metal traffic bollards and a Yamaha bike with a broken kickstand.

The short, stocky man got out of the car and stood with his legs apart as though he was practicing his putting stroke. The sound of him unzipping his fly was obscene in the silence.

"In your professional experience, think you could take me all the way to the root? Don't rush—think about it. If you say yes now and later you want to change your mind, we're going to have a problem."

To and Bluesuit laughed, thick nasal snorts that made it sound like they'd been smoking cigars before they came down to the parking lot.

Junko turned away, and the short man caught her by the hair and yanked her head back.

Aki gripped the gun in her purse. It felt long and stupid and the sound suppressor caught on the strap as she tried to pull it out.

"What the fuck are you looking at?" the short man turned to ask her as she stepped out of the shadows, which seemed ridiculous coming from a man with his semi-erect penis wagging out of the front of his slacks in a public parking lot.

She fired, blasting a hole in her bag and sending lumps of patent leather and lipstick flying about. The shot went wide and punched a finger-hole clean through the rear passenger window of a Subaru. It didn't web up like in the movies, but fogged as if somebody breathed on it up close.

"I said 'What the fuck are you looking at?'" he asked again. Penis deflating, less sure of itself now. Was it possible he hadn't seen what just happened? The gun seemed so loud to her, even with the suppressor. The sound boomed out of the bag and rolled up the walls on all sides. Felt like somebody pounded sheet metal right by her head.

He took an even tighter grip on Junko's hair, making an audible creak. The two in the car didn't move, mouths wide like they were watching it all unfold on a screen.

Aki aimed her purse, resigned to the fact that it was lodged for the duration. She squeezed the trigger twice. She didn't see where they hit, but he bent from the waist and fell down shuddering all over.

To's car grunted to life and the headlights kicked

on high beam, blinding her. She emptied the gun into the windshield in the time it took for the tires to squeal towards her. The wing mirror clipped her on the way past. Something hot and wet ran down her forearm. Her brain tried to make sense of it—*screen wash? Oil?*

The car slammed into the wall and climbed up it until the front wheels were off the ground. The rear tires kept spinning, crumpling the hood and coughing out smoke that cast the streetlights in slanted beams.

Aki forced herself up, hobbled towards the crippled car. She reached over her head and popped the driver's door with the gun raised, hoping they'd be too dazed to know it was empty.

To struggled behind the blood-spattered airbag.

"Mk ..." he said. "Blop ... Hups ..." More blood spurted out of a bullet hole in his jaw. Aki wrestled the silver gun out of his hand and shot him twice more in the chest with it.

She looked across his ruined body just in time to see Bluesuit's golf shoes disappearing over the side of the seat and flopping into the stairwell beyond.

She walked around the car as if she had all the time in the world, followed the blood trail down the wet concrete steps. *Had she hit him already? Did he get hurt in the crash? Did it matter?* She caught up with him curled against a padlocked door at the bottom landing and put four bullets in his back. His blood looked like spilled pots of India ink on the fabric of his suit.

"We've got to go now." Junko grabbed her by the shoulder and dragged her away.

Shibuya, Tokyo – Three Weeks Later

Aki answered her front door with tears streaming down her cheeks and a butcher's knife gripped in her fist.

"What happened?" the Widowman asked.

"Oh," she laughed. "The onions are stronger than usual today."

"Well, now I feel very foolish." One of his hands had gone for his gun. Aki was well aware that it wasn't normal to find that sort of gesture touching.

"No need. Come in, I'm making Jingisukan. I've never learned to cook for one."

"I couldn't possibly intrude."

"Stop it. You wouldn't be intruding. It would be good to have some company for a change."

He looked as red-faced as her. He swung his satchel around onto his hip. It bulged with envelopes, many more than usual.

"Honestly, I've thought about it. If I did, I wouldn't be done with these until midnight. Seems they didn't learn from their last war. Some fool's started another."

"That's terrible."

"It is."

"Nobody profits."

"Except the widows," Aki said.

"You don't mean that."

"Maybe I—"

There was a bang. Yamagawa's circular scar burst outward and he stepped neatly aside in the doorway as if letting an elderly lady off a train. Then he slumped down dead as his hands clutched at something only he could see. Whether he was warding it off or embracing it, it was hard to tell.

Aki shook her head from side to side. Droplets of his blood flew from her hair tips. Junko stepped from the elevator, silver gun still trailing smoke. She kept it trained on Aki as she pulled his bag from his shoulder and slipped it onto her own. Millions of yen worth.

"Is this what it was all about?"

"Yes."

"Money?"

"Yes."

"Did To really kill my husband?"

"He had a wife and three mistresses. I chose him to add as much as I could to the pot. That's all. Who knows, maybe he really did do it." She walked backwards to the elevator, bag pulling her shoulder down. She shrugged. The doors closed.

Aki ran for the stairwell, kicked the door open. Down two flights so quick the automatic lights didn't come on before she burst out onto the twenty-first floor. Along the corridor. She jabbed the elevator call button a hundred times.

The light above the door hung at twenty-one. If it had already passed, she'd never catch up to her. If the doors opened, she'd get a few swings in with the knife before she could fire.

THE ENVELOPE

by Linda L. Richards

It lay between them like a live thing. A thin gash of creamy white on the dark, battered table. So bright, it sucked the light out of the room. Not much light.

He'd pulled the curtains closed when he came home, eyes bright. She'd watched him curiously as he did it. Had anyone asked, she would have been quite confident he didn't even know they had curtains, yet here he was, operating them like an old hand.

The curtains were still closed now. The day was bright outside though. Light spilled through a hole—something a moth might have made—right near the center of one of the thick draperies. *Seventies thick*, she thought with distaste. Heavy and dark. Earth tones. Her heart yearned for pastels, even chintz. But that would be a different life.

Light seeped through the dark curtains and pawed at the dust motes that danced toward her as she sat on the faded sofa. A song she recognized on the radio. Nena. A German accent. All about red balloons and it sounded so happy, but she'd listened to the lyrics closely a couple of times and it had struck her that the pretty, airy song wasn't about red balloons at all. It was about war, maybe. And things ending. Big things. Bigger than she was. She'd had to stop thinking about it after a while. They were things outside herself. And she barely had room for what was there.

She watched the dust motes intently for a moment: listened to the song, trying not to focus on the words. Just listening to the pretty, airiness of it. Respite from that light-sucking envelope. And what it contained. Something else to think about. His voice brought her back.

"So Calgary, Bonnie. This would get us to Calgary, easy. Give us a few months, probably more. But I'm being conservative, eh? It would give us the chance to pull our feet under us, and then some. It could make all the difference, Bon. It could make all the difference in the world."

She pulled herself back from dust motes. Curtains. Red balloons and unknown battles. She refocused with difficulty on the business at hand.

"Why Calgary?" she asked. Not that it particularly mattered. There was always another where. And why? Because that where was better than here.

"Oh Bon," he said enthusiastically. If he was aware of her ambivalence, he'd long ago learned how to block it out, "Things are booming there. I could get something on the rigs, eh? Or construction. All those oil millionaires need houses. Somethin's happenin' every which way you look in Calgary."

Oil. Building houses. "I think that's all over Ryan. That was all a few years ago. It's not what it was anymore."

"That's not what I hear," Ryan said obstinately, like a kid hunkering down into his belief in Santa Claus.

"Anyway," she persisted. "Even if you're right, what about us, Ryan? How do we fit in? What's it all got to do with us?"

"Dontcha see?" In his enthusiasm, he'd plucked his hat off his head. International Harvester. Bright red, with a black bill, custom-formed by his hands into a sharp "U". One of the last things he had left from his family farm. She wished he'd get rid of it. It seemed to her it probably meant more than he knew.

He twisted the ball cap between two meaty fists, then rubbed hard at the place where his hair didn't grow as well as it had just the year before. He'd let a rattail grow this last while, and she hadn't minded this attempt at fashion. Less hair here, more there—it didn't have to feel like overcompensation. More like fitting in, the long lock in back of his head curled down between his shoulder blades, bright gold where the sun had kissed it, not showing even a sign of grey.

"All that activity there, there's bound to be stuff for us to do. And with this here," he poked one cautious finger towards the creamy envelope—as though either of them had been able to forget it was there—then cast his eyes back to her pleadingly, like he hadn't said all of this to her a million times before.

All but the envelope, of course. That was new.

"Can we just stay here?" she asked, wanting the words in the air between them, even if she figured she already knew the answer.

He looked at her fully then. The look chilled her. She'd never seen his features composed in quite that way before. Handsome features still, sure. She could see the boy she'd known in high school somewhere in them. The depths of the sparkling blue eyes, the high cheekbones and craggy chin. Ten years from high school, it was all still there. Still recognizable. But something was different—in both of them, if she was pushed to admit it. Something was different now when after a short ten years you might expect it to be the same. But it wasn't the same. They *weren't* the same, either of them. It wasn't something they talked about.

"We could stay here," he said, perhaps sensing the thing in her was taut, close to breaking. "We could stay here…"

"But …" she filled in, prompting.

"Well, there's that, isn't there?"

The nudge again. The envelope.

She nodded. Agreeing.

"Yes," she said, "there's that."

"It changes things. You know it does."

"It *could* change things," she corrected. Gently. It was the first time she'd introduced the idea.

Now it was his turn to look at her for longer than was strictly necessary. She found her attention wandering again. Perhaps not unintentionally? But she noticed things. The dark hiss of the radiator that did little to fend off the cold in the room. *Radiator! Who even* had *those anymore?* They did. And she noticed the soft layer of dust that blurred the outline of their outdated, seventies-model TV. And she noticed the smell, suddenly unbearable. The smell of the take-out they'd shared for their evening meal.

And the envelope? Its contents had the power to change all of it. At least, for a short time.

She waited for his answer, but it was possible that neither of them needed the words. Finally, he spoke them anyway, though he was unusually succinct.

"Not 'It could,'" he said, his voice surprisingly strong, sure. "It *will*."

"Will it?" She wanted it to be true. Wanted to

believe.

She'd always wanted to believe.

He nodded. Uncharacteristically confident. She caught a glimpse, again, of the boy he'd been. He surprised her too, by leaning across her now, plucking the envelope from its place on the coffee table. She thought it looked dangerous in his hands. Like a serpent, maybe, in danger of waking. And she? She was a tiny mouse, heart beating too fast, perched at the tail of the snake that now slept in their shared cage.

When he pulled the contents of the envelope out in a single, unexpected movement, it took her breath away. She had wanted to let it all sleep where it lay.

Just say no. The words jumped into her mind unbidden. The words of the US President's wife. Nancy Reagan was talking about drugs, Bonnie knew, but the words were everywhere. She figured this was almost the same thing. Not something you are, but something you ingested to become something else. Something that promised to change your life. To change you for the better, though it never worked out that way, did it?

Just say no.

But she didn't have the words. She didn't even know where to get them.

Now, it was out of its envelope. He held it in front of her like he had before. She didn't want to look at it again, but found it impossible to pull her eyes away. The rich, creamy envelope produced a check on similar, creamy paper. Her name was printed on it in large, clear letters. And the impossible sum: $9,563.07. It was enough to pay rent on a nice place for a year or two with enough left over to buy a car.

"I don't get the seven cents," she said, aiming at

levity. Failing. She could feel the failure in the way the words lay still in the room.

He shrugged. The mechanics of the thing held no interest for him. It was the end result he cared about. She could read that in his eyes. So much, really, in his eyes.

"It might not even be a mistake," he said evenly.

She met those eyes again. Caught the light there. It was a mistake. Of course it was a mistake. It was disingenuous of him to pretend otherwise. Though maybe that was for her sake. Maybe he thought that if she believed it was all as it should be, it would go down easier somehow.

"It's a mistake," she repeated quietly, but with confidence. "Why would Hydro have cause to send me nearly ten grand?"

And she was right. Of course she was. Even so, she hoped that he was right and she was wrong: that there was some easy, perfect answer.

"Some kind of rebate, maybe?" They both knew how thin that sounded. She could see he knew by the way he held his face and the hope that stood in his eyes. Those eyes.

"Rebate for what?"

He didn't respond. What response could there be? Even a big company—a Tim Hortons or a Sobey's— probably wouldn't get a rebate that big from the power company. She was not quite thirty years old and didn't even own a car, never mind a house. What kind of rebate did he really think she'd get?

"No, it's a mistake," she said as though he'd asked. "It's a mistake, sure as shit. We should just send it back."

His face didn't move when she said this, but she could see the panic land there with her words just the same. It fluttered there, somewhere, light as a flame. And it wouldn't take much to fan it to a different place. She knew him well. She could see him contemplating the loss of something he had yet to hold in his hands.

He pushed himself up from the hard chair he'd been sitting in and plunked himself on the sofa beside her. Took her hand. He was going to start with a softer approach. She recognized it from long use.

"They've beautiful restaurants in Calgary, Bonnie," he said, as though they'd never left the topic behind. "And there's a neighborhood close to the city, right on a lake. A lake Bonnie. Imagine. We could live there. You and me. We could live there," he poked the check. Moved it closer, still, to her. "With this."

"On a lake?" she asked.

A smile from him now. It lit his face as though a light were shining from inside. It almost lit the dim room.

"That's right," he said, nodding. "It's beautiful. Like a park. I saw it on TV."

"But they'll find us, Ryan. In Calgary. They'll find us. Make us give it back."

"But that's the beauty, Bonnie. Dontcha see? It's not like we've done nuthin' illegal, right? Hydro sent you a check. Big deal. They sent my mum a check too."

"They sent your mum fifty-seven dollars, Ryan. It's not the same thing at all. This is enough to buy a house."

"But it is, it *is* the same thing." He was adamant, and he believed his words. She could read that too, in his face. He'd made himself *believe*. "That was a rebate check, just like this one. I seen it, Bonnie. I told you before, I'm not making it up."

"Still, that's a big difference." She laughed then, despite herself. "What would I have to have done to get a rebate check that big, Ryan?"

And he laughed too. They shared it. It spread through the room in a warm wave. And that too, was like old times.

"Heated a swimming pool?" He was still laughing, trying to think of an enterprise that would generate enough power that it would warrant electricity bills the size of the national debt. "The biggest swimming pool in Orton Park? Outdoors, but kept heated all year round so all the little kids could swim and be warm even while it was snowing."

She laughed at the thought of it, then sobered. "Still, you'd have had to pay for a lot of power to get a rebate like that." The laughter was gone now, but she could still taste it on her tongue.

"So, Calgary?" he prompted, perhaps seeing the laughter as a place to slide in his advantage.

Calgary.

It simmered in the room with them. Bright sun on a snow-filled day. Light on a lake once seen on TV.

"Calgary," she said with a faint nod, as though making a pact on a dream.

MEANTIME

by Will Viharo

*Night. Heat. Sweat. Stakeout. Ennui. "Silent Running"
by Mike and the Mechanics on the radio.*

"I'm tellin' ya, Rico, it was like the goddamn
Fourth of July in Hell," Crockett said as they sat in his
black Ferrari about a quarter mile from their
surveillance subject, peering now and then through
binoculars at a quiet blue and green Art Deco mansion,
waiting for something to happen. His pink sleeveless
shirt was soaked with perspiration beneath his heavy
white jacket. He dragged on his cigarette with cool
aplomb, as if impervious to the humidity.

"I can't believe you never told me about this,"
Tubbs said, loosening another button on his black silk
shirt, wondering why he'd worn a purple Armani suit
in this sweatshop of a city, even if it *did* fit his
undercover profile. "You sayin' you helped take down
Tony fuckin' Montana?"

Crockett nodded. "I was there, dude. I haven't been
in a firefight like that since 'Nam. It even beat that
melee up in New York a couple of months ago. We've
been in some serious situations before, you and me,
since you relocated to the Sunshine State, but this one,
Jesus, just thinking about it makes me wanna crap my
pants."

"That wouldn't look so good in them faggoty white trousers, man."

"Yeah, no shit. So to speak. Not into earth tones, anyway."

"So tell me about it. We got nothin' else to do on this stupid-ass stakeout." Tubbs turned down the radio.

"Hey, I like that," Crockett said, turning it back up.

"I thought you were a Jimmy Buffet guy."

"We ain't exactly in Margaritaville at the moment, pal."

"I hear that. Though I wouldn't mind me a tequila sunrise right about now."

"Hang tight. It'll be dawn soon enough. Not any bars open yet for the breakfast of champions. You'll have to settle for a shot on my boat. And I only stock the cheap stuff, sorry."

"As long as Elvis doesn't mind. That gator is one jealous bitch. Anyway, c'mon man, song's almost over. What was it like tradin' bullets and bad words with motherfuckin' Scarface?"

"I fired one of the kill shots, pal. At least I'm pretty sure I did. Odds are in my favor. I was kinda far behind the first wave of attack."

"Yeah? How many shooters are we talkin' altogether?"

"Hell, it made *The Wild Bunch* look like a goddamn game of PAC-MAN. Rico. I'm tellin' ya, dude was standin' up at the top of the stairs takin' direct hits to his vitals like a fuckin' zombie. He was completely coked out of his skull. Shoulda just aimed for the head but he was jerkin' around like a piñata in a hurricane, so we just shredded his torso. I don't think the fucker had a heart, or else he woulda keeled over after the first barrage. I'm tellin' ya, he looked like a dancing taco!"

"I've heard of guys whacked out to the point where they could take a couple to the chest, but this sounds like you were up against the Terminator, man."

"He obviously thought so. After he got nailed a few dozen times, he dropped what looked like a grenade launcher and let us use him for target practice until some badass with shades and a shotgun stepped up out of nowhere and blew a hole in his back the size of Cuba."

"How many other cops were with you?"

"Not just cops. FBI, DEA, pest control ... Damn, *everybody* got called in for the bust. It turned into your classic interagency clusterfuck. We lost all sense of coordination. There was a mob of Bolivian hit men mixed in with some of the undercover ops. Switek and Zito were hanging back like, half a mile away, and our wires got crossed in the maze. Nobody knew who anyone was once we got to the mansion, but there was no time to ask any of the players for ID. Montana was armed up the ass with a frickin' military arsenal, and the party had already started. The Bolivians had led us to Montana's mansion, see, after we found his old partner and his sister dead in their home. They were newlyweds, for Chrissake. Word on the street was Montana had the hots for his sister. He was one sick, twisted bastard."

"I heard she was some fine piece of ass too."

"She was, till somebody chewed up that bodacious body with an Uzi."

"Bolivians or Montana?"

"Not sure. It didn't matter. Nobody with a Latin

accent walked out of that place alive."

"So the Bolivians beat you there, obviously."

"Yeah, which was part of the plan. We were hoping they'd do our dirty work, then we'd mop up after, including them. It almost went down that way, except Montana turned out to be a much harder target than anyone anticipated. I mean, this was one fuckin' guy against a goddamn army, Rico. Unbelievable. I'd never seen anything like it. Good thing we had plenty of backup."

"It's almost like the Bolivians were working with you. Only they didn't know it. Sweet."

"Common enemy, anyway. They were sent by Sosa. You know, the drug lord down in Bolivia that got nailed last year."

"Yeah, yeah, Alejandro Sosa. Too bad he had to get popped in the raid. His inside intel would've taken down whole networks, maybe even a couple of the Cartels."

"Don't believe everything you hear, pal. I got a source inside the DEA that told me after a few beers that the cartel got nervous about all the noise down here and actually hit Sosa right before our boys arrived on scene. Those swingin' dicks stole bragging rights for this takedown just to make themselves look good to the suits upstairs. Rah-rah-rah, go team, all that nationalistic, pseudo-patriotic crap. Meantime, everyone on this side of the fence knows that Dutch Reagan is funding the rebels in Nicaragua through some covert arms deal. This was just another way to deflect attention, but I bet that dirty little secret, if true, is about to float to the surface too. Nobody can hide the truth forever."

"Just until it's too late to fix it."

"We're both singin' those vice-cop blues again, pal. Sorry I bummed you out."

"You kiddin'? I got a raging boner just hearin' about all this."

"Yeah? Well, save it for Elvis. He'll be hungry for a little sausage snack by the time we get back to the boat."

"Ha ha, motherfucker. You couldn't even measure my manhood with a ruler, you'd need a yardstick. But I catch your drift. We should just call it a night before it turns into a day again, Sonny. This is gonna be a bust all right, but not the good kind."

"Not if Izzy's tip is any good, and they usually are since he knows better than to fuck us up. Apparently this Frank dude has been operating down here ever since he left the Windy City with a bunch of bodies and blown-up buildings in his wake. He only reached our radar a couple of months ago, but apparently, he's been a Miami operator for some time now, after a brief stopover in Palm Beach."

"He's just a thief though, right?"

"Not just a thief, but yeah, that's his main gig. Lately he's been bolder, whacking out any dumb rich crook that happens to walk in on him holding an armful of ill-gotten gains, mostly jewels. I really don't mind him takin' out the garbage for us. Saves us the trouble, but still, it's against the law and shit. This so-called thief's become a regular vigilante now. I almost wish we could just let him do his thing."

"So tell me again why Vice is on this, when it sounds more like a Homicide or Robbery case."

"Because for one thing, that pretty little palace

down the block belongs to a known associate of the late Tony Montana."

"You're kiddin'."

"See, Rico? I was waitin' for just the right moment to relate this particular anecdote. Now seemed like the perfect time. This dude we're on, Enrique Salazar, he pretty much picked up right where Montana left off. In fact, we have another common enemy, meaning Frank and us. That's one reason we're hangin' so far back and peepin' the score through binoculars instead of up close and personal."

"So this cat from Chicago is another of your unwilling allies in the fight against crime, Crockett?"

"I don't know about 'unwilling.' He's been making quite a tidy little profit ripping off our friendly neighborhood drug dealers for the past few years."

"That's what I call a retirement plan."

"Well, I'm afraid his AARP membership is about to be revoked."

Time crawls by. Insects buzzing and biting. Wang Chung on the radio.

"Hey, speakin' of outrageous stories, you hear about that crazy shit that went down in L.A. last week?" Tubbs asked Crockett after a few quiet moments.

"You mean when the undercover FBI agent got popped?"

"Yeah, and the freeway chase after. Those chumps drove the wrong way up a ramp to escape. And they *did* escape, after causing quite a traffic jam, even by L.A. standards."

"Yeah, for now. I heard they got a line on those bat-shit bastards inside the Secret Service."

"What the hell? You're kiddin'."

"No shit, pal, from what I hear ..."

"You should not sit on a stakeout with your radio on, dumbfuck," a strong, low voice from behind Crockett suddenly said. Feeling the hard steel of a .45 automatic muzzle on the back of his skull, Crockett stopped talking and lifted his hands.

"Lose it," the voice commanded Tubbs, who reluctantly tossed the sawed-off shotgun from his lap out the open car top into the nearby weeds.

"Don't tell me. Your name is Frank," Crockett said without budging or blinking.

"So you're not entirely stupid. Good for you," Frank said. He was tall, muscular, and tan, with a perpetually stern facial expression. He was dressed casually in jeans and a Hawaiian shirt. He pressed the gun to Crockett's temple and cocked it. "But don't try to get smart with me. I doubt your dry cleaner can get brain stains out of a pink T-shirt."

"Best back down while you got the chance, chump," Tubbs said, eyeing Frank with practiced intimidation. "You don't know who or what you're messin' with here."

"Actually, yes, I *do*," Frank said. "You clowns have been tailing me for weeks. What, you think I am an amateur? That I can't spot a couple of cops dressed like dandies? You're like a couple of walking neon signs, for Chrissake. What I cannot figure out is whether you are on to me or just the score."

"Both," Crockett said.

"Well, I can help you with one, and it's not gonna be me, *that* you can put in the bank."

"Help us?" Tubbs said.

139

"Yes," Frank hissed. "Though I am now having my doubts since it was so goddamn easy to get the drop on you fuckin' idiots. Makes me wonder if you can handle the situation."

"What situation is that, Frank?" Crockett said, keeping his cool, but simmering beneath the surface. "Besides this one, I mean."

"Well, while you girls are sitting here gossiping like two queens in a coffee klatch, inside, there is an epic orgy in progress, with enough coke and paid prime pussy lyin' around to make your year's quota in one fell fucking swoop."

"That sounds like a set up," Tubbs said. "Our source told us the house would be empty. Until you showed up to clean out the closets, that is."

"So it is a surprise party," Frank said. "Deal with it."

"We should call for backup," Crockett said.

"I *am* your backup, slick," Frank said. "Now both of you, get your pansy pastel asses out of the car, hands in plain sight."

Crockett and Tubbs obliged, standing pat with their arms raised as Frank carefully trained his cocked .45 on both of them.

"I will let you go get your weapon on one condition," Frank said to Tubbs. "You both go inside first, after I give you the layout, make your bust while I cover you, I get what I came for, then I'm out of here."

"We can't let you continue your little shopping spree in Miami, pal," Crockett said. "It's our sworn civic duty and all that jazz, ya understand, not to let criminals roam around plying their trade on our dime. Tax payers tend to frown on that sort of thing."

"Then they need to take their grievances out on all the goddamn crooked politicians running the goddamn show into the goddamn ground from behind their cushy goddamn campaign offices," Frank said. "Me? I'm just another non-tax payer trying to make a dishonest living like everyone else. But like I said, I am done after this, at least in this godforsaken city. I clean out this asshole's safe, then I am out West where the sun does not shine by the time that fucking fireball sets on this muggy shithole again."

"So you'll agree to leave town," Tubbs said, unimpressed. "That's it?"

"That is a bonus on top of all the powder and whores inside, but yeah, that's it, slick. Take it or leave it."

"We like package deals," Crockett said, "but you're the big prize, pal. Chicago PD has been bugging Miami Dade to mail you back, in a box if necessary, for way too long to just let you skate. I admit, it was downright magnanimous of you to take out so many of your fellow public enemies up there, same as you've been doing down here, even if it wasn't for purely altruistic reasons, more like a private vendetta that just happened to benefit society at large. I'm sure you'll get a good citizenship medal from the mayor of Chicago. Ours too. You can keep it nice 'n' polished up in your prison cell."

"I did my time, slick. Not going back into a box. Ever."

"Maybe we can get you a deal, but we'll have to go through proper channels, Frank. Sorry."

"Then we most definitely do not have a deal," Frank said. "I will walk away right now, take my stash with me, and you will never see me again. And you will walk away with nothing."

"What's to prevent us from tracking you down again?" Tubbs said.

"Because I will be way outside your jurisdiction, Prince."

"Prince?" Crockett echoed with a grin as Tubbs grimaced. "Dude, I'm actually starting to like you. Okay, since you're holding all the cards at the moment, tell you what. Let me confer with my partner here, and ..."

"No time, cowboy," Frank said. "The party inside is almost over. I also heard it would be at his South Beach fuck club, leaving his house unguarded, but they switched gears and decided to stay in and order pizza at the last minute, which complicated my agenda. Otherwise I would have been in and out already, and you would still be sitting here sharing your little paranoid sour grapes conspiracy theories."

"Not polite to eavesdrop, Frank," Crockett said with a wince.

"You kept me entertained, so I figured I would cut you in on this action, since you look so sad and bored. I felt kinda bad about letting you go home empty handed. Not really, but you accidentally fit into my "Plan B." Together, we can take them all down. Works out for everybody. But split us up, his designated drivers will definitely get the upper hand."

"Designated drivers?" Tubbs said. "You mean his sober torpedoes standing guard while they fuck around."

"That is correct. I already cased it. They got way too many pistoleros on standby to take on without at least three of us. No more time to bullshit. You in or out?"

Crockett looked over at Tubbs, who looked back, paused, then nodded.

"Let's do it," Crockett said.

Tubbs retrieved his shotgun and the three stealthily approached the mansion, sticking to the street shadows.

Once they arrived, Frank led them to a secluded basement window behind some palm trees swaying gently in the soft night breeze, and motioned for them to peer inside. The basement was crowded, smoky and dimly lit, but the general scenario was evident.

Copious copulation. A sensuous sea of nude, premium female flesh. Mounds of uncut cocaine. Cash. Booze. Guns. Lots of everything.

"I count six shooters," Crockett said.

"Figure at least two more on post upstairs," Tubbs said. "Though we didn't see any from our discreet vantage point."

"Three," Frank said. "Already checked. Right inside the front doorway, out of sight, laying low to maintain the illusion nobody is home. See? I did your recon for you, so you already owe me. Discreet, my ass. Okay anyway, you two should go in the back way, around that corner, kick it in and go straight down the stairs. I will take care of the goons up front, then meet you down there."

"Wait a minute," Tubbs said, but Frank was already gone.

"Shit," Crockett said.

"We got enough firepower for this?"

"I'd say between us we got about two bullets for

each body, so we gotta make 'em count." Crockett checked the chamber of his Bren Ten 10mm. Full clip.

"From what I can see, Salazar and his boys aren't in fighting shape," Tubbs observed. "Dig those chicks, man. I feel exhausted just looking at 'em."

"We'll let them go," Crockett said. "They'll take off once the fireworks start. No room for petty prostitution perps in the paddy wagon."

"They're too hot to pop any way but one way," Tubbs said.

"Keep your dirty little mind on your job, Rico. This ain't gonna be a cakewalk."

As instructed, they crept around the back, where they found one dead bodyguard already, a casualty of Frank's exploratory visit. They got ready to rock.

"Cue the music," Tubbs said. They kicked open the door and went inside, guns drawn.

Inside it was very dark, but the sounds of hedonistic revelry beckoned them downstairs. The 12-inch extended dance mix of "Fade to Grey" by Visage blasted from a high-end sound system below.

There was no door to open once they arrived at the foot of the staircase. The air was thick with the heady aroma of unbridled sex. A fog machine from inside the basement room blew fake fumes, combined with actual marijuana smoke that billowed into the outer hallway, making the human images within somewhat hazy. They were illuminated by the swirling lavender colored lights of a whirling disco ball hanging from the middle of the low ceiling. There was a big screen television in one corner showing XXX porn with the sound off, which paled in comparison to the real-life debauchery on display. The bulky shadows standing pat on the sidelines of those wallowing in wanton indulgence were obviously the professional bystanders, packing heat. The eerie atmosphere and ominous sense of danger was exhilarating, like an ambient narcotic. Or maybe it was just the second-hand pot smoke. Didn't matter.

Showtime.

"Miami Vice, freeze!" Crockett yelled as they burst inside. The stoned guards only froze momentarily due to shock, then immediately responded with massive volleys of gunfire and expletives, which was almost (but not quite)0 drowned out by the pulsating synthesizer beat of "Fade to Grey." There were several other naked, unarmed men wallowing in sleaze, but they only cowered in fear, not posing a threat, and probably not worth any extra bother; random customers caught in the wrong place at the wrong time.

Dozens of shots and screams ensued, beautiful bodies nearly caught in the crossfire. Blood burst from heads and chests onto hysterical high-class hookers, all nude except for shiny, dominatrix-style pumps, their bouncing breasts suddenly red and sticky with gore, but not their own. Crockett and Tubbs let the women as well as their johns run past them and back up the stairs as the two intensely focused cops continued moving quickly forward through the room, literally taking out targets left and right.

A couple of the high-heeled hookers slipped and fell on the cocaine spread across the floor like flea powder, whipping up minor dust clouds, though most of it was now mixed with various bodily fluids and guts, giving it the consistency of thin, well-whipped pancake batter.

They found their main objective, Enrique Salazar, his nose covered with what looked like flour but wasn't, standing in front of a well-stocked, garishly-decorated Tiki bar, totally naked except for a gold medallion, his penis still erect and glistening from recent use.

"Fuck you, maricons!" Salazar shouted, picking up and waving around a .38 sitting next to a bottle of whiskey and pile of cash on the bar behind him.

"Now where have I heard that before?" Crockett said out loud.

"Déjà vu?" Tubbs said to Crockett. Salazar aimed the gun at them, about to squeeze the trigger.

"Including this part," Crockett said as he fired a single round from the hip straight through Salazar's forehead. It was his last bullet. Tubbs had already spent his last shell.

With everyone dead or gone, Crockett and Tubbs looked around for Frank, but he was nowhere to be seen.

Stepping over the cocaine-covered corpses, they went back upstairs to the opulent parlor, and checked out the equally luxurious living room. No one was around.

The adjacent, wood-paneled office was decked out with retro furniture. A safe behind the desk was wide open, and as empty as the rest of the house.

Out front, they found exactly what they thought they'd find. Three dead bodies. But no sign of Frank.

"We've been played for a diversionary tactic all along," Tubbs said.

"You heard what he said earlier, right?" Crockett said, holstering his empty gun. "About heading out west where the sun don't shine?"

"I assumed that meant up your cracker ass, but wrong direction, I guess."

"Where out west doesn't the sun shine, Rico?"

Tubbs nodded. "Want me to drop a dime to Seattle PD?"

Crockett shrugged and sighed. "Nah. Fuck it. Dude helped us nail these scumbags. Let's give him a head start, at least."

"And just call it a night, finally. Righteous enough, all things considered. So what do we tell Castillo?"

Crockett shrugged. "Nothin'. We got here, thought we saw a shadow creeping inside, then somebody watching the house made us and forced us into a confrontation. Frank never showed."

"It's like he was never here," Tubbs said.

"That's how it is with most of us, Rico. We're just killing time until it kills us. Nothing we do matters in the long run. We're just going through the motions until ..." Crockett stared into the dark but glowing horizon.

"Until what?"

"Until it's finally over."

Sirens wail in the distance. Dawn breaks. The stars slowly fade away.

BIG HAIR, BANANA CLIPS, AND THE FIGURE-FOUR LEGLOCK

by Nina Mansfield

Suzanne wanted to be the next Leilani Kai. That was until Wendi Richter managed to win her title back in Wrestle Mania I. Then she was all Wendi. Wendi, Wendi, Wendi. Suzanne was intent on becoming pro-wrestling's next female superstar.

"One of these days, I'll have Cyndi Lauper managing me too," she'd said. "Girls Just Want to have Fun" was her new favorite song.

That's how we ended up cutting class at Roller Alley that Wednesday afternoon. The roller rink was located in Bedwell Plaza, a strip mall off of Route 119, across the street from Carley's Tow & Fix. We went there a lot. There was a Mister Donut, a Ground Round, a Dress Barn. The Caldor's where I worked was down the street. Incidentally, that Dress Barn was the last place nineteen-year-old Andrea Russo had last been seen two weeks before.

I didn't know Andrea, but I'd seen her around campus at Westchester Community College, where Suzanne and I were enrolled. Suzanne had gone to high school with her. "She's such a wannabe. Always has that fucking pink banana clip in her hair. And her boyfriend reeks of Hai Karate," Suzanne said after we'd heard some girls whispering before Basic Accounting class about the disappearance.

"I heard she stole a bunch of jumpsuits from Dress Barn and split," said one girl.

"I heard she ran away to New York to panhandle in the subway."

"I heard she and Gino are following the Dead."

But Suzanne had her own theory. "Andrea a Deadhead? I don't think so. I'm sure she just skipped town with her boyfriend. You know, everyone is talking about how Andrea is missing. Like Gino isn't? But he is. I mean, that's why no one's really looking for them. They're probably driving cross-country in his Camaro, heading to Hollywood to be movie stars. That's totally the kind of thing Andrea would do."

Gino had this totally decked out Camaro IROC-Z. Bright yellow. You didn't have to know him to know the car. He was always revving the engine on campus. I think Suzanne actually thought he was kind of hot, but I was more into guys that wore popped collars and penny loafers than gold rings and cowboy boots. Then again, I was more headband than big hair. More Molly Ringwald than Cher.

But I wasn't analyzing my fashion choices that afternoon. And I wasn't thinking about Gino or Andrea. I was fully occupied making sure I didn't burn Suzanne with her crimping iron. We were getting her ready for her big interview.

She'd seen the ad in the PennySaver. "Aspiring manager looking for female wresting talent. This is your road to stardom." I was with her when she'd made the call. After she scheduled her meeting she squealed like a five year old. I didn't want to stick a pin in her bubble and tell her what I really thought about wrestling.

But that afternoon in the bathroom, I couldn't hold back. "You know it's not real," I said. "Professional wrestling is, like, totally fake."

Her jaw clenched up. "Is that what you think?"

"Yeah. I mean, not that you shouldn't meet with this guy. I just mean ..." I shouldn't have brought it up.

"Have you ever been placed in a Figure-Four Leglock, Laura?"

"No," I admitted.

"Would you like me to put you in one?"

I held up the crimping iron in self-defense. "No thanks."

Suzanne produced a bottle of Aqua Net and started spaying her fully-crimped long black hair into place with a vengeance. "So you're telling me that time Hulk Hogan got his head split open, and the blood was gushing out—"

"OK, yes, the blood is real," I interjected. "But they use razor blades to make cuts."

"So you say." She sprayed her hair one more time, and then started to refresh her blue eyeliner.

"Come on, Suzanne. Don't you think the way Wendi won that title match was, like, totally staged? Leilani Kai had her pinned. And then suddenly, it's all dramatic and stuff. Wendi flips her and bam, bam, bam, we have a new champion. How come none of these matches are ever boring? Real sports are boring sometimes."

I could talk and talk and talk, but I was never going to convince her. A month before, she'd dragged me off to watch Wrestle Mania on closed-circuit TV. She'd been bummed she couldn't get tickets to Madison Square Garden. We were only an hour north of the city, but it had sold out fast. Seeing the event on a giant screen at school was the next best thing. And let me tell you, the place was packed. Whole families out for a day of wrestling falseness. I mean, don't get me wrong, I found it just as entertaining as anyone else. But there was no way you could make me believe it was real.

Still, if Suzanne wanted to seek fame and fortune in the wrestling ring, who was I to stop her? I hadn't felt like going to class that afternoon anyway, and I didn't have a shift at work that night, so the least I could do was help my friend. "Look, what do I know? You're probably right."

"Of course I'm right," she said, ending the conversation.

The truth is, I was kind of jealous. Yeah, I thought wrestling was a scam. But at least Suzanne had goals. Me? I didn't know what the hell I wanted to do with my life. I figured I was gonna be stuck in the shitty suburbs, living with my parents and working at Caldor's forever.

Once her eyeliner was perfect, Suzanne went into one of the stalls. The doors were covered with "Angie Loves Bobbie" and "Debbie is a slut" graffiti. I even spotted a fresh "Andrea and Gino together forever" written in sparkly marker and wrapped up in a bubbley heart that I hadn't noticed the last time I'd been there a few weeks before.

When Suzanne came out of the stall, she was wearing a florescent pink bathing suit and matching leg warmers. Blue bracelets ran up her arm.

"That's what you're wearing?" I asked.

"I can't decide if I should wear my denim skirt or these stirrup pants. But I definitely want to be ready if he wants to see my moves."

We decided on the skirt. It made her look a little taller. Suzanne stood only 5'1", but she was stronger than she looked, and boy was she fast. She was really fit too from doing her Jane Fonda workout video religiously every morning.

We got our makeup packed back into our purses and stepped out of the bathroom. When we'd arrived earlier, the roller rink had been pretty empty. Now, there were kids all over the place pulling their skates on. Others were playing video games. On Wednesday afternoons, it was free admission at Roller Alley. They only charged you if you skated—then they gave you this special hand stamp and stuff—so a lot of kids came after school for the greasy pizza or to catch a game of Ms. PAC-MAN or Space Invaders. The crowd was on the young side, mostly junior high kids.

"Where are you meeting this guy?" I asked.

"He said at the tables in back."

I started to head that way, but Suzanne stopped me.

"You wait here, Laura. You know, bringing a friend to a job interview isn't exactly professional."

"And having a job interview at a roller rink is?" I asked.

"It's an audition," she said, like that made it all better. "Maybe he wants to see me skate or something. You know, that could be my thing, roller skating out to fight. Anyway, he said his office was in back of this place."

Suzanne headed to the back. I got myself a Tab and

went to a little alcove near the rink called "Spectator Gallery." I was gonna sit, but all the stools were either sticky or had gum stuck on them. A bunch of kids were skating around in circles, showing off their moves or pairing off and holding hands. Tina Tuner's "Private Dancer" played as neon lights swirled around the rink. The smell of greasy pizza and buttery popcorn seeped out of every corner.

After a couple of minutes I saw Suzanne's manager guy show up. He looked so out of place that I knew it had to be him. He must have come in through one of the back doors—the ones kids were always trying to sneak through on Friday nights and weekends when they charged a $3.50 cover whether you skated or not. I'd expected someone who looked like Captain Lou— overweight, bearded, rubber bands dangling from his face. This guy was maybe 5'8," wearing a sharp grey business suit and a black T-shirt. He was Phil Collins- bald and on the skinny side. I wasn't gonna stand around and stare at him and Suzanne, and I was bored of watching all the awkward hand-holding on the rink. I wandered over to the video games. Someone was playing Ms. PAC-MAN, and I didn't have any quarters anyway. The junk food stench was getting to me. I decided I needed to get a little fresh air.

Suzanne seemed engrossed in conversation with the manager, so I stepped outside. I wandered around Bedwell Plaza, poked my head into Dress Barn, thought about getting a snack at the Mister Donut. But I didn't know how long Suzanne's interview would be, so I headed back to Roller Alley instead. I leaned on one of those coin-operated rocket ships out front. It was then that I saw the tow truck pull into Carley's Tow &

Fix. It was pulling a bright-yellow Camaro IROC-Z.

And that's when I thought of Andrea Russo.

I thought about how she'd last been seen in Dress Barn. I thought about the fresh graffiti on the bathroom wall. I thought about everything Suzanne had ever said about her, and I thought maybe she'd been the kinda girl to answer an ad in the PennySaver too.

I stepped back into Roller Alley and walked past a short line of kids waiting to rent skates. The DJ was blasting Van Halen's "Jump." Kids were always requesting "Panama," because of the dirty part, but the DJ never played it. The song ended and REO Speedwagon's "Can't Fight This Feeling" started up.

I figured I was just being paranoid. Maybe it wasn't really Gino's car. I mean, he wasn't the only guy in the world with a yellow Camaro. Or maybe he'd sold it to finance his and Andrea's adventure, and they had actually hitchhiked somewhere. Or gone to the city, where they wouldn't need a car.

But somehow I knew none of that was true. And more than anything, I knew I needed to check on Suzanne.

But she wasn't there.

I looked out on the skating rink. It was a little more crowded than it had been before, but I still would have spotted her big, black crimped hair.

Not there either.

And no sign of manager guy in the Spectator Gallery or by the video games.

I practically attacked a puny kid wearing an AC/DC T-shirt who was totally engrossed in his friend's game of Centipede.

"Did you see a girl here, talking to some guy in a

suit?" I demanded.

He jumped back, startled. "Huh?"

I repeated my question.

"I dunno."

"They were sitting right there?" I pointed to the table where I'd last seen Suzanne.

"Oh, you mean the fox talking to that bald guy?"

I nodded.

"They headed back there." He nodded his head toward a hallway back behind the vending machines, the one that led to the back door.

Suzanne had said this guy's office was in back, so that's where I headed. I kept telling myself there was nothing to worry about. I mean, he had advertised in the PennySaver, right?

Concrete and dumpsters. That's all there was in back of Bedwell Plaza. Where the concrete ended, tall grass sprung up, and beyond that, forest. There's no way Suzanne would have followed this guy out into the woods. She was smarter than that. So I headed over toward the rear of the stores, looking for his office.

I started to breathe a little easier after I'd passed the back of Dress Barn. I'd never been in back of Bedwell Plaza—never tried to sneak in through the back door of Roller Alley—but there were actually some offices there. There was something that looked like a travel agency, and another office that was clearly a dentist. The other doors weren't labeled, but the boxes outside indicated there was *some* kind of business venture going on inside. When I got toward the end, I found a rusty metal door with a makeshift sign that read, "Star Management."

At that point, I just kinda stood there, trying to

figure out what to do. I could knock and interrupt what could be a totally legitimate audition, but Suzanne would hate me for that. Or I could wait, and what? What had this guy done to Andrea Russo? What had he done to Gino?

Five seconds. Ten seconds. I needed to make up my mind.

And then I heard the crash. It sounded like something large falling to the ground.

"Suzanne, you in there?" I called out. I pulled at the handle. Locked. I pounded my fist on the metal door.

There was another sound. Something smashing. I thought about Rowdy Roddy Piper smashing those gold records over Captain Lou's head. Suzanne had taped that match on her Betamax, and we'd watched that moment over and over again.

"Suzanne!" I yelled out again. I pulled at the handle, and this time it opened too easily, Suzanne on the other side.

Before I had a second to ask her what was going on, Manager Guy lunged from behind her, grabbing her in a half-Nelson and pulling her back into the room. She kicked her feet and clawed at his arms. She managed to get her hand back around to his head and pull his hair. He dropped her to the ground and jumped on top of her, pinning her down. She responded with a headbutt and was able to throw him off. She was up on her feet before he could get on top off her again, and then, suddenly, she climbed to the top of his desk. Before I realized what was happening, she was flying elbow-out at the guy like Jimmy "Superfly" Snuka. Her elbow caught him square in the eye. Blood spurted everywhere. He got to his feet and stumbled toward me. I grabbed one of his arms and twisted. Suzanne grabbed his other arm. Together, we were able to flip him back down onto the floor.

That's when Suzanne put him into a Figure-Four leglock. And boy, did that dude *scream*.

At that point I had the good sense to pull the crimping iron out of my purse. I wacked the guy over the head with it, hoping to knock him out. But all it did was make him scream louder, so I pulled out the can of Aqua Net and sprayed it in his face. He thrashed harder, forcing Suzanne to unclench her legs. But as he got up, Suzanne jumped on his back and put him in a sleeper hold. Sure enough, the hold put him to sleep.

"He'll wake up in a minute," Suzanne said, pulling off her leg warmers. "We'll use these to tie him up."

We hog-tied the guy and then got the fuck out of there. We ran around to the front of Bedwell Plaza, where Suzanne found a payphone and called the police.

We didn't speak until we were seated at Mister Donut, waiting for the police to arrive. I was shaking, but Suzanne was totally calm. "So what the hell happened? Did he, like, attack you, or something?" I asked.

"Nah. I jumped on him while his back was turned."

"But, how did you know?" I asked. I filled her in on my suspicions.

"Didn't you smell it?"

"Smell what?"

"That room *reeked* of Hai Karate. Plus, I found this." From her purse, she pulled out a pink banana clip.

The police arrived. Suzanne went out to meet them and brought them to the back of Bedwell Plaza. I remember seeing Manager Guy taken away in a police car. I got asked a whole bunch of questions too, but I couldn't tell you what they were.

Sure enough, they found Gino's body out in the tall grass behind Bedwell Plaza the next day. His throat had been slit. They didn't find Andrea until a couple of months later. From what I could figure out from the news, the condition of her body was such that it was hard to tell if she'd been raped or just mutilated.

Turns out, the manger guy was indeed a pervert and a con man wanted in Arizona and Ohio for everything from indecent exposure to breaking and entering. They found a couple of other girls who'd answered his ads in our area. One had gotten a bad vibe and left the interview. The other one had gotten sick and tried to reschedule. I guess she eventually discovered how lucky she was.

There were memorial services on campus for Andrea and Gino. People talked about it for weeks. But life got back to normal eventually, though everything changed for me. I ended up switching my major to Criminal Justice. Thought about applying to John Jay College in the city after I got my associate's. As for Suzanne, she abandoned her dreams for pro-wrestling stardom. In fact, she stopped watching it altogether, didn't even want to talk about it anymore. Which was a shame. Because after what I'd seen her do to Manager Guy, I no longer denied that professional wresting was anything but real.

DUTCH

by C.S. DeWildt

They say you got to pay for your sins. People are always saying shit like that, but I know a lot of people who haven't paid for a thing yet. Kreese didn't pay. He lost some things, sure. But he didn't really *pay*. Maybe there's no such thing as sin. Maybe it's just a lie wounded people tell themselves to sleep at night. But then, that's not to say that what you deserve can't eventually get you. It just ain't the rule. The only way people pay, *really* pay, is when you make them.

I drop off Timmy's money at the diner like I always do Monday mornings after a weekend of collects. I know he's going to make me pay for his breakfast. My penance for talking to him. I sit in the open chair across from him. Roxy stands up. I pretend not to notice her, which is absurd because all three of us know why I'm there. She looks good, as always, a little thinner than I liked her, but late nights call for a bump or two, and a bump or two will take the place of food real quick.

Not caring whether I notice her or not, she gives my shoulder a pat as she excuses herself. I turn to watch her go. She's wearing a short, billowy skirt, kind of like a tutu, over black fishnets. Her shirt is a "Wham" T she found at the Goodwill. She'd cut the sleeves off and slit the neckline so the head hole hangs loose over her shoulder. Her electric blue bra strap matches her hair.

I love the girl and Timmy knows it. When I turn back to face him, he's grinning at me like I'm a sucker, his gold tooth shining. I'm sure he has a real laugh about it with his other boys whenever I'm not around. Me, Dutch, in love with one of his whores. Another of my sins, I suppose.

"Good night," I say as I slide the envelope across the table. Timmy seems disinterested, but he always seems like that. I've stepped into many meetings since I started collecting for him and it's always the same. He stares into his newspaper with a new romance novel next to his plate, or vice versa, depending on his mood. I don't know if he reads the books or just uses them as a test, daring someone to get smart. No one gets smart.

Most of these meetings are with people who owe him money, pleading for time. He listens and then sits quiet long enough to make them wonder if he was listening at all. I don't know if he'll listen to me; this is my first time in the chair. I don't owe him money. But if all goes well, I will.

"Show Timmy your knuckles," Timmy says. It catches me off guard. Like I said, he isn't one to make small talk. I hold up my scarred fists and let him look them over. "You like the work?"

I nod. It beats frying up food at the Jack in the Box. I did that for a while after the rest of the guys went off to college.

"Good," Timmy says. "You're good at it, Karate Kid." Timmy chuckles as he drags a toast point through the yellow yolk of his runny eggs. He knows I hate that nickname. He also knows that I'm going to let him use it. "So tell Timmy what he can do for you?"

He knows damn well what I want. Roxy's been in his ear about it. But he wants to hear me say it. So I do.

"I want Roxy," I say.

Timmy nods, soaking up the rest of the yolk with the toast. "I know you do. But she's mine."

I was afraid of this. Timmy is good at needling a guy and you never really know what's going on in his head, what the endgame is for him. He might kill you or punch you in the gut and drop an envelope of money on you for doing a good job. He's a little inconsistent.

"What can I do for you in trade?" I say.

That gets his attention. He looks up from his plate and smiles. I asked the right question.

"Pay me," he says. Simple. "Timmy need to get paid." He laughs like he made some kind of joke. His life is a TV show where he's the star and the studio audience at the same time.

I wait for him to follow up and I feel like I'm with the guy in Venice who sold me my dirt bike, not wanting to name his price until I give him an idea of how much I have.

The truth is, whatever the price, it'll be too much, and yet could never be enough to match her worth. "How much?"

"What you wanna pay?" Timmy shoots back.

I don't know what to say. $200? *Everything*?

Timmy helps me out. "What do you pay for a night? Now multiply that by every night of your life."

I don't say anything.

"That's a million bucks and change," Timmy says, "assuming you make it to eighty years. But don't fret on that. Timmy don't think she's got more than another five years in her." Timmy does another calculation in his head. He's a lot of bad things: pimp, loan shark, extortionist, dealer, but you can't say he's bad with numbers. "That's less than one hundred Gs."

My heart sinks because it may as well be a million. Timmy laughs again and a small piece of egg shoots from his mouth with the spittle and lands on the cobra tattoo on my forearm.

"Don't look so sad, Dutch! You're a good kid and Timmy wants to help you out." I look at him. He removes his Ray-Bans and looks me in the eye. He's only got one good one, the other put out by a guy he was trying to make his bitch during a stretch in Chino. The punk then took a tumble off the fourth-level tier. That's the story Roxy tells, anyway.

"Timmy'll give her up to you for twenty. How's that sound?"

It sounds a hell of a lot better than a million, or even one hundred grand. But still, the magnitude of that kind of cash is staggering to me since I haven't got it yet. Timmy reads me perfectly. He pulls a red handkerchief from his pocket and wipes his mouth as he stands. "You're a smart kid. You'll figure it out. Pay for breakfast, I'll put it toward your bill."

Timmy leaves me sitting in front of his empty plate. The waitress comes to the table with the check and lays it down in front of me. Ripping open the Velcro on my OP wallet feels like what it is, my skin being ripped from the bone. I'm down to my last seven dollars. The feeling will be good to remember, because now that the deal is made, Timmy will expect the transaction to be completed. The contract is as good as signed. I watch out the window as Timmy meets up with Roxy across the street. He puts an arm around her waist and walks her away from the corner. This time tomorrow, I hope that'll be me instead. Leading her not only away from the corner, but away from this life.

***

I meet up with Roxy a few hours before the job. I wouldn't have approached Timmy if I didn't have some kind of plan. I'm scared, to be honest. We fuck like it's our last time ever. I finish inside her and roll off. We pant, sweaty in the summer heat of the small studio Timmy keeps for Roxy's "entertaining." I snap the condom from my deflating cock and toss it into a trashcan next to my side of the bed.

"Gimme a cigarette?" she says. I roll over and pull one from the novelty dispenser she keeps on the nightstand, a gift from one of a thousand Johns. This one is a pewter-made Mexican burro wearing a straw hat. You push down the hat and a cigarette pops out of the ass's ass. I light the smoke and take a drag. I don't usually smoke, just with her. I hand it over and roll out of the bed. It's usually hot in the Valley in the summer time, but the current heat wave has me ready to pass out. It might just be my nerves. I lift the window.

"Don't do that, this place is going to stink."

"Already does," I say as the slightly-less-hot air cools me. The stink she mentioned is from the exhaust fan of the Thai restaurant below us. It usually doesn't bother me, but tonight it makes me ill. I close the window and flop back onto the bed. Roxy is sitting up with her back against the wall. She's got her notepad on her lap, a journal thing where she writes lyrics and poems and stuff. She was in a punk band before she ran out of money and found Timmy to take care of her.

She's scribbling something new, and I let her be until she's done.

"What you working on?" I say. Roxy smiles and pushes back her blue hair. The sides of her head are shaved close, the same way they were in the Cunt Rage promo pic she keeps on the dresser. That pic was taken only three years ago, but Roxy's face says it was a lot longer than that.

"A letter."

"To who?"

"To whom," she jokes.

"To whom?" I say, sliding into her.

"To youm," she says.

"Let me read it," I say, reaching for the notepad. She slaps my hand.

"Not until it's done. Not until we have the money."

The money. Thirty Gs total. Twenty grand to buy her freedom and ten to start our lives over. The idea is liberating, invigorating, and terrifying.

"It's coming, right?" I ask.

Roxy's looking at me with her black eyes, the way a mother looks at a silly child. The eyes chase away my fear, replace it with shame.

"It's coming, baby, for sure. He was going on and on about it again last night. He's taking delivery of the games tonight at the arcade."

Roxy's referring to a deal she learned about from one of her regular customers, a small business owner getting a shipment of gray-market stuff, cash deal.

"Thirty grand," I say. I lean over and push on the donkey's sombrero. It craps out a smoke and I light it off Roxy's cherry. She leans into me.

"Did I ever say, 'thank you'?" she whispers.

"For what?" I say. She's tearing up the way she does sometimes. The way she did when she told me the story of how she came to belong to Timmy. How he'd saved her from five-dollar blowjobs at the Greyhound station, given her a place to stay. Food, clothing, but more importantly, a reason not to go back to her parents in Michigan. I add, "Babe. You don't need to thank me. I love you."

And then she loses it completely. She burrows into my chest, into the Cobra Kai tattoo Bobby convinced us all to get back when he won the All-Valley Tournament. As if reading my mind, Roxy wipes the tears from the black cobra and looks up at me.

"I'm sorry," she says. "I'm just scared, is all. What if it goes to shit?"

"Don't be sorry," I say. "I *want* to do this. And nothing's going to shit. Trust me. I trust you, but you've got to trust me too."

It's funny. I'm the one who's scared, but the need to make her feel better is the only thing that makes me sure of the plan. So I focus on her. There's no way I can fuck it up if it's about her.

She slides up my body and kisses me on the mouth. "No one's ever been so good to me."

"That's why you're coming with me," I say. Roxy nuzzles in again and I stroke her hair.

***

I never carry a piece but Roxy loaned me this one for the job. I don't know where she got it, maybe off some John. I should probably carry one of my own, but the bullshit code I try to live by won't let me. It's stupid, but it's about the only thing I have left. There was only one time I really wished I had one, a time a guy pulled his on me when I met him to collect. He saw me for what I was, still green in the game, thought he could scare me with it. But soon as I saw the barrel, the "No Mercy" mantra flashed in my mind. That, and Kreese's hand-to-hand techniques he brought back from Nam. Instinct kicked in and the next thing I knew, I was busting the guy upside the head with his own gun. Before I left I took what he owed off of him.

Tonight though, I need the piece, not to shoot anybody, just to put a scare into the clerk so he'll give up the cash.

I sit on my dirt bike waiting in the dark parking lot as the last of the kids leave the arcade. The blue-and-red open sign goes dark. Hard to believe I was one of these kids only a couple years ago, my biggest worry if I was going to flunk a math test.

The gun weighs heavy in my pocket. Something tells me to leave it alone. Go get Roxy and leave this place forever, figure out the money part someplace else. But no. Gotta do it right. We have to make good with Timmy, or else. He once had a guy killed in Vegas over five hundred bucks. The kind of money we're talking tonight doesn't have a safe distance to hide from.

I'm in, I say to myself. *All in.*

I leave the bike out front, walk around the back of the strip mall, and find the loading entrance for Flipper's Arcade. I hop up a small staircase and rap my knuckles on the metal door. There's nothing for a long time. I keep knocking.

"What you want?" a voice calls from behind the door. I look into the peephole and try to look non-threatening, but not friendly either.

"I'm the guy," I say.

Another pause and I wonder if someone's tipped him off. Maybe he's been ripped off before.

"Bullshit. Where's the truck?"

I look off into the direction of a phantom truck. "It's down the block. I need to make sure the money's there. When I tell the driver it is, he'll come down with the truck."

The guy doesn't answer, so I lay it on a little thicker. "C'mon, man. We got a guy at Golf N' Stuff ready to go if this falls through. Let's just get this done."

More silence, and I'm afraid I overdid it. Then I hear the deadbolt click, and I step into the small warehouse area behind the arcade. The cool air hits me in the face. After the heat of the evening, it makes me want to strip down naked with Roxy and have a nap in it.

"C'mon, c'mon," the little guy from behind the door says. He's short and balding and I realize he's not at all what I expected from the harsh and deep voice behind the door. Nerves again, making me think the worst. I follow him, putting my hand on the loaded .38 revolver in my jacket pocket, into the rear of the arcade, the games asleep now but the neon lights still throwing a rainbow glow over the patchy pastel carpet.

Little Man leads me down a hall next to the snack bar and finally into a small office, nothing to it but a desk, a potted fern in the corner, and a heavy floor safe. Little Man crouches the best he can and spins the combination dial left and right. I hold the gun in my pocket, ready to pull it. Then suddenly Little Man is spinning the dial faster than I'd imagine he could.

"Gonna rip me off, huh?" he says. Little Man has a

gun of his own, shaking in his hand. He's scared, but the anger in his eyes is real. "Little shit. Pull out your piece. Slow."

"I don't have —" I begin.

"Fuck you! Pull it out!"

I nod and pull my left hand first, show it's empty. I pull my right, the cold steel turned hot with body heat, wet with my sweaty palm.

"Hurry!"

I pull the gun free from my pocket and hear the shot. My ears ring. I think about Roxy. *Where did he get me?* The man is gone now. *Am I already dead?*

Gun smoke hangs in the air of the tiny office. My ears are still ringing, but my pupils recover from the gun flash and I see the open safe. I'm not dead. I'm not even shot. I step forward and look over the small desk. The little man is lying there on the floor, blood weeping from a small hole above his left eye, beginning to pool on the carpet around him.

I'm still piecing it together when I feel the eyes on me. I spin.

"Nice shot," Timmy says. "Made things easy for Timmy."

"What the hell you doing here, Timmy?"

"Come to get the money."

One of Timmy's guys, Big Black Vern, steps out from the hall and I think he's coming for me. I keep my hand on the pistol. Vern moves past me, toes at the little dead man to make sure he's dead, and then crouches at the safe and begins pulling out the bundles of cash. There's much more than thirty grand in the safe as far as I can tell. Vern takes all of it.

"I was here to get your money anyway," I say. "The

hell is this?"

"This is the way it is," Timmy says. I think he's going to go on, but he doesn't. Whatever "this" is, it isn't good for me.

"Where's Roxy?"

Timmy grins, flashes that single gold tooth. "Working," he says.

And then I get it, kind of. My request of him got me a new position: fall guy.

I don't think. I just rush him and before I get two steps, my knee explodes and I'm on the floor. I remember when Tommy wrecked that Larusso kid's knee at the tournament. I wonder if it felt like this. I can feel the hot blood pooling into my shoe.

Behind me, Vern wipes down the gun and returns it to the little bald man on the floor. Then he steps over me and I try to grab his leg. He kicks my hand away as he draws his own piece and holds it on me.

Timmy squats next to me. He smiles. "She's a good girl. Earner. And you crazy you think I'm gonna give that up. Timmy don't give up *shit*, you understand? Timmy takes what he want. Timmy keeps what his."

My knee throbs. "I'm gonna kill you," I say through my teeth.

Laughter. "Nah. You gonna do some time though. And if you want Roxy to keep that pretty face pretty, you gonna do it quiet. Timmy know a boy or two that pay up real nice for the chance to cut her up good. You think about that."

I curse him, but they're already gone. I roll over and use the desk to pull myself to my feet. I try the bad leg, but it screams at me as it gives out. I clench my teeth and hop out of the office, back through the arcade and into the small warehouse, dragging my bad leg and dripping blood the whole way. I need to get to my bike. Maybe I can still catch Timmy.

Outside the warehouse sits the truck the bald man had been waiting on. The driver is laying on the concrete, his throat cut, dead. I continue hopping through the lot, huffing, sweating. The endorphins and adrenaline allow me to ignore the pain, but that doesn't make my mutilated knee any more useful.

I stumble a few times, manage to get back up to my good leg. I see the bike the same time I hear the sirens. The bike comes closer as the sirens grow louder. I just need to get it started and I'll be gone. If I can make it to Encino Wash, I can lose them. I can get rid of the piece and get some help for my leg. And then, Roxy. The sirens grow louder. There's no mistaking their destination, no mistaking who alerted them.

The latter is confirmed when I see my bike on its side, tires slashed, the bloody blade still sticking out of the rubber. I see Roxy's face in my mind and I continue to hop. I'm exhausted, and the blood loss isn't helping me move any faster.

The last thing I see are the flashing read and blues reflected back to me. I hear the barking dogs, the orders to "freeze." More dogs barking as I'm knocked to the ground. I close my eyes and I suddenly don't know anything, don't know Timmy, don't know my knee is mangled, don't know the Valley heat, don't even know Roxy. And I must say. For a little bit there, it's nice.

***

Two years later and my knee is healed for the most part, healed meaning the joint moves with about half the mobility it once did, but it supports weight. I guess

I should consider myself lucky. Ha, funny what you consider good luck after a real string of bad.

I'm reading a Louis L'Amour in my cell when the letter is delivered by one of the screws. It's already opened, standard procedure inside, and I recognize the handwriting on the envelope immediately. I spread the envelope and smell inside. I smell Roxy. I pull out the pink sheet of folded paper. It's the first I've heard from her in all this time.

***

Dear Dutch,

I love you. I do. This is weird writing to you when you're right next to me, but I suppose it makes sense. Maybe I'm hoping you'll happen to read this before you leave tonight, but then, I also know what kind of guy you are and if I tell you to wait, you'll wait. I don't know how this is going to play out, but I know it isn't going to be good, not for either one of us. I feel like a shit for choosing Timmy in the end, but what can I say? I met him young. He saved me first. I'm his.

God I wish I'd have met you first. Or better yet, known you when I was younger. Gone to school dances with you, dates at Golf N Stuff, became a woman under your touch instead of, well, you know ...

God, I want that so much, just to know you when we were kids, before I became the kind of person that would fuck somebody over this way. The only person who really cares about me. I know you care, Dutch, and I still care about you, as weird as that seems now. I hope you don't hate me. I know that's stupid. I hate me, so how could you not? But I hated myself before I loved you, and old habits are hard to break. Just know that I think about you all the time, that if I'd had a

173

choice, I would have chosen you.

Love always,

Roxy

***

I stare at the ceiling as my knee throbs with twenty-four months of wasted emotion. I lift my bad leg and bend it. I grab the shin and lace my fingers, force it beyond comfort, beyond its stopping point, until the pain becomes too much. I stretch it out again, let it settle. I grab the letter again, look at her signature, a heart in place of the "O". I crumple the note and toss it into the stainless steel toilet. I realize now that everything I thought about sin was true. The only people who pay are the ones that are made to pay. I know that now.

IN THE SWIMMING POOL

by Jen Conley

It was evening, still light out, and the air smelled of hotdogs, chlorine, cigarette smoke, and liquor.

We were in Jimmy's rectangle-shaped swimming pool whipping a yellow plastic ball around, trying to outdo each other, although I was the weak link. I never could throw a ball like the boys because I was a girl.

"You suck, Andie," they said. I told them girls aren't as physically strong as boys. They came back with an entire list of females from school who could kick ass. I told them to shut the F up. It was Michael, Jimmy, and Jimmy's cousin Sean from Keansburg. They were twelve, maybe thirteen, like me at the time. I had friends that were girls, but I was a late bloomer, or maybe just odd—I wasn't into makeup or drooling over Rick Springfield or John Stamos.

It was a party and there were a slew of adults lounging in chairs, sitting at the tables, all of them down for the day from Jersey City, Yonkers, maybe Queens—that's what Jimmy said. The music was all the old stuff, Doo-Wop crap and the crooners. "The soundtrack of my teenage years," a lean, muscular man named Alan announced. Alan was wearing a red bikini-bottom bathing suit, strutting around the backyard in an open linen shirt and aviator sunglasses, the red bikini catching the eyes of some of the women.

The other adults nodded along with him wistfully.

"I bet he does porn," Sean sniggered. Alan was very hairy. We giggled and mocked him, calling him Magilla Gorilla, Michael making monkey noises and saying shit like, "Hey, catch the ball before Magilla gets it!" followed by, "Oo, oo!"

I don't know if Alan heard him. I think he did even though the party was pretty loud. Jimmy had some other cousins and family friends there, and they were running around the grass screaming at each other as they weaved through the tables and the horde of people. "Come Go With Me" floated from stereo speakers perched in the back windows of the house. I heard Alan singing along in a big sonorous voice like a disc jockey. He took off his aviator sunglasses and pulled off his linen shirt, placing both on empty chair, then slipped out of his flip-flops and strolled over to the edge of the pool. He dove in with a sloppy splash, waves traveling through the water, crashing against my stomach in the shallow end. Jimmy and Sean were in the deep end, both using small tire floats to keep above water. Michael was across from me, also in the shallow end. We stopped throwing the ball and watched Alan swim underwater, cutting through like a shark, heading straight for Michael like a torpedo.

There was a gentle splash when he came up. "There he is!" Alan said to Michael.

Michael backed up as Alan stood tall and waded towards him. He circled Michael, who hadn't grown into the wiry, tough man he would one day be. Back then Michael was skinny, knobby, smaller than Sean and Jimmy, but he was quick. He ducked left, then right, disappeared under the water. Alan laughed, but his face darkened. With one leap, he jumped on top of Michael and snatched my friend up like sea monster. Michael squirmed, but Alan was too much. He got Michael into a choke hold and a second later, hoisted Michael into the air, his right arm hooked around Michael's torso and arms, Alan's other arm around the waist.

"Should I do it?" Alan shouted.

"Stop!" Michael cried out.

I looked at where Alan's left hand was — it was on the top of Michael's trunks. He was threatening to pull them down.

"What do you think?" Alan's loud voice echoed in the yard.

The noise from the party lowered as all attention turned to the drama.

"Do it!" some guy called.

"Yeah?" Alan said, his fingers clasped on Michael's waistband, inching the trunks down, below Michael's tan line.

"Don't!" Michael shouted and squirmed more, but I saw the tendons in Alan's hairy arms tighten.

"Should I do it?" Alan shouted again.

"Yeah!" a woman at one of the tables yelled.

"Do it!" another called.

"Alan, put him down!" another woman screamed.

Alan laughed at her and then said, "I'm gonna do it!" He inched the shorts down again, revealing more white skin. Another bit, Michael would be exposed. I looked across the water at Sean and Jimmy, who had moved to the sides of the pool, their floating tires rocking on the small waves, their eyes glued to the scene. Even the little kids who had been running around were still, holding their little toys and staring at Michael, not quite understanding.

"I'm doing it!" Alan shouted. Michael whimpered.

"Stop!" I screamed.

Alan's head twisted towards me.

"Stop it!" I repeated.

"Stop it," he mimicked.

I looked to Jimmy and Sean for help, but they were frozen.

"Stop being a jerk!" I shouted. That got a laugh from the crowd.

"Yeah, Alan, stop being a jerk!" a man yelled out, mocking my girly voice.

Alan scowled and I knew I had crossed the line— he could drop Michael and go after me.

Michael sobbed and begged Alan to let go. There was no chance of escape, and fighting back meant risking exposure to the entire party.

"Alan!" Another guy called from the bar area. "Get out of the damn pool, you hairy bastard. We've got drinks up here!"

Alan huffed, hesitated, then readjusted his hands and tossed Michael away. Michael hit the water like he'd fallen from a building.

"Assholes," Alan grumbled. He climbed out of the pool and made his way to the patio where the drinks were.

Michael swam to the far end and pulled himself out. I did the same, and so did Sean and Jimmy. Sean handed Michael a towel and I found one for myself. There were some folding chairs in this corner of the yard and we all sat down, huddled with our towels. I didn't know what to say. I looked at Sean and Jimmy.

Jimmy shrugged. He didn't have anything to say either. The little kids walked away and the party people returned to their conversations. The music switched to that stupid crooner song, "Venus," and I heard Alan singing again.

The sky had dimmed and dusk loomed over the yard. Jimmy's mother staggered over and switched on the huge, monstrous bug lamp with a long neon purple bulb that hung on the fence near the pool. All the kids loved when the beetles or huge moths flew into it, getting themselves electrocuted.

"I know you guys like the bug light," Jimmy's mother mumbled to us. She stumbled a bit and giggled, muttering something about too many drinks.

We sat quiet and waited for the bugs to get zapped. Michael let out a half smile when a moth got caught and sizzled for a half minute.

After it died, Michael told me he wanted to go. We were damp, covered in Jimmy's towels as we slipped out through the back gate. We walked down the block to my house, both of us wearing sneakers. Michael didn't want to go home because he had a dickhead father who was probably drunk — it was Saturday night, after all. So we sat in my family room watching TV and eating Doritos. We were in dry clothes now. My brother was a couple years younger than Michael, but he still could wear Brian's clothes. That's how small Michael was. He had the body of a fifth grader.

Michael sat quietly on the couch, taking a chip every so often. It was strange because he was normally running his mouth, starting shit with some other kid, taking a punch, throwing one. Michael was used to dealing with his mean-ass father, but his father wasn't a pervert and Michael wasn't used to dealing with the shit he'd just dealt with in the swimming pool.

My mom was in her bedroom reading. She wasn't one for neighborhood parties. When I'd come in, after I had sent Michael into the bathroom with Brian's clothes, I went into see her, relaying what had just happened in the pool. I wanted to tell someone. I wanted someone to do something.

But all she did was press her lips together and shake her head. "Disgusting," she mumbled. There wasn't much she could do.

***

An hour later, while we were watching TV, my grandfather showed up.

My grandfather lived with us because my dad was gone and my mother needed help with the mortgage. Grandpa had been at a Ladies' Supper, some weekly thing over at one of the several retirement villages in our township. He was sixty-eight and a big deal with women in his age bracket—handsome, sturdy, able to lift things. My grandfather had lived a hard life. He could either be charming or ruthless. I adored him.

Grandpa left the kitchen and I fidgeted, wondering if my mother was still awake and whether she would tell him the story before he went to bed.

Five minutes later, my grandfather called for me. "Andrea!" He wasn't calling me Andie, so I knew he meant business.

He was standing in the hallway, arms crossed against his wide chest.

"Your mother told me some asshole tried to pull Michael's pants down?"

I swallowed and told him the story. I also added

the part about why — that we were making fun of Alan. It was always best to get the entire story correct for my grandfather, even the parts you didn't want to tell him. "He was wearing a red bikini and he was hairy, so we were calling him Magilla Gorilla. You know how Michael gets."

"Michael was calling him a gorilla?"

"Not to his face…" I said. I was starting to regret I had even told my mom the story.

"But," Grandpa went on. "Michael called him a gorilla and this man held him up in the pool and tried to pull his pants down in front of everyone?"

I nodded.

Grandpa grimaced. "And Michael was crying and asking to be put down?"

"Yes."

"Your friend gets himself in some peculiar situations, you know that?"

"His dad is mean."

Grandpa raised his thick eyebrows. "What the hell does that have to do with anything?"

I had learned on an episode of Donahue that boys who had abusive fathers had tendencies to partake in risky behavior. I communicated this information to my grandfather.

"Are you planning to be a psychiatrist someday?"

"No."

He huffed and rolled his eyes. "Where is the kid?"

When we got into the family room, my grandfather said to Michael, "Take me to that man."

Michael eyed me, connecting the dots.

"It doesn't matter," Michael said, leaning back against the couch and staring at the TV. "I don't care."

"Yeah, you care," Grandpa said. "So show me."

Michael looked up at him for a moment, deciding if he should go ahead with it. Then he wiped his eyes and stood. We walked out of the house, down the street, trailing after my grandfather. I let him know the guy's name was Alan.

"Alan," Grandpa repeated.

I could hear the oldie music playing and people talking and laughing as we approached. We followed my grandfather through the back gate and along the meandering path that led to the pool area. It wasn't that dark with the spotlights glowing, so we could see. None of the kids were around anymore, probably inside playing Atari. A few adults noticed us, but they were drinking and that seemed more important.

My grandfather stopped in front of a table and turned to us. "Point," he ordered Michael.

Alan wasn't far, just two tables away. Michael couldn't, or wouldn't point. So I did. I pointed out the man who had humiliated my friend in the pool. "That guy," I said.

Grandpa nodded and walked over to the table where Alan sat. "You Alan?"

Alan's head turned to my grandfather. "Yes."

Grandpa snatched him up by the arm like a doll and punched him in the mouth. Alan stumbled backward, his linen shirt floating like curtains in a window. My grandfather went after him again, punched him once more. People jumped out of their seats, yelled. From the corner of my eye, I saw some men coming forward. Grandpa hit him once more, then stopped, leaving Alan standing in his red bikini and linen shirt, his face a mess with blood.

My grandfather stormed by me and put his hand on Michael's shoulder, pushing him forward. "Go," he ordered.

As we walked along the path towards the gate, an insect got caught in the bug zapper and sizzled. Michael stopped and swung around to face me. He was grinning. "You hear, it Andie? You hear it?" His voice popped and bounced happily. "I love it!"

It was such a sudden switch — he was his old self, the kid who cheered on the bug zapper. My grandfather didn't seem to notice. "Get going," he said.

Michael started walking again. "It's just great. I love when that happens!"

When we reached the gate, Grandpa held it open with his left hand and rubbed his right hand against his chest. It was obviously hurting him.

"You kids are a pain in my ass," he said as we passed through.

And then we were out on the street, walking through the summer night. Michael didn't thank my grandfather for avenging him. But he did mimic Grandpa's punches.

"You Alan?" Michael said to nobody as we walked. Then he threw a swing into the air, following it up with a *Bam!* sound. He did this the entire walk home.

GETTING SECONDS

by Greg Barth

When *The Phil Donahue Show* cut to the live press conference, Pardo was at the kitchen table putting his pistol back together. It was a cheap .32 automatic, and it was prone to jams if he didn't keep it good and clean.

"Ah fuck, man. I wanted to see that break dancing shit." Pardo scraped his nails across his scruffy chin. He kept the dark stubble on his face the same short length as the hair on his head.

Bobby was lying on his back on the couch smoking a Vantage, glass ashtray filled with butts on his chest, like he did pretty much all day, every day. Lean and scrawny, Bobby was tall and had curly dark hair that spiraled out from his head in every direction. He jerked his head and squinted at the TV screen. "Look at this, man. It's fucking her."

Pardo looked over at the screen. Standing next to the man at the podium was Britney Jackson, the girl who had been shot in the head during an armed robbery.

"No fucking way," Pardo said. "Turn it up man. If she's gonna speak, I gotta hear this shit."

Bobby pushed himself up from the couch and placed the ashtray on the cluttered coffee table. He crossed the room, turned the volume knob until the sound from the TV set filled the room.

The man standing at the podium was County Sheriff Brad Daniels. "Before Britney says a few words, I would like to remind everyone that the fugitives who committed this horrific crime are still at large. If anyone out there has helpful information—any information at all—that would aid us in our investigation, I encourage you to call the anonymous tip line at the bottom of the screen today."

"Damn. She still looks pretty hot, don't she?" Pardo said. "Even with all her hair gone. That's a pretty scarf."

Bobby sat back on the couch. "Shut up, man. I want to hear this."

On screen, the woman wearing a red scarf covering her head stepped up to the podium. She moved in jerky, awkward steps, as if every move required deliberate effort. She flashed a big smile and waved at the unseen crowd. Her eyes lit up, bright and glassy. There was the sound of applause.

"Britney Jackson, Shooting Survivor" was printed across the bottom of the screen.

Britney was dressed in a white blouse. She had pretty features—prominent cheekbones, sparkling green eyes, a long, delicate neck, and full lips. Her eyes glowed when she smiled.

Another woman stood close by her side. She was a bit heavier than Britney, and didn't look as happy. Her face carried a look of concern. Her mouth was flat and her eyes had little life in them. Minus the facial animation, she looked a good bit like Britney. They could have been sisters.

"Who's the other chick there?" Pardo said. "She looks kinda damn familiar."

"No idea," Bobby said. "Wonder if she's got a big scar under that scarf from the bullet? You think?"

"Hell, I doubt it. They can do so much with plastic surgery nowdays. Probably not even real skin and shit under there."

"What the hell do you know about plastic surgery?"

"I watch TV," Pardo said. "They can make anybody look like anything."

On screen, Britney spoke. "Thank ... you ... all ... for being here ... today," she said.

"Still recovering," Pardo said. "Speech all fucked up. Bullet must'a hit the vocal part of her brain. Still, she's hot."

"Just be glad you got a piece of it when you did," Bobby said.

"Shit. I'm already thinking about seconds. She don't gotta be able to talk. Better if she don't."

On screen Britney said, "Kessie ... she's like an... angel. Kessie say ... says ... Kessie says ... now, Britney, don't you ... don't you go ... getting sad. Everybody ... is here to ... help you. Everybody loves ... you."

The crowd applauded again. "We love you Britney," someone shouted.

Britney flashed her big smile again. "I love ... you too," she said. "I want ... to thank ... everybody for ... your con ... constant support. And I want ... to ask ... if anyone ... can ... help ... bring the ... horrible men ... that did this ... to justice. The police ... need ... your help. Thank you."

"Hear that?" Bobby said. "She called us horrible men."

"Kessie, Kessie, Kessie ..." Pardo said over and over

under his breath. "Shit. Holy shit! I fucking got it, man."

"What?"

"Kessandra Jackson?"

"Yeah?"

"Fucking PO, man."

"Huh?"

"Kessandra Jackson was my brother's fucking parole officer."

"So?"

"That Kessie on TV? That Britney was buh-buh-babbling about? That's Kessandra Jackson. I *knew* I recognized her. That's gotta be Britney's sister."

"Sure. Small world, huh?" Bobby said.

"Nah, man. You just don't fucking get it. That hot little Britney? I'm going to get me some more of that shit." Pardo pointed the re-assembled .32 at the TV and sighted down the barrel at the woman on the screen. He was wearing a black tank top. His arms were the kind you got from five years of push-ups in the state penitentiary. The tattoos covering them were of the same origin.

"You're just asking for trouble. You gotta stay away from that shit," Bobby said.

"When have I ever stayed away from something like that when I wanted it?"

"You just ain't right in the head, man."

"That bitch will help me get right. You wait and see."

"So you know who her sister is. That don't mean you can find them."

"Know who she is and where she works," Pardo said. "Just a matter of time and effort to get the rest."

***

Bobby had been feeling antsy on the drive over that night. He needed a fix in the worst way, but he was all out. Out of smack and out of money. Out of everything with no fucking-good way to get any more.

But then Pardo had had this idea that he shared in the parking lot inside Bobby's piece-of-shit Chevette.

Bobby pulled into the strip mall from the side and parked along the dark lane leading around behind the building.

"That's good," Pardo said. "Nobody's going to see us way the fuck over here."

Bobby didn't think anyone would be watching to begin with. First of all, this was a rundown, shitty part of town. Second, this strip mall was ancient. Most of the storefronts were closed and boarded up. Only the check-cashing place and the laundromat were open. It was only 5:45 PM, already full-dark in late November. Many of the bulbs were burned out in the lot, leaving it heavy with shadows.

There were only two cars in front of the check-cashing place. Bobby figured those belonged to the women that worked inside.

Bobby turned down the volume on the cassette player, cutting Mick Jagger off in the middle of "Undercover of the Night."

Pardo was babbling on and on about his plan. "So the fact that it's Friday evening and the first of the month is a good thing. It's a rare occurrence, man."

"How is that a good thing again?" Bobby said.

"Weren't you fucking listening to a goddamn thing I said?"

"I might've zoned out there for a second. Man, I

got, like, a bad brain cell or something. I should sign up to get a check for it. You know if Social Security covers that shit?"

"So people get paid on Fridays, right?"

Bobby thought for a moment. He nodded his head. "Yes. They do."

"And when do government checks come? First of the month. You sign up, that's when you're gonna get that check for your dead brain."

"Still, it don't connect for me. I don't mean to be so slow getting up to speed on this."

"So this is their busiest day. Like, e-ver. It's like a double hit that only comes up in a blue moon. People have had checks written out until payday. Today is payday. People have checks held until the first. Today is the first. They come in and pay off their checks. So they got extra money in there now. From both of those events on the same day. It's like a fucking two-for-one lap dance."

"But it's not the first of the month," Bobby said.

"Yeah, dipshit. It's not the first. The first falls on Sunday. So, the government don't do shit on Sunday. So for them, today's the first."

"But don't most of them re-write? Mom always does. All the money's going to be gone."

"Not true," Pardo said. "Here's why. They start today with a lot of cash on hand to cash out payroll checks and make loans, right? But when everybody comes in to pay off their payday loan, sure most of them re-write, but it's still a net gain for the store. They bring five hundred and eighty dollars in with them and walk out with five hundred. See?"

"No man, I don't," Bobby said. "The store's five

hundred lighter when they leave, right? So end of day, they've got nothing."

"No. That ain't right. See the person that is paying off the loan brings the five hundred in with them. It's not like it was already in there. If it was, we'd have gotten up early and hit this morning. They bring it in and they take that five hundred right back out the door with them. But the store, on the other hand, is up eighty dollars. They keep the eighty. You do that all day long, it adds up."

The light came on for Bobby. "Yeah, I fucking see, man. I get it. This is good. You've got a good idea. And the timing, man—fucking brilliant." Bobby grinned, flashing his brown teeth.

"Right? So we hit them last thing on a Friday, a Friday that happens to be the first of the month, and we come out with a lot of green. It's got to be today."

"But what if they go to the bank throughout the day and make deposits?"

"That's the beauty of it. I've watched this place. Only two girls all day long. Can you believe it? Fucking *chicks* run this place, man. Easiest fucking job on the planet. And one of 'em's got a piece of ass on her. Wait 'til you see. Most days, one will go out and get some food and come back. She don't go to the bank. She goes to get that shitty McDLT like fucking Webster, or to some Chinese joint. Any other down time they got is spent standing behind the counter smoking. All fucking day like that. Smoking and yak, yak, yaking. Walk in there, it's like a fucking smokehouse, man. But on Fridays and firsts of the month? They are fucking heads down, working all day long. No breaks hardly. They don't even got time to fucking smoke."

"So what do you need me to do?"

"Put this on." Pardo handed him a knee-high stocking. "When we go in, flip the sign to 'Closed' and stand by the door. Turn your back to the room and watch the lot."

"Got it," Bobby said.

"I'll do all the talking. I'll get the money, and take care of the girls—tie 'em up or something—and then we get the fuck out."

"How much do you think we'll get?"

"Shit, man. You'll be able to buy enough smack to be a dealer if you want to."

"Nah, man. That's too much like work."

"All I'm saying is, you got money, you got options."

"Let's go," Bobby said.

***

Gina was counting money, banding it, and putting it in the safe while Britney went on and on about her fiancé. She tried to block out Britney's voice as she counted, but she didn't ask her to be quiet. Gina had worked with Britney long enough to know that she was going to have to let her talk this one out.

"... and I told him I knew he'd slept with her because I could smell it. I could *smell* her on him. He said I was full of shit. I told him I knew what a girl's kitty smells like. I've had one my whole life, you think I've never smelled it, and he was like, 'Well I'll just take that ring back then,' and I was like ..."

Gina stopped counting at the right number, bundled up another stack of bills, and put them in the safe. She was too tired to make a run to the bank that evening. Her daughter needed her to pick up a book on her way home. Something she was doing research on at school. Then it would be a late dinner. TV dinners again. Friday night. That meant they would watch *Miami Vice*. The money would keep in the safe. They opened the check-cashing place for a few hours on Saturday mornings, and she would make the run to the overnight deposit then.

"... I don't need me no man," Britney was saying. "I keep a fresh supply of batteries on hand. I know how to get where I want to go, and I can do it a whole lot better than he can anyway. And there's less to have to clean up afterward too. Truth is, he ain't worth it. And if he thinks he can just ..."

Gina saw movement in the parking lot. Somebody was walking up to the door. She glanced at the clock. 5:55. This would be the last customer of the day. *Thank goodness*, she thought to herself.

"... so I told momma that I was not gonna send out all the cancellations. People would just have to spread the word ..."

"Customer, Britney."

Britney looked up.

The bell above the door rang as the door pushed inward. Two men walked inside.

"I can get you right here, honey," Britney said as she walked up to the counter. Then she gasped.

Gina heard and looked up. *Oh shit.* The men wore stockings over their faces. One of them stood by the door. He flipped the lock bolt and turned the "Open" sign over to "Closed." The other man approached the register.

The safe was under the desk, well back behind the counter. The front of the desk prevented anyone standing in front of the counter from seeing the safe. Gina nudged the safe door closed with her foot.

The man at the counter had a gun pointed at Britney.

No one spoke.

Gina placed the bills she was counting on top of the desk and walked around the edge of it. She approached the register. Her mouth was dry. "Can I help you, sir?"

The man pointed the gun at her. "Open the safe. Give me everything. Nothing funny."

Gina drew a deep breath. "The safe is on a timer, there's no way I can open it right now. But if you want—"

The man shot her in the chest.

Gina felt an icy sensation spread throughout her body. Adrenaline surged through her. She looked down at her chest. She was wearing a low-cut blouse that showed the tattoo at the top of her left breast—a hummingbird hovering in front of a lily—and a ton of milk-white cleavage. A trickle of blood drained from the hole above her right breast. *Oh lord, I've been shot*, she thought.

Pain blossomed around the entrance wound and then exploded throughout her chest. She fell to her knees, feeling the blood drain from her face. Black dots danced in her field of vision. *Am I going to be okay?* she thought. She looked around. Britney's jaw hung slack, her eyes wide with horror. Her hands covered her mouth.

Gina felt the room spin and she saw the floor rise up to greet her.

***

"Stupid fat cow," Pardo said. "You alright back

there?"

"Uh, yeah," Bobby said. "I thought we wasn't going to hurt 'em?"

"Well now we are," Pardo said. "Try to keep up with what's happening here. Keep an eye on the door."

The girl standing by the counter turned back to him. She was tall and thin. Pardo could tell she had nice, firm boobs under her shirt. He liked how she kept her long brown hair looking pretty and shiny. The other woman was ugly as hell and had a mouth on her. Now she was dead. The girl in front of him was something else. She was young and fit and prettier than any woman Pardo had ever been with. He wondered what she would look like under all those clothes. The brass nametag on her blouse said "Britney." Well Britney looked like she was going to either scream or faint. Pardo couldn't tell which. He turned the gun to point at her. "Don't you fucking tell me there's a timer on that safe, you hear me, cunt?"

Britney opened her mouth but didn't say anything.

"Nod yes," Pardo said.

Britney nodded. She looked scared shitless.

Pardo chuckled. "Now, I'm coming over there with you to make sure you do this the right way." He opened the waist-high door at one end of the counter and stepped through to the other side.

"You piss your britches?" he said. He gestured toward the large wet spot on her pants.

Britney looked down at herself.

"It's okay. You can change them when we leave. Now, where's the safe?" Britney turned and pointed a shaking hand at the desk behind her.

Pardo walked over and knelt down on one knee,

keeping an eye on Britney. He felt under the desk and found the door. It was closed but unlocked. "Well looks like you've already got it open for me. Empty those cash drawers and bring me all the bills inside. Leave the change."

Britney did as commanded. Her hands shook as she brought the bills over and pushed them into the bag.

"Now get everything out of the safe and do the same. You can keep the fucking checks."

Britney got down on her knees. Pardo walked up close to her, looking down at the top of her head and enjoying the view. He felt something stirring in his pants.

Britney cleaned out the safe and stacked the bundles of bills on top of the desk. She started to stand up.

"Unh-uh," Pardo said. "Stay right where you're at."

Tears rolled down the girl's cheeks. "Please don't hurt me," she said.

"If you don't want me to hurt you, then you're going to do what I want you to do like your life depends on it," he said. "'Cause it does."

***

Kessandra was exhausted by the time she got home. She had taken all of her sick leave to help Britney with her recovery, but now she was back at work and Britney was out of the hospital and staying with her. It was just too much.

Britney's recovery had been miraculous. One of the thugs had used her in a horrible way and then shot her in the head. Somehow she had survived both the GSW and the surgery. Once the bullet was removed, she was able to recover beyond what anyone had expected. It would take time, but she was getting a little better each day. Kessandra was hopeful that her little sister could have a good life again.

But in the meantime, it was exhausting to work all day and also care for Britney. She needed so much. Their mother had moved in with them to help out, but Mom was not doing so well herself. This week, she was in the hospital, getting over a tough bout of pneumonia. Everything was left to Kessandra.

Britney's fiancé bailed early and hadn't been heard from in weeks.

Britney was childlike in many ways. She no longer seemed to know what kind of behavior was appropriate versus inappropriate. She would just do, well ... anything that came to mind. Some of the behavior was embarrassing. Some of it was, quite frankly, disturbing.

For one thing, she was sexually preoccupied in an innocent way. Kessandra had to set boundaries. She didn't want anyone ever taking advantage of her sister again. Britney was also obsessed with "fixing" things. If she perceived that something was broken, she felt it was her duty to fix it.

Kessandra had a small puppy. It was a tiny, fluffy little thing that was just as sweet as it could be. She'd thought about getting rid of it to ensure she had no distractions while caring for Britney, but she hadn't. Then Britney was home and she took up with the damned thing.

Kessandra wasn't as attentive to the little dog as she had been in the past, and there were the occasional accidents. One evening when she was especially tired and had to mop up dog pee on the linoleum, she made the offhand comment, "If you don't stop this, I'm going to have to get you fixed."

Britney overheard and said, "Is puppy broken?"

"No. Not that kind of fixed. Fixed another way."

Then came the day that Kessandra heard the dog yelping from Britney's bedroom. She went down the hall and opened the door. She was shocked by what she saw. The puppy was on the floor on his back. Britney was on her knees holding a bloody screwdriver in one hand. The dog's fur was matted with blood.

"What is going on?" Kessandra said.

"Oh, I fix puppy," Britney said, her voice filled with childlike innocence. She looked up and smiled, eyes lit up, her face seeking praise.

Kessandra made every effort to hide the horror she felt. Britney could not help what happened to her. Her mind wasn't the same.

That was the worst, but Kessandra's heart filled with dread every time she opened the door, afraid of what she might find.

As Kessandra stepped into the house at the end of the day's work, she hoped she wouldn't be walking into another grisly scene.

Kessandra was a field Parole Officer, meaning she worked outside of the office as much as inside. She spent a good bit of her time visiting the homes and places of employment of her assigned parolees. As such, she had been sworn in with full powers of arrest and issued a .357 service revolver. She was weapons-qualified but had never fired her pistol in the field.

She grabbed a sack of groceries from the back seat

and fumbled with her keys on the way to the front door. As she stepped inside, she saw another car pull up.

Probably the neighbors, she thought.

***

When Kessandra went inside the house, Pardo jumped out of his car and pushed his way in behind her. He had his pistol out and ready.

"What the—" Kessandra said.

"I'm *ba*-ack," Pardo said.

"Who the fuck are you?" Kessandra said. "Get out of my kitchen."

"I'm your sister's boyfriend. Is Britney home?"

"Oh you *motherfucker*," Kessandra said. She dropped the sack of groceries and went for her pistol.

Pardo leveled his .32 at her and squeezed the trigger. The shot hit Kessandra in the throat.

Kessandra was still arcing her Smith & Wesson. The bullet had not stopped her.

Pardo pulled the trigger again, but it didn't fire. He looked down and saw the breech was jammed.

"Shit," Pardo said and tried to move out of the way. Kessandra fired. The bullet caught him in the arm below his elbow. "Fuck!" He pushed past her and ran through the kitchen.

Kessandra lined up and fired another shot. The .357 magnum slug hit Pardo in the back right between his shoulder blades.

He fell face-first to the floor.

Kessandra lowered the pistol. She leaned forward, put both hands on her knees, and tried to breathe. She coughed. The blood in her throat choked her. A large amount pooled on the floor between her feet. She felt dizzy and wanted to sit down.

She pitched headfirst onto the floor. Her world faded as her blood spread across the linoleum.

***

There was the sound of a door opening.

Pardo tried to look up. He couldn't move. He felt a painful jolt of electricity go through his arms and legs when he tried to budge them. The second bullet must have caught his spine. He could wiggle his head just a little. He lifted his chin from the floor and saw feet moving toward him. There was something wrong with one foot. One would take a step, and the other would drag up to it. Then the good foot took another step, and the other foot dragged up again. Step by painstaking step, the feet moved toward him.

Pardo heard a thin, soft voice. The words spoken terrified him.

"I ... will ... fix you," the girl's voice said. "I fix you."

***

Britney sat at her vanity table staring at her reflection in the mirror. She held a long-shank screwdriver in her hand.

Below the edge of the scarf, her brow wrinkled as she thought.

One of her doctors had told her that part of her brain was missing. A bad man had shot her in the head. The bullet had done extensive damage.

Britney thought her thinking was slow and muddled because her brain was out of balance.

She looked at the screwdriver.

The doctors couldn't fix her brain, but Britney

thought she could.

If ... I can ... just ... push some brain ... to the other ... side ... of head. My head. Thoughts ... could run ... smooth.

She leaned toward the mirror. She took the sharp point of the screwdriver and pushed it into her ear.

She felt resistance. Her hand shook as she repositioned the screwdriver to enter her ear canal from another angle.

The tip slipped in further. There was a burst of pain. Britney winced and jerked the screwdriver away.

Must be ... another way.

She stared at her reflection.

She'd already tried entering through her nostrils and her mouth. Neither had seemed to work.

Think.

And then it hit her at once.

My eyes.

She leaned closer to the mirror.

The dark spots in the center of her eyes. The pupils. The round black dots looked like holes. Holes that gave direct entry to her brain.

She picked up the screwdriver.

It was difficult holding her eye open. She kept wanting to blink while she fought to steady the screwdriver with her trembling hands. Looking not at the tool in her hand, but rather at her reflection in the mirror, she lined the tip up with her left pupil and slowly pushed it closer and closer to her eye.

And then she heard Kessie come through the kitchen door.

Britney lowered the screwdriver.

She heard voices from the kitchen. Kessie's and someone else's. Kessie was talking to a man.

Britney startled at the first gunshot. A loud *POP!* And then there were more shots, her body jerking reflexively at each one. She raised a trembling hand to cover her open mouth.

Britney pushed her chair back from the vanity, stood and started toward the kitchen. She walked slowly, dragging one foot along with each step. She had not recovered full use of the leg, maybe never would, but she could get around well enough.

Kessie lay on the kitchen floor in a pool of blood.

Britney knew from fixing the puppy that Kessie had lost too much blood.

A man was on the floor also. He was much closer to Britney and there was very little blood near him.

The man looked familiar, but Britney couldn't recall where she'd seen him before.

Britney held the screwdriver out to show the man.

"I ... will ... fix you," she said. "I fix you."

Britney sat on the floor next to the man. She pushed his shoulder until he rolled over on his back. The man's head jerked but his body was limp.

His eyes widened when he looked up at Britney. His lips quivered.

"Shh. Shh. Don't ... talk," Britney said.

She held up the screwdriver and smiled.

The man's face was a mask of terror.

"It's ... okay," she said. "See? I ... will fix you." She smiled again.

"Call for help," he said. "Please. I think I'm paralyzed."

"If ... your brain ... is hurt." Britney shook her head. "Doctors ... can't help. But I know ... a way."

She leaned toward the man and put the tip of the

screwdriver in front of his eye.

"No. No," Pardo said.

He closed his eyes tight.

"Open ... open your eyes. Show me ... black dot."

"Please," he said.

Britney used her thumb and forefinger to pry open the man's eye.

"Stop ... squirming."

"What are you — "

"Show me black dot."

Britney pushed the tip of the screwdriver into Pardo's eye.

He screamed. He jerked his head.

"Stop ... moving."

Pardo screamed louder.

Britney pushed the screwdriver deeper into his eye. When she felt resistance, she took the screwdriver in both hands, pushed harder and twisted the shank back and forth. There was pop and the tip plunged deeper into the man's head. A spurt of blood erupted from his eye, and a crimson tear streaked down his temple.

The man's tongue protruded from his mouth, wedged tight between his teeth. A pool of urine spread across the linoleum from underneath him.

"Does that ... feel better?" Britney asked.

CAUGHT ON VIDEO

by Brian Leopold

Roberto Razetta's appliance repair shop was less than five miles from Hollywood, close enough to see the neon glow at night. But the dingy brick canyons of Koreatown were about as far removed from the glitz and glamour of L.A. as you could get. Roberto's dank shop was only about as wide as the beat-up front door, with security bars that pulled down when the place was closed, or when Roberto got sick of dealing with customers — something that happened on an almost-daily basis.

A hand-painted sign bolted to the outside wall read, "Razetta's Hollywood Appliance Repair." Roberto had the sign installed when the place first opened in '85, hoping the name would attract rich Hollywood types, along with their fat wallets. Since he specialized in cameras and video equipment, he had visions of doing repair work for the big studios. But no dice. Three years after the grand opening, the original, hand-painted sign remained and Roberto's clientele consisted almost entirely of old people and hopeless Asian tightwads, all trying to squeeze Roberto out of every last dime.

The dented cardboard clock on the door claimed the shop opened at nine, but Roberto seldom unlocked the doors before ten, not that it mattered. One spring morning though, he arrived at the shop at his usual time to find a customer already waiting for him out on the sidewalk, some preppy douchebag who looked like he might actually have some money. Every muscle of the yuppie's face was taut, ready to snap. His head bobbed from side to side. *The guy's wired on coke,* Roberto thought.

The preppy wore Topsiders with no socks, and the sleeves of his blue-striped oxford cloth shirt were rolled up to just below the elbow. He even had the trademark light blue sweater tied around his neck. He was in full uniform, a preppy right out of Central Casting. The preppy clutched a Safeway grocery bag in one hand, and from the expression of sheer panic on his face, Roberto knew what was inside the brown paper bag. His pulse quickened. *Maybe this was going to be a good day after all.*

"I need to get something repaired immediately," the douchebag said, even before Roberto could pull out his keyring.

"Hold on, dude," Roberto said as he worked at the nest of locks and deadbolts. "Let me at least get the place opened up." He took his time, turning to watch the traffic stream past on Vermont Avenue before finally pushing the door open. Roberto hated preppies. They were all privileged, trust fund assholes who looked down on working guys like him. But he liked their money.

It was a nice camera, a Sony, almost brand new, equipped with a good lens, capable of recording in the latest mini-cassette format. Roberto thrust out a hand to take the camera, but the preppy seemed reluctant to hand it over. The two of them stared at one another for a long time before the guy finally relented. There was a long, angry gash down one side of the plastic body, just above the tape carriage.

"Well," Roberto said, trying to mask his delight. "What happened here?" He sighted along the scarred camera body like it was a rifle barrel.

"I wasn't watching where I was going and I ran into a wall," the preppy said. "I dropped the camera and it hit the floor"

Yeah, right. You ran into a wall, Roberto thought, but what he *said* was, "You'd be surprised how often that sort of thing happens. I see it all the time." He continued spinning the shoe-box-sized camera slowly in front of his face. "At least you didn't shatter the lens."

"Here's the thing," the preppy said, unable to meet Roberto's eyes. Another dead giveaway. "There's a tape stuck inside that camera, and I need to get it back immediately."

Of course you do, Roberto thought, powering up the camera while simultaneously pressing the "eject" button. The camera whirred, sputtered, groaned in protest, and an electronic beeping began. It was obvious that the tape carriage had been severely damaged.

"What's so important on the tape?" Roberto asked, trying to make it sound like idle conversation, an innocent question. He had to stifle a smile at the look of unmitigated terror his question generated. The preppy's reaction verified what he already knew, what experience had taught him. Trapped inside the camera was almost certainly another sex tape for his collection. Roberto could hardly contain his glee. The young man swallowed hard, shifted his weight from one boat-shoed foot to the other as he stared down at his empty, open hands.

"I just finished taping a sales presentation for work," the young man said. "My presentation is at one o'clock, and if I don't have that tape, my CEO is going to kill me."

"I see," Roberto said, moving with even greater lethargy. He pretended to peer through the smoked Plexiglas insert in the tape carriage and let out an alarmed whistle.

"Wow," he said. "I can't guarantee I can get that tape out of there without damaging it." He met his customer's eyes. "It's wrapped around the capstans, and when that happens, the tape usually ends up crumpled like Saran Wrap."

Roberto powered down the camera, and turned it on again. He hit the rewind button. "Hear that?" he said. "That's another few inches of tape getting sucked up into the mechanism. That's never good." The preppie grimaced in pain at the sound, like the twisted, mangled tape was one of his own fingers.

"So, do you still need that tape back?" Roberto asked.

The preppy's eyes went electric. "Yes, yes," he said. He made a desperate grab for the camera, but Roberto pulled it out of his reach just in time. He carried the camera through the Indian print curtains that separated the front lobby from the workroom.

"Don't worry," he called over his shoulder. "I'll get what's left of the tape out of there for you, no problem." The preppy's desperation served as Roberto's final confirmation. *Definitely a sex tape*, he thought. *Everybody's making them these days.*

There were two orange plastic chairs pushed up against the wall in the lobby, but the preppie didn't sit down. Roberto could hear his footsteps on the dusty Formica floor, pacing back and forth in the tiny waiting room. Four steps, turn, four steps, turn, walking faster all the time.

Roberto sat down at his workbench. He moved aside a toaster that wouldn't toast, a can opener that refused to open cans, and a Bunn-O-Matic that resisted all efforts to brew a decent cup of coffee. He set the camera on his workbench and began removing machine screws from the plastic cowling. He turned on the television in the back room to serve as audio subterfuge. Now the mark could only hear what Roberto wanted him to hear. Some game show was on Channel 2. There was lots of cheering and shouting.

Roberto gently pried the tape carriage forward, recognizing that the actuator arms had been badly bent. He did his best to straighten them before detaching the tension springs. The tape carriage didn't move easily, but with steady pressure, he was able to lever it just wide enough to grab hold of the tape cassette with a pair of needle-nosed pliers. Slowly, silently, Roberto extracted the cassette from the camera and set it on the counter in front of him.

"Oh shit, that is not good," he announced to the curtain, and heard the scratchy footsteps in the lobby slide to a stop. Roberto took a small mallet from a hook on the wall and began pounding the wooden counter with it. "Damn it," he said, way too loud. While he was pounding, he opened a drawer containing more than fifty blank videotapes. He sorted through the plastic rectangles until he found a tape that closely resembled the one he'd just taken from the camera, same manufacturer, same label.

He popped the access door on this new cassette, grabbed hold of the raw tape and stripped fifteen feet of it from the cartridge. Tape spooled out onto the floor. He wadded the loop of exposed tape into a ball, squeezing it between his hands like he was wringing out a wet sponge. He took scissors and snipped the tape in two, then wound the loose ends back onto the take-up reels, leaving about six inches of mangled tape dangling from either end of the cassette. After a few more sharp raps from the mallet, he walked back out front.

"Sorry, dude," he said, holding out the violated videocassette. "This baby was tied up in knots inside your camera." Tatters of tape trailed behind the black plastic case like twin kite tails. "I did my best, but the tape had already snapped inside the transport. You can only stretch that oxide so far, you know?" The young man snatched the cassette from him greedily, just as he'd expected.

"Sorry about your presentation," Roberto said.

"Presentation?" the preppy said. "Oh yeah, right." He jammed the tape deep into the pocket of his jeans and glared at Roberto again. "Is the camera all right?" he asked.

Roberto shook his head. "The tape transport is in pretty bad shape. It got mangled. These new video cameras are extremely fragile. They don't like to be dropped."

"Damn," the preppy said. "I borrowed that camera from a buddy of mine, and I promised I'd have it back to him tomorrow. We're supposed to have lunch together, and if it's not repaired by then, I'm going to have to buy him a new one."

Well, well, here's a bonus, Roberto thought. *A little monetary gravy.* He nodded across the counter. "First thing tomorrow?" he said. "I don't know. I'm pretty booked up." He let his voice trail off.

"I'll pay you double your usual rate," the preppy said. Desperation burned in his eyes and his pupils were the size of pinpricks. Roberto pretended to consider the offer.

"Tomorrow's just a bad day," he said. "I've got people who are expecting to pick up their repairs first thing in the morning. I'd be here all night."

"All right, I'll pay you *triple,*" the young man said. Then, as though he thought better of it, added, "Unless, of course, the repairs are going to run me more than the camera is worth."

Roberto scratched his head, doing imaginary math. "Let's see," he said, as if talking to himself more than the client. "A camera like this will probably run you at least fifteen hundred new, but I'm going to have to replace the entire tape carriage assembly. Until I do that, I won't know for sure if there's any damage to the rest of the camera or the CCD. Hmm." He drummed his fingers on the glass counter. "I'm just guessing here, but at triple my normal labor rates, this is probably going to run you six or seven hundred bucks." Roberto knew the point at which most people opted for repair over replacement; forty percent. *No use pushing it,* he thought

The young man agonized over the decision for a moment. Then, just as Roberto expected, he said, "All right, but not a penny over six-fifty."

"I'll see what I can do," Roberto said, determined not to let his glee show. He reached for his receipt book. "Let's write up a repair ticket, and I'll need to run your charge card as a deposit."

The preppy reached for his wallet, chose a charge card and handed it across the counter. Roberto forced himself not to smile at his good fortune. The two men's eyes met, and the preppy gave Roberto an embarrassed smile. An odd feeling came over Roberto, like déjà vu, but not really.

"Have you been in here before?" Roberto asked.

"Me? No," the preppy said, casting his eyes at the floor. His expression said, *Normally, I wouldn't be caught dead in a place like this.*

Roberto checked the name on the charge card, Preston Martin. The name wasn't familiar, but the face was.

***

Randy Cox had the toothiest shark smile Roberto had ever seen. He'd entered the repair shop one day wearing a three-piece suit and Ray Bans, even though it was pouring rain outside. Rainwater dripped off him onto the floor, forming a small, greasy pool. Even the rain didn't want to get too close to him.

"I'm from Vivacious Videos, out in the Valley," Cox announced, pushing his sunglasses up onto his forehead as he strode up to the counter, "and I'm here to help you get rich."

"I'm listening," Roberto had said. Which was all Randy Cox needed to hear. He reached into his pocket and extracted a fat wad of hundred-dollar bills.

"From time to time, in the course of your work,

Razetta, you might come across a videotape ... of an *adult* nature. I'm not talking about professional stuff here: what Randy Cox is looking for are totally amateur videos, if you know what I mean?"

Roberto didn't know whether to be embarrassed or not. He knew *exactly* what the guy meant. Anyone who repaired video cameras did, but he feigned confusion at first.

"I produce a little series called *America's Horniest Home Videos*. My movies sell like gangbusters, especially over in Japan. I shit you not, those people over there absolutely love the amateur videos: not porn stars, but Mr. and Mrs. Everyday American doing the nasty." Randy Cox leered. "The nastier the better, if you catch my drift." He jiggled his thick wad of bills. "In the event you did happen to stumble across any videos like the ones I'm describing, I'd be willing to pay a hefty ... *finder's fee* for the tape. Thousands of dollars, as a matter of fact."

Roberto's mouth fell open. He felt as if the heavens had just opened up. The rain hurling itself against his shop window suddenly seemed green and foldable. He already had two tapes in his personal collection that fit Cox's description.

"Now, I know what you're thinking," Cox had said, "but let me ease your mind. I only market my movies in Japan and a few other Pacific Rim countries. There's no way anyone caught on one of these tapes is going to recognize themselves back here in the States. And let me assure you of one other thing, Roberto—a Randy Cox payday is nothing to sneeze at." He tossed the rubber-banded bills into the air, caught them and stuffed the wad back into his inside jacket pocket.

213

Roberto made over ten thousand dollars that first week, all in under-the-table cash, completely off the books. He'd called his connection twice since then, and each time, he'd walked away with a tidy profit. And now, he was about to score again.

Roberto waited almost a full hour before allowing himself the pleasure of viewing the preppy's tape. He let the anticipation build in his mind like a flower about to burst into bloom, a flower made of money. In the meantime, he fixed the guy's camera.

Finally, when the electricity running the length of his spine became so intense he could hardly sit down, Roberto gave in. He went to the front door, turned the "Open" sign around so it read, "Out to Lunch." He spun the red plastic clock hands to three o'clock. If some old biddy brought in a broken blender, she could just wait. He was about to make some real cash, maybe score a month's income in one day. He killed the florescent lights in the lobby and pulled the curtains behind the counter closed. Back in the shop, he powered up his cassette player and a video monitor. The monitor hummed expectantly.

He knew Randy Cox was going to love this latest tape. The preppy was young and good looking. Roberto was almost certain he'd have a super-hot girlfriend. Maybe they'd do some kinky stuff, blindfolds and handcuffs, a threesome with the girl's sister, sex out by the pool where the neighbors could watch. A bit of kink, if it wasn't too much, always earned Roberto a bonus, maybe as much as five hundred extra dollars. Before he hit the play button, Roberto squeezed his eyes shut and allowed himself to contemplate how he was going to spend his windfall.

His heart raced in giddy anticipation. He opened his eyes and shoved the plastic cassette into the machine with trembling fingers.

An image appeared on the monitor, but before Roberto could make out what he was seeing, a raucous explosion of crimson light burst on the screen, followed by blackness. "I guess that's where the camera hit the floor," Roberto said. He pressed the stop button, and hit rewind. The tape wound, began moving in reverse, slowly at first, finally starting to pick up speed. As the tape sang through the transport, Roberto watched the digital counter: one, two, five, ten minutes back. "All right," he said. "That ought to do it." He hit stop again.

"Okay ... Preston Martin," Roberto said, remembering the name on the charge slip. "Show me what you can do." He pressed play, and an image appeared on the monitor.

He recognized the young, handsome preppy immediately, standing on the far side of a large walnut desk. Unfortunately, Preston Martin was completely dressed. There was someone seated at the desk in the foreground, a middle-aged man, but only a blurry suggestion of the second man's head was visible on camera. Preston Martin was clearly visible though. He was holding a silver-plated revolver in his outstretched hand, and he looked deathly afraid.

"Shoot me?" the man with his back to the camera said. "You can't shoot me, you dumb shit. Don't you know who I am?"

"I know who you are, Langone," Martin said, "and I don't give a shit. After what you did to Amy, you deserve to die."

"Amy?" the man in the foreground said with a self-satisfied laugh. "Was that her name? I never even bothered to ask."

Martin looked as if he wanted to climb over the desk and strangle the guy instead of shooting him. "Stand up," he said, gesturing with the gun.

"Stand up, my ass," the man behind the desk said. He turned and for an instant Roberto could make out the side of his face. Langone had the looks of a boxer, one who'd gone to seed. He was solid, but jowly, over forty-years-old for sure and starting to go gray. The stub of a cigar was clenched between his teeth. But there was something else about Langone. His face looked even more familiar than Preston Martin's had.

He's some kind of mobster, Roberto told himself. *I'm sure I've seen him on the news. Maybe he was on that new show I was watching,* America's Most Wanted?

"I know your schedule, Langone," Preston Martin said, waving his weapon in the air carelessly. "I've studied you. I know your weaknesses. Every week at this time, you drive down to your place in Palm Springs. You like to be alone, to spend the time decompressing. If I take your car and drive it out of here, how long do you think it will be until your boys realize you're missing?"

Martin reached into his pants pocket and pulled out a set of car keys. He dangled them in Langone's face.

"If the police find your body with a few bullet holes in it out in the desert, do you think they're going to spend a whole lot of time trying to figure out who did it?" Martin laughed and shook his head with a ragged smile. "They're not going to look for your killer, Langone. They're going to throw a party. One less asshole on the planet."

Langone laughed too, but Roberto could see he was badly shaken. *He's looking for some way out,* Roberto thought. *He knows he's in deep shit.*

You think we're alone, but we're not," Langone snarled with false bravado. "If you shoot me, my boys will be on you like a pack of wild dogs. They'll tear you limb from limb, leave pieces of you from here to Tijuana. My boys will do you just like they did your girlfriend. She was a real screamer."

Furious anger flashed in Preston Martin's eyes and he took a quick, involuntary step forward. Langone leapt up from his chair and made a desperate grab for the gun. The video image became a gray blur as Langone's lurching body blocked the camera lens. Something large, maybe a chair, fell with a thud as the two men wrestled violently. There was a much louder crash, then the sound of a single gunshot echoed through the room.

One of the men let out a bellow, followed in rapid succession by a high-pitched scream. The two men continued struggling and a second gunshot rang out. A flailing arm reached into the air. Langone fell through the camera frame, tumbling to the floor. There was an earthshaking thump, like someone pounding a bass drum. Langone's cigar remained smoldering on the desktop, but the man was gone. The camera showed an empty room.

Preston Martin reappeared in the camera shot, getting haltingly to his feet on the far side of the desk. He stared at Langone lying out of camera range on the floor. Martin was still clutching the silver revolver. A thin trail of smoke wafted from the barrel.

He took a quick step back, pointed the gun at Langone again and fired two more shots, as if he was expecting the man to jump to his feet again. After a long moment frozen in shooting position, Martin seemed to snap out of a trance and tucked the revolver back into a shoulder holster concealed beneath his Members Only jacket. That's when he noticed the camera. A quizzical expression crossed his face and quickly turned to disappointment. "Shit," he said, staring straight into the lens.

Martin hurried around the desk, disappearing from view. When he reappeared, his face filled the frame. "He was right," Martin said. "They'll know it was me, and they'll hunt me down." An out-of-focus hand took hold of the camera, but it wouldn't budge. The hand withdrew, and Roberto could see Martin's face again, even closer to the lens now, a blurry Cyclops eye with the eyebrow wrinkled in confusion. Martin studied the camera then reached forward. The picture jostled violently, but once again, the camera didn't move. "The damn thing is bolted to the bookcase," Martin said.

Martin grabbed a leather-bound book from an off-camera shelf and drew it back. He swung with all his might, and the red and yellow explosion Roberto saw when he first powered up the camera flashed on the screen again. The backroom of the repair shop went dark.

Roberto stared at the blank screen, incapable of movement. A staccato thunderstorm of blood pounded in his ears. "What the fuck have I gotten myself into?" he asked himself aloud. His vision narrowed to the circumference of a drinking straw. "If this Martin dude realizes I swapped tapes on him, I'm a dead man." He saw himself laying on the floor, just like Langone, with a bullet in his head.

The sound of frantic pounding broke the silence. Someone was at the front door, trying to get in. *It couldn't be*, Roberto thought, but then he heard Preston Martin's voice, clear as a bell.

"Open the door, Razetta. I know you switched tapes on me, you bastard. Open this goddamn door." He heard the sound of breaking glass.

Without thinking, he snatched the telephone off the wall and dialed.

"911?" he said. "I need to report a murder."

***

The police arrived in a flurry of sirens and squealing brakes. Five black and whites pulled up on the sidewalk outside the shop, all of them with their lights going. They had Preston Martin up against the outside wall. The front door glass was broken out, but Martin hadn't managed to get into the lobby.

"That jerk switched tapes on me," Martin shouted at the policemen. "He took a video tape out of my camera and kept it. It was my personal property. God knows what he was going to do with it. I just figured out what he did to me, and I want that tape back." Martin was holding a tape cassette in his hand, which he offered to the police.

"Keep your hands up," one of the cops shouted and Martin complied.

"This is the tape he claims he took from my camera and there's nothing on it," Martin screamed at the cops. "The guy scammed me."

Roberto skulked out from behind the counter and unlocked the front door. Broken glass was scattered across the lobby floor. Police officers poured into his place, guns drawn.

"Someone called 911 about a murder," one of the cops said, pointing his weapon at Roberto now.

"That was me," Roberto said. "I own this store."

The cops all looked at him with skepticism. "He's a thief," Martin shouted from the street.

Three officers rushed back into the shop area. "There's no body in here," a voice called through the faded curtain. "It's all clear."

"Was there a murder here or wasn't there?" the cop holding Roberto at gunpoint asked. The cop looked exasperated. It pissed Roberto off. *Typical L.A. cops*, he thought. They see some rich, prepped-out pretty boy arguing with a hardworking shop owner who's just trying to eek out a living and who do they listen to?

"Yes, there was a murder," Roberto said. "It was caught on video. I have the tape in the back. I can show you."

"And where did this tape come from?" the cop asked.

"From the video camera that guy dropped off for repair," Roberto insisted.

The cop pursed his lips. "So, the guy is right. You took his tape."

"He's a murderer," Roberto shouted. "He killed somebody. He put three bullets through some mobster's head. Who cares about some stupid five-dollar video cassette? Take a look at the tape, for God's sake."

They all adjourned to the back room. The cops traded dubious looks at the spider web of unwound wire, electrical meters, alligator clips, vacuum tubes, and spatters of solder scattered across the workbench. Once Roberto played the tape, the cops finally realized he wasn't some sort of lunatic. They made phone calls, and soon there were a half-dozen new officers crowded into the shop. Roberto had to repeat his story over and over again.

Everyone watched the murder several times. No one recognized Preston Martin or Langone, and that seemed to bother them. They ran the charge card and discovered that Preston Martin was actually a seventy-year-old widower who lived in New Hampshire. That news, at least, seemed to comfort them. It was the first detail of the crime that struck the cops as believable. They went out into the lobby and began talking among themselves, leaving Roberto alone in his shop. After several minutes by himself, Roberto's heart began to pound inside his chest, realizing how close he'd just come to dying. He flipped on the TV at the end of the workbench, hoping to calm his nerves. It was some soap opera now.

After what seemed like forever, the lead detective pushed back through the curtain. He looked at Roberto from the far side of the workbench like he was some sort of riddle that needed to be worked out.

"So, let me get this straight, Mr. Razetta," he said. "A murderer brings a camera into your shop with an incriminating tape stuck inside, a tape that shows him gunning down another man."

Roberto nodded in agreement.

"Then, once he has his tape back, or thinks he does, he leaves the camera here with you to be repaired. He just walks out and leaves the evidence behind."

Roberto nodded again. He held up both hands in

submission. "I know, crazy, right?" he said.

"And the guy tries to pay the repair bill with a stolen credit card?"

"I don't know what to tell you," Roberto said. "You saw the tape."

A uniformed officer pushed through the curtain. There was a woman standing behind him. "Detective? Can I see you for a minute?" the uniform asked. "I think you're going to want to hear this."

Roberto and the woman made eye contact. She was a middle-aged woman, fairly attractive, but dressed like she was out for a run. Her hair was pulled back into a ponytail, and she was wearing a baseball cap from Stanford. *I know your face too*, Roberto thought, *but from where?* It was like a jigsaw puzzle with half the pieces missing. There were familiar glimpses, but the whole picture just wouldn't come into focus. The woman and the two police officers filed out of the workroom, leaving Roberto alone again.

The lobby grew strangely silent, no longer filled with the urgent voices of police officers. Roberto shuffled through the broken glass to the front door. Most of the cops were clustered together on the sidewalk, standing in a tight huddle. They had Preston Martin in the backseat of one of the squad cars. He looked scared out of his mind. *Good*, Roberto thought. He returned to his shop. The police seemed to have forgotten him.

The television was still on, still tuned to the same soap opera. A man and a woman exchanged a passionate, forbidden kiss. The background music swelled to a powerful crescendo, and the show went to commercial break.

It was a commercial Roberto had seen a hundred times before, working back in his shop, one he'd never really paid much attention to, a commercial for home owner's insurance. A woman has her house broken into while her husband is away on a business trip. Midway through the commercial, Roberto's eyes went wide. He looked again. *What the hell*, he thought. The guy breaking into the woman's house was Langone. He shook his head in disbelief. Then, in the final shot of the commercial, the one where the husband returns, happy to discover that the insurance company has replaced all his stolen belongings, Roberto got a second shock. Preston Martin was the husband. *They're not mobsters. They're even not murderers*, Roberto thought. *They're actors. What the hell does this mean?*

Three uniformed officers rushed into the backroom. One of them was holding a set of handcuffs. "We're going to need you to come with us," he said. They cuffed Roberto roughly, wrenching his arms painfully up behind his back. They read him his rights and led him out onto the street.

A small crowd had gathered out on Vermont Avenue. Roberto recognized a few of the faces, fellow shop owners. None of them seemed particularly surprised to see Roberto being led away in handcuffs. A cop put a hand on the back of Roberto's head, and tried to force him into the car, but Roberto twisted away at the last minute. "This is police brutality," he announced to the crowd. "I am an innocent man."

That's when he saw Preston Martin standing on the sidewalk, a smug smile on his face. Their eyes met. Martin smirked and gave Roberto a discrete wave. He elbowed the man standing next to him, a big man with a baby face. It was Langone. The heavy-set actor was puffing a cigar, wearing an amused grin that matched Martin's. They were standing next to the woman with the Stanford baseball cap.

Where do I know that woman from? Roberto asked himself. Is she some kind of actor too? He wracked his brain, but his memory refused to cooperate.

The familiar woman took a step forward. "Yeah, that's right," she called. Her voice sounded just like Roberto knew it would, low and throaty. "Who's the smart guy now? I guess you're not such a hot shit with those handcuffs on, are you, Razetta?"

Then, in a horrible rush, it came back to him. Roberto's jaw fell slack. She was the star of one of the amateur videos Roberto had sold to Randy Cox. He remembered her clearly now. She'd been a little kinky, into bondage and a bit of mild torture.

"You messed with the wrong person, Razetta. You ruined my life. When my husband found out about that tape? When my *family* found out? That's something I can never forgive."

A rough hand shoved Roberto into the back of the squad car. The door slammed shut and Roberto slumped dejectedly in his seat, unable to process what had just happened to him. The car seemed to sit there for hours while everyone outside reveled in his humiliation. Then, just as the black and white pulled from the curb, Roberto glanced out the window. On the sidewalk, a man holding a camera pivoted slowly. Channel Two News. Two other television cameramen stood next to him. All three cameras followed the police car as it pulled away from the curb, catching the whole scene on video.

FLECKMAN'S FIX

by Preston Lang

The sweaty man in the plaid suit got out of his seat to stand closer to the TV screen. Overweight and nearing sixty, he was of a generation that still dressed up to gamble on a Sunday afternoon.

"Come on, Joe Montana, you god-damned San Francisco candy ass."

The line got a good laugh, but it had taken most of the breath out of the man. Rose gave him a quick glance. She had $8600 in her pocket, and she wanted to get in and out of the Gryphon Sportsbook as unobtrusively as possible.

"8500 on Buffalo to win outright," she said to the man at the counter.

The Bills were nine point underdogs, but you could also take them to win at five-to-two.

"8500?"

"Your limit is twenty, right?"

The counterman called his manager over—a red-haired guy with pretty features.

"She wants to bet 8500. Buffalo to win."

"Is the line moving anywhere else?"

"Not that I've heard."

"We'll give you two-to-one," the manager said.

"You got it listed at five-to-two."

"Two-to-one is what you get, dear." The redheaded

manager gave her a tight, little smile.

Rose sighed. "Fine, let's do it." *And I'll be back to take seventeen grand off you, Annie Lennox.*

Just after Rose got her ticket, the man in the plaid suit hit the ground hard. Security tightened up immediately, but they didn't move to help the man. Instead, they checked the exits and scanned the room for any other suspicious business. Was it really that common for a guy to fake a heart attack while his friends robbed the place? Give them smoke, liquor, and stress, and what did you expect to happen?

The other patrons watched with interest, though a few kept one eye on the screens as Joe Cool converted a third-and-eleven. No one moved towards the prone man. Great. Time for Dr. Rose Fleckman—delicensed physician—to jump into action.

"Call 911, for God's sake," she shouted.

The man wasn't breathing. Rose had always been bad at finding a pulse, so she didn't even try. She went straight to CPR, pumping efficiently, tasting stale bread and whisky. And then he came back to life, his eyes dazed and not quite human, but he was definitely taking in air. He stuck his tongue out and in and out again, like he was trying to be cute. Finally, a guard came over.

"What's the situation, ma'am?"

"Cardiac arrest. Thanks for all your hard work."

She continued to monitor the guy, who was still silently working his tongue, until the paramedics showed up.

"We'll take it from here, miss."

Please do. She left by the back exit into the relatively fresh air.

"Hey, you just saved a life," said a man with a ponytail.

"We'll see. A guy like that—nine times out of ten he won't make it through the night."

"Give me nine-to-one, I'll bet he's alive tomorrow."

"I've got to go."

"You're a nurse?"

"I'm a doctor."

"You know, Doc, there's some nasty folks looking for you. Lucky I found you first."

"I feel lucky. Have a good afternoon." She turned to leave.

"I can let them know where you are, what you look like, where you've bet. Or you can have a drink with me, and we can figure out how to keep you safe and get you rich."

***

Earlier that morning the phone had jarred Matt out of a deep sleep. It was Vin.

"You can help me with something, find something. A woman."

"You need me to find you a woman?"

"A certain woman. We think she's a nurse. She'll be at the sportsbook."

"Which one?"

"We don't know."

"What's her name?"

"We don't know. But we think it's a woman. And she might be a nurse. She's from Oregon. We think." Vin pronounced it "Ore-goan."

Matt's hair was tangled and unruly. He was going to need to get it wet and pull it back if he was going to get any work done today.

"She'll be putting down a lot on Buffalo-Cincinnati. That's a late game," Vin said.

"Which way is she betting?"

"You don't get to know that. Give you two hundred to try. If you're the one who finds her, you get a thousand."

Not long ago, Matt wouldn't have cracked an egg for two hundred bucks. Things were different now, and Vin knew it. If there was a lady putting down big money on the NFL, it shouldn't be that hard to find her. But there were two things he was going to need first—an eight ball and a really good rubber band.

***

Rose followed the man to a bar two doors down from the Gryphon, watching that ponytail bounce up and down. She couldn't say exactly what she had against a ponytail on a man. Men should be free to express themselves—yadda, yadda, yadda—but she couldn't get into it. It used to mean you were a hippie. Now it could mean anything: Wall Street guys and construction workers had long hair.

She ordered a rum and coke.

"So your boyfriend calls you up at three in the morning and says drive to Vegas and bet every nickel you can get on a football game? That's what happened?"

Pretty much. But it left out the ride over to Dr. Carranza's house, climbing around on furniture gathering the cash out of his crawl space. It also left out the serious temptation to just take the money and head up to Canada. But Carranza had sounded so confident on the phone, and she knew his connections were real. *And wouldn't it be a hell of a lot sweeter to drive up to*

Canada with three times the cash?

"Here's what they know," he continued. "The man they work for—Bellisario—fixed a game. Someone who wasn't supposed to know—probably your boyfriend—found out about it. He called a woman in Oregon, a nurse. That's you."

"I'm not a nurse, okay?"

"Fine. You're the goddamned surgeon general, but you put down a ton of money on one game, right?"

She wasn't going to answer that either.

"But you still have to collect. And in the three hours you have to wait, they'll get themselves better organized."

"Who are these people I have to look out for?"

"A man like Bellisario has people in Vegas. Problem is, they're idiots with a history, and sometimes they get thrown out of casinos on sight. One of them called me because I know how to behave myself in public. Promised me a few dollars if I found you."

"But you'd rather work with me than with them?"

"More money, better company."

Yeah, he was into her. If she could just get that stupid ponytail off his head, she'd feel a lot better about the whole situation.

"So we have to figure how to slip your money out from under them," he said.

"Why would I trust you?"

"Because you can't do it alone. No offense, but you're an amateur. And if you blow me off, I'll just take the reward from Bellisario's people. How much did you bet total? Hundred grand? More?"

"So what would our deal be?"

"Partners. Fifty-fifty. Think of it as me getting your

boyfriend's share."

Maybe it was better to have this guy's help. He looked like the type she could handle. And there was one good thing you could say about a guy in Vegas with a ponytail: he probably had coke back in his hotel room.

***

Matt had gotten just enough flake to make it through what was going to be an active day. Turned out that's what reeled her in. Some things he just knew when he was with a girl: when she was getting cold and needed your coat, when to put on the George Michael, and when to ask if she wanted to fade into Bolivian.

She went with him to his room. The girl may not have been a professional gambler, but she knew how to get the most out of a small bag of cocaine. That left nostril was finely calibrated, the kind of thing NASA would use to keep the instrument panel clean.

There were some problems with the TV's vertical hold, but they watched as the Bengals quarterback fumbled once and threw two interceptions.

"So it's Yerkovich? He's throwing the game?" Matt asked.

"I have no idea. I didn't get any details."

"Who's your boyfriend? Is he a hood, or is he, like, Yerkovich's sushi chef?"

She shrugged—smart enough not to tell him what he didn't need to know.

"Whoever he is, he's toast."

"Why do you say that?"

"The leak pointed to you, didn't it? That means they know who told. Right about now, your boyfriend's probably getting the flesh whacked off his face. Do you care?"

She leaned in closer: blond, compact, with just a little tang in her voice that said New York.

"Yes and no. I mean, I saw in the papers a few weeks back this guy in Corvallis cut his wife's head off, tossed it from a bridge. That's horrible, but I still got myself a frozen yogurt that night."

"So he's not your boyfriend?"

"Especially if he's got no skin on his face. I can't date that guy. So I'm pretty much back on the market, right?"

Yeah, the high was coming out clean and cynical in this girl. But it wasn't killing her sway one bit.

"I'll lay it out for you, cowboy. You let me cut off that ponytail, I will fuck you raw. That's a promise."

"Yeah?"

"I learned shit in my neurology rotation that'll freak you the hell out. You'll be lucky to leave here with any spinal fluid."

He should've been concentrating on the job, but there are things that a man who lives in a ratty motel room can't turn down. She wasn't a surgeon, but she did a pretty good job with his pocket knife. The back looked almost even.

"That's about fifty times better, man."

She threw the furry mess in the trash and things got pretty crazy then. It didn't take long, but it was loud enough that the guy in the next room kicked the wall a few times. When they were done, Matt reached over her for her jeans.

"What are you doing?"

"I just want to see how much you bet."

She grabbed his arm. He was still for a moment, but knew she wasn't strong enough to hold him back like it was a game. If he went for it, the only way she could stop him would be to try and hurt him. He pulled back his arm.

"I'm not robbing you. Calm down," he said.

"You want to see the tickets? That's what you want?"

"How many are there? What books did you go to?"

She reached into her pants and pulled out her wallet. Her car keys also clanked on the floor. She gave him the five tickets. The biggest was from the Imperial. If the Bills won, she stood to make $87,000 just from them. He studied the rest of the tickets carefully for a full minute.

"You really drive a Yugo?" he asked.

There was a knock.

"You in there?" Vin called through the door.

They both jumped out of bed and started putting on clothes.

"Who is it?" she whispered.

"Someone who's looking for you."

Rose went into the bathroom. Matt was a little embarrassed about the place—the stained shower curtain and the rusty fixtures. He heard the faucet running as he opened the door.

"What are you doing here?" Vin asked.

"The game isn't over until after four, right? She's not going to be stupid enough to show her face until then."

"She might. She's some ditzy nurse from Oregon. And we know what she looks like."

"You saw her?"

232

"We got a description. She's about five-five. Skinny. Blond."

"Natural blond?"

"Who am I, Miss Clairol? Her hair is yellow and shiny. I'm paying you, so get back out there."

"If you're in my room instead of out looking for her, I know you don't have faith in your other guys. *Three* grand if I find her."

"I can't go that high."

"If you're going to jew me around, I'll hold out for more money when I've got her in hand. Three grand's fair. Let's be gentlemen."

Vin didn't say anything for a moment. Then he let out a quick laugh.

"So what happened—you finally went to a barber and now you think you're a man?"

"Three grand—what do you say?"

"I'll give you five hundred if you get out there now. *Two* grand if you find her."

Vin was getting a little desperate. He wasn't a man who could improvise this kind of operation on a moment's notice.

"Deal," Matt said.

Vin handed him five hundreds and glanced at the bathroom.

"You got a girl in here?"

"I'll get rid of her and get to work."

"I don't get a peek?"

"No. *Murder, She Wrote* comes on tonight. Wait 'til then, and you can get off on Lansbury."

Once Vin left, Matt knocked on the bathroom door.

"Why did you haggle with him if you're not going to give me up?" she asked, coming back into the room.

"I have to play it like it's real. Otherwise he'd get suspicious."

"You said he was an idiot."

"I don't take chances. You could hear everything from in there?"

"Yeah."

"Hey, you're not Jewish, are you?"

"I'm a doctor from Queens. You figure it out."

"You're really a doctor?"

"Lost my license, but yeah."

"Why'd you lose it?"

She nodded to the little spoon and straw on the table.

"While you were treating patients and everything? Didn't you take an oath?"

"I also took an oath to the Girl Scouts of America. Then I stole their cookies and traded them for leather pants and Bowie tickets. Don't get moralistic with me. You're getting high, and you're at work, aren't you?"

"I *am* at work. And here's what we're going to do: you'll call all the books and ask if they'll give you your winnings in chips in the main casino."

"Because the casinos want me to gamble the money right back to them?"

"Yeah."

"And your idiot friends will only watch the sportsbooks?"

"Yeah."

"You might earn your keep after all."

***

The Bengals took out Yerkovich in the fourth quarter, but it was too late. The Bills won by ten. Rose called the Emerald Casino first.

"This is Rose Fleckman. I placed a bet on the Buffalo Bills earlier today. I'd like to pick up my winnings in chips inside your casino."

"Uh ... hold on one moment, please."

Four of the books went for the deal, but the Imperial — the big cheese — wouldn't.

"Then I'll be by later to pick up my winnings," she told the manager.

"What time will you arrive, ma'am?"

"At a time that is convenient for myself." She hung up the phone.

They took his car to the Emerald Hotel and Casino, where they got the chips without much fuss. Matt played a little blackjack while Rose bet red a few times on roulette. At first she felt anxious as hell — it was a lot of money to flip over in twenty minutes or so. But then she saw an old man in a tux give his young wife a fistful of thousand dollar chips; a guy in a burnoose bet five grand at craps; finally, there was Gladys Knight herself, drinking club soda and laying out two thousand a hand at baccarat. *Somebody had better get me a real napkin, because this motherfucker is not particularly absorbent.* Rose's winnings weren't exactly the attention-grabber she'd thought they'd be.

All told, they lost about a hundred dollars in four casinos. Even without the take from the Imperial, they were up big on the day.

"This is all pretty sweet, but you *do* understand that once Bellisario gets the grownups on the job, things are going to get a lot rougher, right?" Matt said.

"How long until the grownups get here?"

"Hard to say. But there's more to it than that. You can't go back home after this."

"What about you?"

"If I get the sense I'm burnt, I'm running as far away as I can."

She hadn't really considered the danger when she put the money down. The cash wasn't stolen and the bets were legal, but that didn't mean some hardnosed individuals wouldn't be very angry at her. Still, there was no way she was leaving the big money behind. She was feeling too good for that, even better after they did another bump in the car.

***

Matt peeked into the sportsbook at the Imperial. There was Vin, sitting on plush, red cushions next to a huge, muscled-up kid. Matt toyed with telling security that the two had tried to sell him coke, but he tossed the idea as the kind of thing that would get him on the wrong kinds of radar.

He went back to the lounge where Rose was waiting. The piano player was doing a Twisted Sister medley as dainty light jazz. High as she was, Rose really seemed to be digging it. Matt looked around for an attractive blonde in her early thirties. There she was at the bar—not a dead ringer, but she'd do on short notice—sitting alone and drinking wine.

"You think that girl looks like you?" he asked Rose.

"A little, maybe. She's not wearing a bra."

"I don't see that as a problem."

He walked to the bar and gave her a smile. Then he turned to get the bartender's attention.

"So. Hey. Las Vegas, right?" she said.

"It's something. What do you play? Slots? Roulette?"

"No, I don't gamble. I just come in to see the

shows."

"Really? What do you like?"

"Magic."

"No kidding? You're not going to believe this. I just saw Doug Henning in the sportsbook. Guess he bets on hockey or something."

"Yeah, he's from Winnipeg. They love their hockey in Canada."

"He was really cool, actually. Down to earth. Signed a few autographs, but wasn't acting like a big shot. I think he's still there."

"You serious?"

"You want me to show you?"

He walked her down the hall towards the sportsbook while she told him what he needed to know about the modern magic scene.

"And I like Roy a lot, but Siegfried has some very complicated neuroses to work through," she told him.

"Yeah, I can see that." Matt reached for his pocket. "My pager just went off. Mind if I catch up with you in a few minutes?"

"Your pager? What do you do?"

"I'm in sales. The sportsbook is just through that door."

She hesitated, but the thought of meeting Doug spurred her on through.

Rose and Matt found a spot behind a full-sized cutout of Charo where they could watch the traffic in the hall. Five minutes later, the blond woman came back outside, looking like she'd just been let down by her favorite illusionist. Vin and the big kid followed about half a hallway back. Once they were out of range, Rose slipped into the sportsbook.

***

"How about those Bills?" she said, putting her winning ticket down on the counter.

"I'm going to need you to come with me, ma'am," the agent said.

"What's going on?"

The counterman brought her into an office where she waited for twenty minutes all alone. Maybe it had gone rotten. The truth was, she knew almost nothing about who was involved or how. All Dr. Carranza had said was get the cash and bet. Maybe she should take what she had in hand and run. But the money at the Imperial—*her* money, goddamn it—was too great a pull. She drummed her fingers on the walls and tables until the manager and another man came back into the office.

"We'd just like to talk a bit," the manager said. "This is Detective Rusk of the Las Vegas Police Department."

"Just here to observe," Rusk said.

"When do I get my money?"

"We know that you bet quite a bit at a few other establishments."

Rose said nothing.

"You understand if there are irregularities, we need to look into it."

"What are the irregularities?"

"Why were you so confident the Bills would win?"

"So if you win, you collect; if you *lose*, you guys call the police?"

"Tampering with a professional football game is not something we take lightly."

"What do you think I did—spike the Gatorade?

The Bills were awesome. End of story."

"No, the Bills were *not* awesome. The Bengals were accident-prone. You'd better be very careful — "

"Please, Miss," the cop interrupted, genuine but sleazy, "just tell us everything. It'll be better."

"You want to know why I bet so big on the Bills? You guys see the interview with Yerkovich on Thursday?"

"No. Why?"

"Last week he took a big hit to the head. A little slow getting up. It happens, right? I saw him on the news, one of those dumb press conference deals. He's talking and I can see he's got slight ocular displacement and his left hand has a subtle tremor. He's got Hackford's Syndrome."

"He's got *what*?"

"Do you keep up with recent literature in neurological studies?"

"No, I do not."

"Well, I do. Hackford's is a specific reaction to head trauma. It can have a profound effect on motor skills over an extended period of time. I knew it was going to be a disaster when he had to play a full game."

"Because of this Hackford's Syndrome?"

"That's correct."

"What are you — some kind of doctor?"

"Yeah, the neurologist kind. What I did is take publicly available information and make a guess. On this particular Sunday, I was smarter than all the bookmakers in Nevada. You can't welsh just because you don't understand science. I won. Pay me."

"You buying this?" the manager said to the cop.

"Do you have any proof of a fix?" the cop asked.

"Did you watch the goddamned game?"

"I'm not a neurologist. Maybe she's right. And you can't say the NFL is crooked without proof. I listened to her like you wanted. Now I suggest you pay her."

Rose walked out of the sportsbook with all her money and an off-duty Las Vegas police detective as an escort. As she made her way through the room, she saw one of the hoods—Vin probably—sitting there, glaring, then looking away.

"Can you do me a favor, Detective, and give me a ride to my car?"

"Sure. Actually, I was going to suggest we have a bit of a chat myself."

They went to his car—a brand new BMW. Rusk insisted that she put on her seatbelt.

"They thought having me there would scare you. The last thing they want is for people to think the NFL is fixed. They were hoping you'd break down and leave your money on the table. But you were a pretty Solid Sadie in there."

"If I were you, I'd bet against the Bengals for the rest of the season."

"I haven't followed football since they started wearing helmets."

"You're not that old."

He gave her a quick look in the mirror.

"You're really a doctor?"

"Went to medical school and everything."

"You want to see a show tonight?"

"I've got work Monday morning. Got to get on the road."

"You can't take a day off? You just made, what, two years' salary? Stay. We can have dinner, talk things over. See Liberace, Phyllis Diller. Who do you like?"

"I do like Phyllis Diller. A lot. But I have to get back."

"Hey, you did a little blow today?"

"I just won $87,000. My heart rate is up a bit."

"We see a lot of cocaine use, of course. We take people in on public intoxication all the time. Controlled substances. The word of a good cop is hard evidence."

"I say no to drugs, detective."

They'd made it to the lot of the Emerald Casino.

"Look, I don't really care about dinner or Phyllis Diller, but some people are a little more grateful for law enforcement."

"I am very grateful for law enforcement. Is there a fund I can contribute to? A benevolent society?"

"We don't always go for that kind of bureaucracy here in Nevada."

"Would six thousand dollars help the force?"

"An even ten would probably get us where we need to be."

She gave him ten grand. For a second she thought something else was going to happen—a request for more, an arrest, a sloppy kiss. But he released the lock, and she got out of the car.

***

Matt lay on his side—knees up to protect his midsection, left hand over his face. The big guy was working him pretty good with kicks that rattled his entire body. On the recoil of the last kick, Matt reached for his knife. He'd get one shot at this. He managed to pull it out of his pocket, flip it open and stab the kid in the leg all in one fluid motion. Then he pulled it out and pushed it back in three more times. The kid crumpled. Matt ran. He shook off the knife, closed it, and put it back in his pocket as he made it out of the alley. He didn't look great, but at least he wasn't dripping blood as he slipped back into pedestrian traffic.

He knew a few things. The first book she'd bet at was the Emerald, and all the others were walking distance from there. The Emerald's parking lot was a fifteen-minute jog. It was full of cars, some of them pretty fancy, but he was looking for the bright orange of an Oregon plate on a Yugo. He only found one.

It wasn't long before Rose showed up with a suave older man—*a cop?*—in a BMW. But she got rid of him and walked over to the car. When Matt stepped out from behind a Datsun, she was only mildly surprised.

"You get in a fight?" she asked.

"Yeah. So we have to get moving. Did you get the money?"

"Yeah. How did you find my car?"

"I'm smart. You were going to run off on me?"

"I wasn't going to poke around all night looking for you, no. Let's go."

The boxy thing drove like a toy, but it got them out of town and into the desert.

***

The little girl sat still while the doctor explained to her mother how much and when to give her the drugs. The doctor spoke a bad mix of English and Chichewa. "Let her rest and the antibiotics will see her through." The woman listened carefully, holding up fingers to verify the dosage, then she put the girl back on the bike and pushed it along the dirt road. That was it for the day. When Rose got home, there was Matt, back from

Bophuthatswana, laying in the hammock next to a stack of recent issues of Newsweek that he'd bought for her.

"There's a weak dealer at Sun City," he said. "We go back at the end of the month—take them for maybe two-hundred grand."

"I don't know."

"I can't do it alone, Doc. Come on. Rod Stewart is going to be playing the Bowl."

"I hate Rod Stewart," she said, kissing him. "And South Africa—it's just wrong."

"Don't get all moralistic on me."

"Apartheid and all ..."

"We're taking their money, aren't we?"

"I'll think about it."

She ran her fingers through his hair. It was getting a little too long in the back. Time for a cut.

LAST DANCE AT THE GLIMMER LOUNGE

by S.A. Cosby

Chaz sat his last crate of records down beside the bandstand. He had ten new singles and four new albums. It was lot of synthpop mostly, but he had sprinkled in some new wave with the shiny pop melodies. Chaz liked to mix it up, and the owner of the club didn't mind as long as the kids were buying liquor and filling the joint to the rafters.

Norman Pittman was a former southern lawyer who had been disbarred sometime in the late seventies. Lucky for Norman, he came from old money and was able to whine and complain to Mommy until she bought him the club to get him out of her hair. The building had formerly been a tobacco warehouse, then a honky-tonk. Norman's nineteen-year-old girlfriend had convinced her thirty-three-year-old boyfriend to make it a dance club. Skeptical, Norman had hired some painters to throw some teal green and rose wine pastels on the walls. A few fog machines and suspended dance cages later, and the Glimmer Lounge was born. Six months after that, Norman was wiping his ass with ten-dollar bills and using the hundreds for coke straws.

Chaz had been the house DJ since September. He had previously worked at a disco in California and after that, he had spun records at an AM station in

Maryland before following his now ex-girlfriend to Richmond. She had broken up with him after only a month in the Cap City, having discovered she liked girls around the same time he had landed this gig.

"Hey Chaz, you're early," a voice said. Chaz looked down from the bandstand. Terry Sanders was wearing the latest in his endless supply of soft-hued T-shirts under a white sports jacket. The sleeves were rolled up tight to his elbows. Terry was the bar manager. He and Norman were old friends from their college days. Terry had a degree in philosophy, which explained why he was managing a nightclub.

"Yeah ... didn't really have anything going on so I decided to come in and set up. Got some new stuff for tonight," he said, resisting the urge to look down at his watch.

"Well, you don't get paid until we open. Just saying."

Chaz smiled. This prick really just said that to him.

"I know, Terry. Don't worry, I won't punch in until the first spoiled debutante with pink hair falls off a barstool," he said. Terry rolled his eyes and looked down at his checkered loafers.

"You holding anything? Just need a little bump for later," Terry whispered. Chaz looked around. There was no one else in the club. None of the bartenders were even there yet. It was just him and Terry. Why was Mr. Cotillion whispering?

"An eight ball for one fifty."

Terry frowned. "A little out of my price range. What can I get for forty?"

Out of my fucking face, Chaz thought. "Less than an eight ball," Chaz said.

Terry smiled. *"Touché.* Alright, fuck it. I'll get the eight."

"I'll grab it in a few minutes. Meet me in the office," Chaz said. He had to get the coke out of the spare tire compartment of his van where he had it buried in a jar of peanut butter. Peanut butter was supposed to throw off drug dogs. An old hippie turned drug lord in Florida had taught him that trick. This was the last of his supply though. That's why he was charging Terry so much. Plus he really didn't like the bleach-blond bastard.

"Hey, you're not gonna play any of that slow new wave shit are you?" Terry asked. "Brings the mood down. Kids start thinking about their lives. Nobody wants that."

Norman didn't care what Chaz played, but Terry had no love for Sixousie and Banshees or the Smiths or Echo and the Bunnymen. Chaz shrugged. "Just gotta feel it out Terry," he said.

Terry nodded.

"Alright. Well I'm gonna let you get ready. See ya in a few." As he walked away, Chaz pulled out one of the single 33s he picked up at Tower Records. It was "The Love Cats" by the Cure.

"You will be the second song of the night," Chaz murmured.

Once Terry had disappeared behind the "Employees Only" door, he took a look at his watch. *Where was she?* The whole reason he'd come in early was to go over the plan one last time before tomorrow. His stomach felt like it was hovering somewhere around his knees. He needed to calm down. He wished he had a lude. Not every day you plan on ripping off the boyfriend of the hot bartender you're secretly screwing ... *Especially* when that boyfriend was connected to the Philadelphia Mob.

***

Lydia watched Tommy do a short line off his dresser with a rolled up fifty-dollar bill, then rub his finger across the lacquered surface and against his gums. She was dressed and ready to go to work, but Tommy was taking his sweet time. He snorted two or three times before shaking his head like an enraged bull. He was built more like a bear. Big broad shoulders with a slight paunch that was hard as rock. A shaggy shock of black hair that he never bothered to comb covered his head. She checked her watch again.

"Tommy, we gotta *go*," she said. Tommy turned his massive head and leered at her. She could tell he wanted to fuck her again before he dropped her off at the club. The coke made him horny, but it also made him quick. Not quick enough for a romp though. She was already late.

"What, you in a hurry to see your boyfriend? Don't worry, his candy ass will be there to follow you around like a good little puppy all night," Tommy said. Lydia rolled her eyes.

"It's not like that and you know it, Tommy. Chaz is good people. Otherwise he wouldn't be going in on this with us," she said.

"I still can't believe his punk ass came up with the money." Tommy's Philly accent was thick.

Lydia pulled a cigarette out of her purse. She lit it and took a deep drag. "Well he did. Now you just gotta come through on your end."

Tommy ran a meat hook of a hand over his bare

chest. "I got my end, don't you worry sweetie. My Uncle Harry will look out for me. We're getting a great deal on that brick. Uncut, pure Colombian snow." He walked over to the bed and stroked Lydia on her chin. "Why don't you put out that cigarette and put something that's good for ya in your mouth?" he said.

Lydia wondered how he would feel if she put out her smoke on the head of that thing he was so proud of. Lydia didn't hate Tommy. He was cute and funny and good in the sack. He was also tiresome, a cokehead with a hair-trigger temper and a penchant for punching her in the gut if he was on a binge. Her daughter Julie had told her teacher how her mommy puked up blood all night after Uncle Tommy hit her. So now Julie got to live in foster care while Lydia tried to figure out a way to get Tommy out her life.

"I'm late for work," she said, blowing a cloud of smoke over her left shoulder.

***

Chaz saw Lydia come in five minutes before the club opened. Tall, leggy brunette with a thick pile of tresses sweeping up and over the right side of her face. It hid her eye just enough to make her look mysterious. She was wearing a tight, off-the-shoulder electric-blue top and tight black-leather pants that showed off her dancer's thighs. She once told him she had studied ballet as a kid, but adult Lydia had learned pretty fast that stripping paid better. She quit stripping when she got pregnant, took up bartending instead. "They're a lot alike," she'd added. "Either way you're giving a horny guy what he wants, a smile or a wink or a come-on. Only now I don't have to show them my tits. "

Chaz hopped down off of the bandstand and

hustled over to the bar. Lydia had squeezed past the other two bartenders, Cindy and Mike, and was signing her time sheet.

"Hey, can I talk to you for a second?" Chaz asked. Lydia licked her top lip before answering.

"You only got a few minutes before Terry turns down the lights," Cindy said, winking at Lydia. Chaz and Lydia fucking around was the worst kept secret in the club. As if there are any well-kept secrets in a place that served alcohol.

"Alright," Lydia said. Chaz headed for the "Employees Only" door and Lydia followed. They entered a short, dark hallway. The manager's office was to the right and the utility room to the left. They headed left. Once they were inside, Chaz closed the door. Lydia grabbed him by his spiked belt and pulled herself too him. They kissed hard, like only secret lovers and conspirators do. Finally they came up for air.

"You ... is everything good to go?" Chaz asked.

Lydia took a deep breath. "Yeah. His uncle's guy is meeting you two at the bus station. Tommy vouched for the money, so you guys are just gonna switch bags," she said.

"I shut off my electricity last night. Cleaned out my bank account. My buddy Isaac says we can get four hundred grand for the brick once we get out to Cali." Chaz cleared his throat.

Lydia stared into his eyes. "What?" she said.

Chaz clucked his tongue against the roof of his mouth. "Just ... what if Tommy comes after us? We're leaving him holding the bag. Literally."

Lydia kissed him on the cheek. "I told you, Tommy isn't gonna come after us," she said. Chaz felt the cold fury in her voice charge the air between them like a high-tension power line.

"Yeah, I know what you *said*, but ..."

"Tommy vouched for the money. His people have never seen either one of us. By the time they figure out what's going on, we will be on the other side of the country. Then in Acapulco. Just me, you, and Julie. And nephew or no nephew, son or no son, Tommy will be taken care of." Lydia grabbed Chaz and kissed him again. When she released him, his lips were stinging.

***

By the time they came from the back, Terry had turned the incandescent lights down and the neon lights up. The Glimmer Lounge shone like a ruby in the gutter. Black lights, illuminated posters behind the bar decorated with tigers and zebras. Over the bandstand, a neon sign in the shape of a blue diamond pulsed like a beating heart. The dance floor was illuminated from beneath by bright red, blue, and green lights that shone through the Lucite squares. Portrait lights shone down on Patrick Nagel prints that Norman's nineteen-year-old girlfriend just loved. They looked like zombies to Chaz. When the crowd was jumping and the air was full of smoke and sweat, it reminded him of what his bible-thumping father had said Hell was going to be like. Chaz figured out early on the difference between Heaven and Hell was just your perspective. Heaven to the spider was Hell to the fly.

As the crowd began to pour into the club, Chaz suddenly felt a wave of melancholy wash over him. Watching them shimmy and undulate like a living organism on the lighted dance floor, he realized he was going to miss spinning tunes. In addition to cutting off his utilities and cleaning out his bank account, he had sold all of his personal stereo and DJ equipment two weeks ago. That was the only way he could come up with the money to pay for the kilo. Or what *looked* like the money for the kilo.

Chaz put on a fast dance record. He spoke a little patter into the mic and took sip of his drink. His friend Isaac had promised him and Lydia half of the profits after they cut and sold the kilo. He had cleared enough from his checking account for the drive. This was going to work. He rubbed his palms together and changed the record. Some DJs were switching to cassettes, but Chaz still liked the sound of the needle hitting a record. Terry had tried to convince Norman to upgrade the sound system, but Chaz had already outflanked him and told Norman it would be too expensive. If everything went well tomorrow he would be in Acapulco sipping piña coladas by the end of the month. Sound systems and fog machine machines would be rapidly fading memories.

***

Later, as the club was winding down, Chaz came out of the bandstand and got a drink from the bar. He had just put on a song by Phil Collins. The former Genesis front man was spinning a dark tale of revenge and retribution. Lydia poured him a gin and tonic. She wouldn't meet his eyes. Maybe she was just really busy. Maybe she could feel it coming in the air tonight. Was she scared? Somehow he didn't think so. Chaz killed his drink.

By the time the house lights came back on Chaz had a buzz going. He thought about taking a bump, but then remembered he'd sold the last of his product to

Terry. He moved to the bar to get one last drink. As he threaded his way through the crowd, a soup-bone of a hand fell on his shoulder.

"You not gonna bail on me, are you Charlie?" Tommy asked. Chaz turned around.

"Hey Tommy," he said. Tommy's face was slick with perspiration, and his eyes were as big as saucers. The motherfucker was higher than a goddamn kite in a tornado.

"So you gonna fucking bail Charlie?" he asked again, "Or do you have some cojones? You in the big leagues now." Tommy was smiling so wide Chaz could see his wisdom teeth. Chaz hated it when the asshole called him Charlie.

"Tommy, let's be cool, okay? I got ya back, alright?"

Tommy snaked his arm around Chaz's neck and pulled him close to his chest. "Aw, I'm just fucking around with you, Charlie. Biggest thing you had to do was get the money. We'll be farting through silk soon enough." Tommy squeezed Chaz's neck tight and whispered in his ear, "Just don't try to fuck me, Charlie. I'll feed ya your own fucking nuts." Tommy released his neck and pushed his way to the bar.

Chaz headed back to the bandstand. He didn't want to watch Tommy pawing all over Lydia. It wasn't jealousy, just simple abhorrence. He wasn't a fan of watching vultures feeding either, but he didn't have anything personal against the birds. It was just disgusting.

Lydia found him before she left for the night. He was packing up when she came up into the bandstand. "Tommy is in the car. Everything cool?" she asked.

"As cool as it's gonna get," Chaz said.

Lydia cocked her head a few degrees to the side. "You ready for this?" she asked.

"Well, since I haven't won the Publisher's Clearinghouse Sweepstakes in the last hour, yeah, I guess I'm ready."

Lydia smiled. "It's gonna be fine. And once I get to Cali, I'll send for my girl and get her out of that fucking foster home," she said. Her green eyes were clouded like imperfect emeralds.

"You mean when *we* get to Cali," Chaz said.

Lydia ran her tongue over her teeth.

"That's what I meant," she said. Chaz thought she believed that he believed it.

***

Tommy's connection was coming in on the seven o'clock bus. Chaz wore his aviator sunglasses and a light tan blazer over a simple white T-shirt, his longish-blond hair pulled back in a ponytail. Tommy was wearing a leather jacket, black shirt, and jeans with a pair of battered loafers. Chaz felt about as conspicuous as a fat kid near a cookie jar. Tommy was even more jacked up than he had been last night.

"You get any sleep last night?" Chaz asked. They were leaning against a row of lockers near the rear of the bus station. A blue nylon duffel bag sat on the floor between them. Chaz was pretending to read a paper. Tommy was so keyed up he was vibrating like a tuning fork.

"Nah. Lydia kept me busy. Why the fuck you care?" Tommy said without looking at Chaz. He was staring at the bank of pay phones on the opposite side of the bus station. A few people were milling around, checking their pockets for change.

"Just asking. You seem kind of tense," Chaz said.

"Don't worry about me, Charlie. While you were still playing with Hot Wheels, I was in the street making my bones. You just watch the fucking money."

Chaz glanced at him again. The big man was sweating like a whore in church. Yes, the money. Sixty grand. Six-thousand dollars per bundle. Ten bundles in the bag.

Or so it appeared.

In many ways, fooling Tommy about how much money was in the bag was the scariest part of the whole plan. Chaz had sold damn near everything he owned and cleaned out his savings to come up with six thousand dollars. It had been Lydia's idea.

"He's so fucking gacked out he won't look very hard. He needs this just as much as we do. His dad sent him down here to get clean and handle some business at the docks. But he ain't getting clean. He's tooting every day of the week, and twice on Sundays. Spending money from his dad's trucking company like it's his own. He's scared to death that his dad's crew is gonna find out what he's been doing. He just needs to see one bundle with six grand. The rest of the bundles can have a hundred dollar bill on top and ones underneath. He'll believe 'cause he has to. I'll be right there to distract him. Between my tits and the coke, he won't know what's happening. I'm telling you Chaz, he's coming un-glued"

"This isn't your first time running a scam," he had said, not a question. Lydia ran her finger along the underside of his penis. The sensation had made him buck and shudder.

"I don't have a lot of first times left of anything, baby," she whispered in his ear.

And damn it all if she hadn't been right. Tommy checked the first bundle Lydia handed him and gave the rest a cursory once over. Chaz's asshole had been tighter than the eye of a needle while Tommy counted it. If he'd farted, only a dog could have heard it.

"Those two guys over there. By the phone. They're staring at us," Tommy whispered. He turned his head left and right like it was on a swivel.

"Tommy, they're not even looking this way," Chaz said. He was nervous himself, but Tommy seemed as ragged as fresh road rash.

"Nah, fuck that. They're looking right at us, I'm telling you," Tommy growled.

"Tommy, be cool. No one's paying any attention to us. We're just two guys waiting on a bus."

Tommy's face had become a tapestry of tics and spasms. It was like his cheeks were messaging someone in Morse code. Chaz peered over the top of his paper. There were two fit-looking guys standing by the phone bank. Just standing. They weren't rifling through their pockets for change, or looking toward the door of the station. They were slowly scanning the area. Their heads moved left and right with a small delay, like water sprinklers. Chaz felt his balls tighten and crawl up somewhere around his ears. *What if the cokehead was right?*

No. Not possible. The only people who knew what they were planning were Tommy, Lydia and Chaz.

"I'm gonna get a soda from the machine," Chaz said. God he wanted a Quaalude. Or some weed even. Anything to take the edge off his nerves. After the exchange they were supposed to go back to Lydia's, where she would distract Tommy with her pussy and Chaz would slip out, ostensibly to set up the meeting with his connection. Lydia would get Tommy to pop a couple ludes to relax, wait until he was snoring, then *poof!* They would dip and be on the road to California. Tommy would wake up and have to explain how he lost the coke and why there wasn't sixty grand in the duffel bag.

"No, you stay right next to me, Charlie," Tommy said. He grabbed Chaz by the arm and pressed his thumb into the crook of the elbow. Chaz almost cried out.

"Fuck man, I'm gonna be three steps away," Chaz said.

"No you're not. You're gonna be right here next to me like a goddamn Siamese twin, right until we meet your connections and chop this brick up," Tommy said. He was grinning that too-wide grin again. Chaz's heart pounded so hard he thought he could see his shirt moving. Had Tommy caught on? What the hell was he doing here? He was a small-time guy. The big bastard had been right. He wasn't ready for the major leagues.

As Tommy gripped his arm, Chaz heard a rush of voices. The Philadelphia bus had just released its passengers. A crowd of weary travelers poured into the terminal carrying backpacks and suitcases and overnight bags. One short man with a face like a catcher's mitt was carrying a blue duffel bag just like the one at his feet.

"That's our guy isn't it?" Chaz said. He cocked his head to his left. Tommy scanned the crowd for a second before he saw him.

"Yeah. Be cool," he said.

Really? He was telling Chaz to be cool? That was like a sailor telling a nun to cut back on the swearing.

Catcher's Mitt didn't acknowledge them. He just headed to the lockers. The plan was for him to put his bag down and Tommy and Chaz to pick it up and leave theirs in its place. Quick and painless. That is, until Catcher's Mitt got back to Philly and counted the dough.

Tommy released Chaz's arm and leaned back against the lockers. Chaz moved a few steps away from him, his arm still tingling. Tommy could probably kill him with his bare hands. Hell, he'd probably wounded a couple of guys with one hand a couple times before.

Catcher's Mitt was twenty feet away from them.

Chaz felt like he was going to vomit.

Catcher's Mitt was ten feet away.

Tommy was breathing so hard he sound like a freight train.

Five feet.

"Excuse me sir, are you Tommy Venucci?" a voice asked. Chaz felt his mouth open like a drawbridge. One of the fit guys had cut around Catcher's Mitt and was standing close to Tommy.

"Huh?" Tommy said. Tremors flowed through his face like he had put his finger in a light socket.

"We need to talk, Mr. Venucci," the other fit guy said. He opened his sport coat just a hair. When Chaz saw the badge clipped to his belt, everything started to go dark. Catcher's Mitt turned around and headed for the exit. As Tommy watched him go, a dark cloud roiled across his sweaty face.

"Oh shit," Chaz said.

Tommy pulled the biggest goddamned gun out of his coat pocket that Chaz had ever seen.

Everything after that was a blur.

Tommy shot Fit Guy No.1 in the chest with the hand cannon, pulling the trigger three times in quick succession. Fit Guy No. 1 crumpled to the floor like a sheet falling off a clothesline. Chaz was shocked that he didn't fly backwards like they did in the movies. Fit Guy No.2 shot Tommy in the face with a chrome revolver. People in the terminal started screaming and running. Chaz joined them.

He scrunched down and ran for the exit. Catcher's Mitt had been confronted by two other plain-clothes cops. He pulled out a small semi-automatic pistol and shot at them. The cops unleashed a fusillade of bullets. Chaz tried to ignore the sharp pops of multiple handguns as he ran for his life. He hit the street and took off in a full sprint. His van was parked on the corner. Flickering street lamps gave scant illumination as his feet pounded the pavement.

Chaz reached the van and sprawled across the hood, trying to catch his breath. He fully expected to see a battalion of cops chasing him like he was the fox in a wild hunt. But when he raised his head there was no one following him. Cop cars swarmed the terminal. A crowd had gathered across the street, made up mostly of survivors from the shootout and gawkers who'd come to view the carnage. Shaking, Chaz climbed in his van and turned the key. He checked the back end to make sure there were no cops hiding back there.

His blue van melted into the traffic like a drop of water falling into a river.

***

Chaz waited for two days in his cold, unlit apartment before he went to see Lydia. She didn't seem surprised when she opened the door and found him standing there. She'd dyed her hair a startling shade of blonde with ephemeral blue highlights. She wore a shredded black top with a black bra and zebra-striped leggings under a red leather miniskirt.

"Hey Chaz," she said. He walked into her apartment and sat down on the couch. Lydia closed the door but didn't move too far from the entrance. An old and battered brown suitcase sat near the door.

"Leaving town?" Chaz asked.

Lydia shrugged. "Shit went south. Thought it best to make myself scarce."

"No, I don't think things went south for you at all. Sure did for Tommy and that other guy though,"

Lydia held her hands out palms up and shrugged again. "What, you want an apology?" she asked.

"No. I want my share of the money. As soon as the cops came up, I knew you'd dropped a dime, but I couldn't figure out your angle. Turning us in didn't help you, unless ..."

"Unless what?"

"Unless you had an inside man. Someone who could get rid of me and Tommy and still get you the coke," Chaz said. He pulled a small gun out of his waistband. He didn't point it at Lydia. He just laid it on his thigh. "A cop. Probably one of the ones who approached us," he added.

Lydia pulled out a pack of cigarettes. She lit up and took a deep drag.

"You're an okay guy Chaz. I don't think you would

ever put your hands on a woman, let alone shoot one." Smoke flowed from her nostrils like a dragon.

"How'd you get the bag out of there? Your friend hide it in a locker while everyone else was doing first aid?" Chaz asked. Lydia didn't speak. "How you plan on moving the junk? Isaac won't touch it if I'm not there."

Lydia smiled. "That's sweet that you think he is that loyal," she said.

Now it was Chaz's turn not to speak. "And if I really had a friend like you say, do you think you should be talking about it? Like maybe you should just keep those kinds of thoughts to yourself."

Chaz just sat there.

Lydia took another drag on her smoke.

Chaz sighed.

"Can I at least get my six grand back?" he asked.

"Bye Chaz," she said.

Chaz walked over to Lydia and put his gun in her free hand.

"You know, I brought that to scare you," he said, nodding at her hand. "But you're scarier barehanded than I could ever be with a piece." He turned around and left the apartment.

***

Lydia locked the door. The surviving cop from the bus station, whose name was Eric, came out of her bedroom carrying a gun of his own.

"You think he gonna talk?" he asked. Lydia took another drag.

"Only to himself when he gets pissed about missing out on the money. If you're worried, I guess you could always take this gun and plant it on him after you put two in his head," she said.

Eric laughed. After a few seconds, so did Lydia. As long they both laughed they could both pretend she had been joking.

NIGHT THIEF

by Michael Pool

I flick my cigarette out of the open T-Top and hammer the 81' Camaro into fourth as the city skyline peeks through the fog beyond the freeway, Survivor's "Burning Heart" pulsing from the speakers. White lines appear and dissolve. My high beams light up the otherwise empty highway as the rotating red and blue lights fade back into the distance.

I had no other choice but to run—the way it goes when you're driving a stolen Camaro with what looks to be a dead hooker stuffed inside the trunk.

I didn't kill her. I didn't even hire her. She was in there when I boosted the car, not that anyone would believe it now.

Killing the headlights, I hit the next exit still running a hot seventy-five. The service road dips down and right. The tires scream as I peel around the curve and down into Harbor Row's collapsing warehouses and run-down automotive shops. The engine groans as I rip through the intersection at Captain's Way. Streetlights blaze by above like little bolts of orange lightning. I dip through an intersection too fast and the car goes airborne, bottoms out in a wave of sparks on the other side as the tires re-grip asphalt and pull a hard left turn.

This is my last night on the job. I don't need this

kind of shit in my life.

It goes like this: locate the right make and model, boost the car, drop it at the dock. Rinse. Repeat. On good nights, I can get four or five catches and be home by two with enough cash to last half a month. Mostly using a slim jim, but occasionally duplicate keys bought off a General Motors sales manager my boss Sven has his talons sunk into, like tonight. On bad nights, I occasionally get mired in some kind of bullshit. But this? This is a first.

I just had to get cute with the T-Top. Same old shit. I pulled off in an empty lot a few blocks from where I boosted the car to take out the inserts. Call it vanity, maybe even a bit of a Burt Reynolds fetish, an overwhelming desire to feel cool like criminals in the movies. In real life, I'm not cool. At best, I'm a lonesome, washed-up car thief who gave nine years of his life to prison yards and cellblocks, but didn't learn much from the experience. Gave up my family in the process. In the movies, things always work out. My life is nothing like that.

When I first found the body, I thought about just tossing the inserts in on top of her and walking away. I probably would've done it too if a patrol car hadn't pulled in the parking lot and lit me up right then and there. No doubt I looked suspicious, but what are you gonna do, dead girl in there and all? I jumped behind the wheel and kicked gravel in Buford T. Justice's face.

Now if I can just get the car to the docks and into a container, this whole mess becomes someone else's problem a few thousand miles from here.

I blow through two more intersections, take another corner on smoking tires and hit another left, hammer straight into an alley and cut up four more blocks. That cop has got to be toast, though the sooner I get off the streets, the better.

It's right about then that banging erupts from the Camaro's trunk. My adrenaline redlines, making my shoulder go numb again. *What the fuck?*

I ease down the next section of the alley and back the Camaro in behind a brown dumpster as the banging crescendos again. I shut off the engine and get out, walk around back of the car looking up and down the alley. A muffled voice yells something from the trunk, but I can't make out the words. My eyes scan the area for people or cops. No one around but a shadowy shape up on the iron fire escape two buildings down that looks vaguely like a person but is probably nothing.

The muffled voice calls again from inside the trunk. I ease my ear down onto the cobalt blue surface. She's definitely moving around in there. She sounds upset, but at least she's alive.

"What?" I say, trying to keep my voice down.

"Get the snout in here," it sounds like she says.

"What?" I say again, my southern accent breaking through now on account of my nerves. She yells so loud that I have to pull my ear away. I still can't make out the individual words, but her tone makes it pretty obvious what she wants.

She lays into the trunk lid again like a one-legged man in an ass-kicking contest. The thumps echo down the alley. *Thump thump thump.* Tick tock, clock's ticking. Too much noise, cops could be right around the corner. Not much choice but to open it and let her out. At least she's not dead. I know, I already said that. It's kind of a big deal.

I slide the square-shaped master key into the slot, hoping to surprise her. The latch pops and the lid starts to come up slow.

She doesn't.

She slams the lid up so hard that it's incredible to think I mistook her for dead twenty minutes ago. It catches me square on the forehead and sends me stumbling backwards into the grimy brick wall.

"You fucking psycho!" she screams as she tears out of the trunk. Her face pauses when she sees me, blood dripping from my forehead where the trunk split it open.

"Who the fuck are *you*?" she says, her tone less certain now that she realizes I'm not whoever she thought I was going to be. "Gino would cut your junk off if he saw you driving the Camaro like that."

"Gino the one who put you in the trunk?" I ask. I take a step back and cover up like a boxer to avoid the punches she gives as an answer. Probably not the time to mention I don't know Gino.

She whips a haymaker at my face but I catch her arm, use her momentum to spin her around backwards, then fold her wrist ninety degrees and twist it up behind her shoulder. I use the leverage to fold her over the open trunk so that her head is back inside, ample ass poking to the sky beneath a red leather miniskirt, those Judo classes I took at the Y as a kid finally paying off.

"Ouch motherfucker!" she says. "Let *go*, that fucking *hurts*. These stupid fucking windows already beat the shit out of me while you were going all Richard Petty back there. Get off me you fucking

Barney."

"Relax," I tell her, surprised she knows who Richard Petty is, and even more surprised I don't know what a Barney is. "I didn't know you were alive. Take it easy."

"Didn't know I was *alive*? What the fuck is that supposed to mean? Now let *go*," she yells.

I look around again, check that shadow on the fire escape, but if it's a person, they couldn't care less.

"I want to let go, but I'm afraid you'll start hitting me again," I say, trying to sound calm when my nerves are kicking into high gear.

"You fucking better be scared. Now LET GO."

I decide *fuck it, let her go*. I release my grip and take a few steps out of range. She flings her arm as she spins to face me, obviously hoping it will slam into the side of my head. It damn near does. I hold my hands out in front of me and say, "Relax, be cool."

"Stop telling me to relax, bozo."

"Just don't hit me, okay? I'm not going to hurt you. Now, what's your name?"

She stands still, hands on her hips, as if assessing me. Her lipstick is smeared a little, and her teased hair is a giant tangled mess from the ride in the trunk. Even in the dark alley the bags under her eyes have a presence. Her leopard print halter-top and red leather miniskirt are so tight they might as well be painted on. Her arms look like a tracked-up road map of her addiction.

"I'm Brianne," she says, her voice hoarse now. "I dance at the club. You one of the new door guys or something? Gino must have a breeding stable for you creeps, seems like there's a new one every week."

I start to ask what club she's talking about, then remember I stole the car out of the Baby Doll's parking lot. "How'd you end up in the trunk?" I ask instead.

She rolls her eyes against the night. "I guess I got a little too high, must have nodded off backstage. Gino gets pissed when I nod at the club, but I'm a good earner so he won't fire me. Sometimes he carries me out back and sticks me in his trunk. The bozo thinks it's funny. Did he put you up to this? That fucking bastard."

"Nobody put me up to anything," I say.

"I've never seen Gino let anyone drive his Camaro, so you must be *somebody*. That creep's obsessed with this car, it's like his child or something." She takes a step toward me, and I step back in turn.

"What's your damage, man?" she says. "I'm not gonna fuck you up. I'm over it. You got a cigarette though?"

The question catches me so off guard that I almost laugh. I dig into the pocket of my Members Only leather jacket and pull out my soft pack of Kools. I tap one free and hold it out to her. She takes it so casually that we might be old friends.

"Of course you smoke fucking menthols," she says, her voice bathed in contempt. "You guys are all the same. Got a light?"

I flip open my Zippo and snap a flame to life as she leans in and lights her smoke. I pull out another and light it for myself.

"So seriously, man, did Gino put you up to this?" she asks.

"I don't know Gino," I say.

"You don't know Gino? Bullshit." The glow from

268

her cigarette highlights her eyebrows as she raises them and takes a puff at the same time.

"Never even heard of him."

"Then what," she says, pausing to pull on her smoke, taking her time about exhaling it, "you, like, *stole* the Camaro?" She laughs, reveals a mouth of better teeth than I would have expected on a junkie I just found passed out in the trunk of a Camaro. "You must be crazy. Gino's a bad dude. No telling what he'll do if he catches you. That why you haven't told me your name?"

"I'm Hawk," I say, thinking that whoever Gino is, he's probably not half as scary as Sven. Hawk's my street name, short for Charlie Hawkins. Not that I tell her that. After tonight, there's no more Hawk, only Charlie. If things go right, I won't have any more use for a street name, especially the one I've been carrying the better part of fifteen years, fucking my life up at every turn.

Tomorrow it's back to Texas to reconnect with my ex-wife and kids, who I haven't seen in years, since she finally did the right thing and left my sorry ass. If it were possible, I would go back in time and leave myself too.

But that's all over, water under the bridge, as they say. Forty-eight hours from now, I'll be sitting in a supervised visitation room seeing my little girls for the first time since I got out of prison. Becoming the kind of father I never had, rather than the kind I did, which is what I've been up to this point. My old man was nothing but trouble too.

The thing is, starting over takes money, and stealing cars has always been my thing, so that's what

I've been doing. And yes, I understand how cliché it is to get out of prison and go right back to doing what got you in there to begin with. I've got my reasons, even if those reasons aren't enough. That's why I'm taking my chances and ducking town on Sven.

After tonight I'll have enough liquid cash to get me down to Dallas, maybe tide me over until I can get something regular going. At least that was the plan before this bullshit cropped up. Sven's gonna be angry, but I doubt he'll keep looking for long.

"So what do we do now?" she asks.

I shake my head. "Who's 'we?' There's no we. I've got to get going, I'm late. For what it's worth, I'm glad you're not dead."

"Jeez, take it easy. I'm not coming on to you. What I mean is, *where* are we?"

"In the warehouse district, just east of the docks," I say. "Far as I'm concerned, you can do whatever you want, so long as you don't mind a good walk. Your club's on the other side of town though. I guess you can call a cab from a pay phone or something. I'm sure there's one around here somewhere."

Her face goes so red I can see it even in this dark alley. "Unh-uh, no way, creep." She pokes me in the chest with her cigarette finger and the ember singes a hole in my jacket before I can back away. She doesn't give me time to protest, says, "I didn't ask you to drag me all the way over here on your little joyride, asshole. Do I look like I can walk all the way back in my condition?"

"Sure you can," I say, still thinking she looks pretty damn good for a junkie I thought was dead twenty-five minutes ago. "You can work something out with the driver, I bet."

"Fuck you, asshole," she snarls, "I'm not some skank-bag hooker, alright? I go to college. At least, I used to. I'm going back soon, for reals. You're giving me a ride, wanna know why?"

I start to laugh, but the look on her face tells me I should keep it to myself. I sigh instead. "Why? What on earth makes you think I would drive you in a stolen car back to the place where I stole it?"

Her left hook catches me off guard, opens the cut on my forehead wider, splattering some of my blood on the alley wall. I cover up and try to circle out with her hot on my trail.

"You want some more, motherfucker?" she screams. "You might think I'm just some piece of trash, but I've got a few tricks up my sleeve."

I dodge a couple more swings before wrapping her arms up. "That's really how you want to play it?" She wraps her arms around my waist and struggles for a minute, then stops without warning and goes slack.

"Take a chill pill," I say. "Cut it out with the violence."

"Okay fine, I'm done," she says, no longer resisting. "Let me go. I'm getting out of here."

I shrug and release her. She walks away as I exhale my relief. They were expecting me at the dock twenty minutes ago, and Sven's not known for his patience. The bacon boys are probably combing the neighborhood too, looking for this car.

Just as I'm getting in the Camaro to leave, Brianne stops under the streetlight, fumbles with something in her hands, and then calls out to me.

"Sure you don't wanna talk this out?" she says.

271

"Positive."

"Okay, that's fine. When I get back to the club I'll just let Gino know that Charlie Hawkins, 1615 Bay Avenue, Apartment B-206 took the Camaro. I'm sure he'll be happy that your picture is on this license, it'll make it easier to know which guy to kill."

I'm too shocked to respond for a moment. Then she waves the object she has in her hand at me and my quick self-pat-down reveals that she's got my wallet. This shit just keeps getting better.

"I don't care what you do with the car," she calls out, "so long as I get a ride to my motel room."

I sigh.

"Alright, have it your way," I say. "Get in."

"What, like, back in the trunk?" she says, smirking a little now.

I stab her with a glare that says not to push her luck.

She nods. "Just take me to my motel and I'll forget we ever met," she says, her voice almost friendly now.

I nod.

"Okay. But first I have to drop off this car. Trust me when I say that whatever Gino would do to me over this car isn't half as bad as what my guy will do if he don't get it in the next ten minutes or so.

"After that I'll drop you off, best I can do. But first you have to make me believe you won't tell your friend Gino where his car ended up. Trust me when I tell you a lot of people could get killed over a thing like that."

She spits on the concrete. "He's not my friend. Gino doesn't have friends, trust *me* on that."

"Can I?" I ask.

Her face gets serious now, and I can see she was

once a normal person, probably a suburban girl who got caught up in drugs. I thought goddamn Reagan was supposed to do something about that, but easier said than done, I guess.

"Yeah," she says, "you can trust me. Hell, all I really want is to go grab my bags. I'm done with that place, and besides, Gino will probably think I stole his car and beat the shit out of me anyway now. Time to bail town, I guess."

I study her reaction, looking for signs of a lie, finding none. "Works for me, I guess."

It's not perfect, but it's the best option I've got right now. Brianne grins and comes over to the passenger side. I hit the electric locks to let her get in.

The engine gurgles as I shift it into gear and pull down the alley with the lights still off. I cross Broadview and stick to the alley, making sure the bacon boys aren't still on the prowl. Nothing but street lamps and pay phone booths in either direction. This is cutting it too close.

I flip the lights on and turn back out onto Harbor Way. One mile to go and we're at the docks. A Ford Bronco eases past us on an otherwise empty street. Brianne takes one of my smokes from the pack I tossed on the dash and puts my lighter to it.

"Help yourself," I say.

"It's all anyone can do," she replies.

"You a philosopher too? Sartre in stilettos, that kind of shit?"

Brianne actually smiles before she can help it, then forces her ruby-red lips back down over her teeth. "I actually did study Sartre in this course I took my last semester at State."

"What'd you think?"

"More than I probably should have, so I stopped."

"I get that."

"I don't," she says, closing the subject.

I turn off Harbor Way and onto Shoreline, flip the lights off and pull off to the side about thirty yards from Sven's freight yard.

"Why are we stopping?"

"You gotta get out for a second. I'll come back and get you in a minute in the burn car my boss lets me use. I doubt you'll be impressed, but you don't want to meet these people."

"Oh, puh-*lease*. I bet I've met worse. You found me in the trunk of a greaser's Camaro. I think I can handle a bunch of car thieves."

"These guys are much more than that, I promise you. But that's beside the point. They don't want to meet *you*. Just hang out on those benches over there on the waterfront, and I promise I'll be back to give you a ride in a few minutes. We're trusting each other, remember?"

It's Brianne's turn to study me now. Finally she shrugs her shoulders, checks herself in the sun visor's mirror, and reluctantly gets out. I reach up and flip the dome light off so it doesn't light up when the door opens. She turns and leans back into the open door.

"You better come back, otherwise I'm telling Gino everything."

"I'll come back. Besides, I get the impression you and Gino ain't all that close."

She shrugs again and starts to close the door, then opens it back up. She reaches in and grabs my pack of smokes and my lighter. "Something else for you to come back for," she says. I smirk and shake my head as she closes the door. Girl's got spunk.

I pull away, leaving her standing next to the concrete benches. As I maneuver the car through the open chain-link gate, I notice activity down by the storage containers lined along the shore. It looks like Sven and his lackey, Carlos, and they look unhappy to be kept waiting. Gravel crunches beneath the tires as I pull to a stop in front of the open shipping container they're standing next to. I leave the engine running and get out.

"Is about time, Hawk," Sven says in that flat tone of his. "Was starting to worry you got picked up. You know how I hate waiting."

"Couldn't be helped," I say, trying to sound relaxed even though Carlos is boring a hole through me with his fuming eyes. "I think I got you a good one here though, real swanky ride, exact one you asked for."

Sven walks a circle around the car inspecting it, leans down and brushes his hand across the front bumper's bottom where it scraped blowing through one of the intersections.

"Pretty good," he finally says. "Yes. Even with scratches, it's perfect."

I nod, relieved, ready to head back to pick up Brianne, and then back to my apartment to get some sleep for the drive tomorrow in the Ryder truck I rented. Hell, I might even leave tonight.

"Glad to hear it," I say. "So can I go ahead and get paid out for the night?"

Carlos smiles, and I know immediately there's more bullshit coming down the pipe. Sven gives him a look that wipes the smile away.

275

"Something I need to know?" I ask.

Sven locks his blue eyes on me, and my blood turns to ice. He's a cold-blooded killer, everyone knows that.

"I was wondering the same thing. Carlos tells me you might be preparing to skip town. Is that true?"

I frown, wondering how Carlos knows that. I haven't said a word about it to anyone, was planning to just go. In fact, I already moved everything out of my apartment except a sleeping bag and pillow for tonight.

"Who told him that?" I say, still speaking to Sven instead of Carlos, who creeps me out with his gold chains and popped-collar suits. That fucking guy needs to get laid.

"Don't worry *who*. All that you should worry about is that I know it's true. You weren't planning on leaving without saying goodbye, were you?"

I was. But I can't tell him that.

Sven sneers. "Don't lie, either. Your stuff is packed into a Ryder truck in front of your apartment right now, I know that for fact. Carlos did some checking and looks like you got a one-way rental. That wasn't our deal when I paid my attorney to handle your parole hearing, Hawk."

If this night was taking a bad turn earlier, it just drove off a fucking cliff. I forgot to mention that Sven got me out of prison early in exchange for the work I'm doing, work I'll still have to do for several years to finally pay him back.

"I don't know what to say then, I guess."

"Why you even try to lie is beyond me, Hawk. You're not good at it. Sooner or later, the lies start to corner you. You know that. You *owe* me, and you'd better start convincing me why I should let you live long enough to pay it back instead of having Carlos drown you in the ocean."

"Alright, that's fair," I say, knowing it's not fair but just wanting to get out. Guys like Sven don't know the meaning of the word "fair." "What kind of assurances do you need?"

Sven and Carlos grin in unison. Sven pauses, lights up a smoke. I wish I could do the same, but Brianne has mine. "I think we can— Who the fuck is this?" Sven says in a nasty voice, looking over my shoulder.

I turn to see Brianne come prancing out of the darkness, one of my Kools drizzling smoke from between her fingers.

"Are you almost done yet, Hawk? I can't be waiting around all night while you—"

Sven's face fills with rage. "You bring someone else to our deal, Hawk?" he bellows, incredulous. "Have you lost your mind?"

"It's not what it looks like," I start to say, but I know that explaining isn't going to work. No new faces, that's the rule. Guys like Sven haven't stayed in business this long by letting just anyone know what they're about.

"Who the fuck are you, buddy?" Brianne replies to Sven. "It's a free country, I can go wherever I want."

Believe me when I tell you that people do not talk to Sven like that. "Now are you gonna give me a ride, Hawk, or what?"

"You think this is a game, don't you Hawk?" Sven says. "Bring whoever you want, quit whenever you want. You forget who I am. Time to remind you." He turns to Carlos. "Kill them both and have the ship captain drop their bodies at sea."

Brianne's face looks shocked as Carlos reaches into his waistband for his Baretta. "Brianne, RUN!" I yell as I barrel my shoulder into Carlos' chest and wrap my arms around his waist. I hook his leg with the back of my knee and yank it out from under him while driving forward. He falls backwards and lands on his ass on the asphalt with me chest-to-chest on top of him. Sven reaches for his own pistol, but Brianne doesn't run like I tell her. Instead, she flicks her cigarette butt into Sven's face. The tip catches him right in the eyeball, a one in a million shot. He drops his pistol on the way to raising it. His hands go to his face instead. "Shit, my eye!" he screams. "You fucking bitch!"

I don't wait on Sven to recover. Instead I focus on Carlos, who still has a pistol in his hands. He fires blind, but the muzzle is behind me so the bullet goes off into space. I pin his gun hand to the ground with my left and start swinging for the fences with my right. A big right forearm connects, and his face seems to evaporate. He makes a valiant attempt to recover, but I drop another big elbow on his forehead, and I can feel him fading.

Just as I'm about to deliver the final blow, a gunshot rings out, and I'm sure it will mean the end of me. But I don't feel anything, so I drop the elbow to Carlos' head and he sinks to the concrete, unconscious. I roll off Carlos and turn to see what's left of Sven's face staring at me from his back, the gun still smoking in Brianne's hand.

"Holy shit, you took half his head off," I say.

"He was about to kill you," she replies. "I didn't have a choice."

She could have run, but I don't say that. "Do you

have any idea who he is?" I say instead.

"Doesn't matter now anyway."

Her calm demeanor is unfathomable for a woman who just shot and killed the biggest crime boss within three states. I wonder if she might be in shock.

"We need to get the fuck out of here."

Brianne helps me to my feet, where I dust myself off. She's still got the pistol in her hand, and I wonder if she's forgotten about it.

"I'll take that, if you don't mind," I say. She hands me the weapon like it's something she's ready to throw away anyway. Ironic, since that's exactly what I plan to do. But first I've got a score to settle with Carlos. I don't need him telling the story of how Sven Chamberlain was killed in his own shipping yard by an ex-con he helped get out of prison. Plus I never liked the motherfucker. I've never cared for killing, but I'm not above it. I put two rounds in Carlos's forehead. Brianne looks away as I do it.

We pile back in the Camaro, both close to hyperventilating as the gravity of our situation kicks in.

"What do we do now?" Brianne asks, finally sounding scared. She starts to shake, manages to shiver another Kool out of the pack and light it, but her hands sway back and forth so much she can barely get it to her lips. "Man, I need a shot," she says, like it's the only thing that ever mattered in the universe. Junkies, man. They all have a one-track mind, and all it wants is escape.

"Stay here," I say, thinking on my feet now. The last thing I need is a dope-sick girl who just helped me commit a double murder twisting off on withdrawals. "I might be able to help you out."

She doesn't respond.

I get out and walk back to the chaos. I stand over Sven's body, his face a distant memory under blood and brain matter and shreds of skin. I pat his pockets and find a wad of cash, probably close to a thousand dollars. I search a little deeper and finally come back with the little plastic baggy of white power. Sven was no junkie, but he always had a thing for China White. Only guy I ever heard of using the stuff responsibly.

I get back in the Camaro and Brianne is still shivering. "Here, snort some of this," I say, passing her the baggie. "But go easy, might be a little purer than you're used to."

"Hey, I can handle my dope," she says, then frowns. "He didn't have a shooting rig on him did he?" she adds, suddenly alert now. Two dead bodies fifteen feet away and getting the best high possible is still the only thing that matters to her. Like I said, junkies, man. I shake my head and she looks a little defeated.

I drive to the yard's entrance and flip the lights up again before making a right. I head straight for the interstate that will take us north out of town.

"Did you have somewhere you want me to take you?" I ask Brianne, who's busy using her Lee Press-On Nails to scoop a couple bumps of the white into her nose. She inhales deep, squeezes her nostrils and swallows hard. When she exhales, I can already see the stress draining from her.

"Nah," she says. "I can't go back there now, not with the car disappearing. Gino will beat me senseless. Plus, we just killed two people. I think it makes sense to head straight out of town."

I'm relieved to hear her say that. I was worried she

might not be taking the situation serious. I have no idea what I'll do with her once her dope runs out, but right now, I could use the company.

I think about Texas, about my girls, Amber and Tanya, not so little anymore. I can't go back there now, chance bringing all this to their doorstep. I'll never be anything but a fuckup, and I realize that in this moment.

The engine barks as I take the on-ramp onto the interstate, not quite sure where we're going yet, and knowing that no matter how hard we try, we'll never outrun ourselves.

We ride toward daylight in silence as yellow stripes snake beneath the Camaro's wheels like little breadcrumbs placed there to lead us out of the woods, or maybe little arrows pointing the way back toward a life we were never cut out for anyway.

ABOUT THE AUTHORS

Kat Richardson lives in Seattle, Washington. Find her online at www.katrichardson.com.

Patrick Cooper lives in Trappe, Pennsylvania. Dig him online at www.patrickgcooper.com.

S.W. Lauden lives in Los Angeles. Stop by for a high five at www.swlauden.com.

Dietrich Kalteis lives in Vancouver, Canada. Find him online at www. dietrichkalteis.blogspot.com.

Sam Wiebe lives in East Vancouver. Discreet inquiries through www.samwiebe.com.

Sarah M. Chen lives in Los Angeles. She can be found at www.sarahmchen.com.

Eryk Pruitt lives in Durham, North Carolina. He parties online at www.erykpruitt.com.

Matthew J. Hockey lives in Northern England. Find him most days at www.facebook.com/MatthewJHockey.

Linda L. Richards lives in Vancouver, Canada and is home on the web at www.lindalrichards.com.

Will "The Thrill" Viharo hangs his fez in Seattle, WA. Swing by his cyber pad for a virtual cocktail anytime at www.thrillville.net.

Nina Mansfield lives in Connecticut. You can find her at www.ninamansfield.com.

C.S. DeWildt lives in Tucson. You can visit him at www.csdewildt.com.

Jen Conley lives in New Jersey. Fine her at www.jenconley.net.

Greg Barth lives in Bowling Green, Kentucky. Find him online at www.facebook.com/greg.barth.75?fref=ufi.

Brian Leopold lives in Mars, Pennsylvania. Find him online at www.brianleopold.com.

Preston Lang lives in New York City. Find him online at www.prestonlangbooks.com.

Shawn "S.A." Cosby lives in Southeastern Virginia. Follow him and his writing at www.facebook.com/blacklionking73.

Michael Pool lives in Denver, Colorado. Cuddle him online at www.michaelpool.net.

LIKE WHAT YOU JUST READ?

Then be sure to check out

CRIME SYNDICATE MAGAZINE

WWW.CRIMESYNDICATEMAGAZINE.COM

www.ingramcontent.com/pod-product-compliance
Lightning Source LLC
Chambersburg PA
CBHW060542180626
46817CB00002B/690